A Falling Friend

By

Sue Featherstone
&
Susan Pape

A Falling Friend

First Published by Lakewater Press 2016
This edition published by Sue Featherstone and Susan Pape 2021

Cover Image by Diana Pinguicha
Cover Design by Emma Wicker

ISBN-1: 978-1-7399460-3-6

For Kevin and Geoff x

Chapter 1

Teri

It was thanks to Peter Heron's love of television that I met Dan.

Peter, Dean of the Faculty of English and Media at this former polytechnic turned university, was not just a corporate know-all, but a TV and radio tart too. Which means, as well as talking a lot of business-speak about empowering the core, he becomes ecstatic whenever there's any topic on which he can spout in the media. He loves being on radio and/or television and will do any interview about academia, anytime. Anywhere.

Somehow, Peter got to hear that *Ridings Today*, the regional TV news outlet, was considering a new Friday night book show and immediately announced his intention to put himself forward as host.

'Who else could do it?' he asked us over coffee in the Senior Common Room. The smug expression on his face suggested he was already fantasising about the books he would feature and the guests he'd invite. Bet he was also wondering if *Ridings Today's* budget would stretch to the ingenue – what was her name? – whose debut novel sparked a media frenzy earlier in the year.

'Really, Peter,' Lee said. 'It's *Ridings Today*. They're more interested in waterskiing piglets and talking horses than intellectual discussion. The only books they'll ever feature are by footballers or celebrity chefs who happen to come from Yorkshire.'

But Peter wasn't to be put off and, shortly afterwards, all of us from the faculty were invited to one of his Widening Involvement in Industry events. It was late November, cold, wet, and dark, but we were promised red and white wine, and nibbles. And surprise, a producer from *Ridings Today*.

Chrissie, from admin, who'd had to issue invitations, informed us Peter had also invited a hack from the *Evening Leader* newspaper, and a youth from local radio to make it look less TV-orientated.

Peter tried to say the event was to 'cross the cultural divide between the televisual and the academic in the digital age', but no one was in any doubt as to the main aim, which was to see our Peter playfully quizzing the nation's literary demi-gods and goddesses in front of a Friday night audience of book lovers.

When I arrived at the event, Peter, dressed in his trademark single-breasted, three-buttoned, dark grey jacket, white shirt, and slim-fit trousers – a tad sombre and formal for a uni boss, I thought – was already monopolising the person I assumed was the producer. Elsewhere there were little knots of people dotted about, but, because I'd only recently joined the University of Central Yorkshire and didn't know many of them, I didn't want to risk getting stuck in conversation with anyone who turned out to be boring.

I spotted Chrissie gazing up at a man who had his back to me. He had light brown hair (not mousy) which was long and floppy and curled cutely over the top of the collar of his pale blue shirt. He had broad shoulders, a slim waist, and a nice, tight bum in black jeans. But I couldn't see his face, and it would be too obvious for me to go over to talk to them. Besides which, Chrissie looked enthralled. She'll be dragging him off to the admin office supplies room before the night is over, I thought.

Lee was talking to two other lecturers – Stella Lastings from history and a tall, dark-haired man I vaguely recognised, presumably having seen him in the Senior Common Room. I went over, and just as Lee was about to say something, I butted in. 'Isn't this a farce – having to entertain these media tarts just so our dear dean can sit in a studio reading autocue?' I noticed Stella's plump face light up in delight. Then I turned to the man and asked. 'Which department are you in?'

He looked at me with a slight smile. 'I'm not with the university.' I felt strangely hot. Stella giggled and Lee looked at me with an earnest expression.

'I'm with the media tarts.' He grinned.

'Oh. And what do you do?' I asked already knowing the answer.

'Oh, this and that,' he said. 'I'm Dan Caine, television presenter, but I mostly sit in the studio reading autocue.'

At least he had the grace to smile.

Lee, bless her, stepped in. 'Oh, Teri,' she gasped. 'As usual, say what you think without thinking.'

Dan laughed. 'You know,' he said. 'It's amazing the number of people who believe that's all I do. Turn up at six o'clock to look pretty in front of the cameras and read whatever's put in front of me. Of course, it's not as intellectually demanding as being an English tutor in a former poly.'

Ouch!

'Of course not,' Lee said, leaning towards him, her red wine sloshing in the glass. 'Anyone could write the sort of stuff you tell us about on the news: "A man was ever so slightly injured when he was hit by a yodelling parrot riding a bicycle".'

'Well, at least we're on to the big stories' – laughed Dan – 'which we wouldn't be able to do if we worked your hours.'

'Our hours? What could you possibly mean?' Lee was getting into her pseudo-indignant stride and loving every minute of it.

'Don't work Mondays as you're travelling to university from your bijou cottage in North Yorkshire,' Dan said. 'Do an hour's teaching on Tuesday. Read an improving book for the rest of the day. An hour's lecture on Wednesday and possibly a tutorial, then an hour's lecture on Thursday and bugger off in the afternoon as you've got to get back to the bijou cottage and prepare for Friday's 'research', which, if I'm not mistaken, is usually into some existential nonsense about *The Creativity of the Sense of Soul: Representations of the Skateboarding Duck*.'

'I'll have you know there's a lot of research to be done into skateboarding ducks,' Lee said.

I do believe the girl was flirting.

I looked from her to Dan and back again. I hadn't seen Lee quite so animated in a long time. She was rosy-faced and giggly and enjoying every minute of this encounter. They were clearly playing with each other. Would they make a good couple, I wondered. Lee in her black leggings and faux-denim smock top, clutching an orange straw shoulder bag that she'd bought at the Oxfam shop, her hair in need of a decent cut (again), and an expression of open worship on her face. Dan, meanwhile, was smoothly good looking, and wearing a light-wool Italian suit in a colour that can only be described as pale biscuit, a dark blue T-shirt, and what looked like expensive Hudson antique leather brogues. Not for him, the comfy old slip-ons that Lee preferred. In fact, that was Lee: comfy. You could go to her with any problem and know the encounter would be comfy. There'd be wine supped while sitting on her comfy sofa in the comfy house her dad built for her; there'd be a comforting ear and comfortable words of comfort spoken.

Examining the expression on her face – *is she imaging herself in the arms of Mr Dan Caine?* – I considered whether she'd be good material for a television wife? All those media parties, mixing with the celebrities, spending the vast fortune these telly types earn? Actually, no.

Much as I love her, Lee hasn't so much let herself go as never got hold of herself in the first place.

I've tried to educate her, which I'm totally qualified to do because people tell me I'm good looking and well-dressed with a good figure. I'm not as clever as Lee, I'll give her that, and I'm not saying she's not attractive, in fact she's quite pretty, but she's not exactly knock 'em dead gorgeous, which I suppose you have to be to be married to a well-known television presenter. Or am I being shallow?

And there we were: Lee flirting like crazy with the only half-decent looking man in the room and the only half-decent looking man in the room thinking I'm a mouthy idiot.

I peeled away from Dan and Lee to visit the loo and repair my lippy, and on returning, saw Lee now talking to the floppy-haired guy in the tight black jeans at the other side of the room, and Dan commandeered by Stella Lastings, who was squirming in a girlish way as though she were an insecure six-year-old. I couldn't bear to watch. The alternatives were to join Peter Heron and the *Ridings Today* producer or barge in on Lee and the mystery man. Funnily enough, something about Lee's demeanour stopped me. She was having what looked like an intense conversation with the guy.

Chapter 2

Lee

I didn't need to turn my head to know Teri was staring at me and Declan. She was hurling so many mental exclamation marks it's a wonder we weren't punctured like pincushions. Declan, who was facing in her direction, inclined his head. 'I think someone's trying to attract your attention.'

I glanced backwards. 'Who's he?' Teri mouthed. I raised my eyebrows, surprised she didn't recognise him. Declan's the son of a family friend. Surely she'd bumped into him at one or another Harper shindig? Teri, who's fluent in the language of eyebrows, shook her head. I raised eyebrows again. *How come?* Teri shrugged and gestured: *I don't know.* I considered. Declan's a few years older than me and left town to pursue a career in journalism the summer I turned sixteen, which would've been just before Teri and I met up. So, no, she'd never made his acquaintance over a burnt barbecue sausage or a Christmas bowl of punch.

But Declan O'Brien, who's newly back home as news editor of the *Evening Leader*, was too much of a mouthful to convey silently, so I flapped a hand to indicate *tell you later.*

She blew a kiss and gave a thumbs-up. 'Dreamy.'

Declan grinned at the soundless word play and raised his eyebrows. 'Is that the Meyer girl?'

'Girl?'

He stretched a hand and tugged at a stray lock of my hair, miming a bell pull. 'Ding-dong. Next stop.'

I glowered. Pulling my pigtails had been a favourite childhood trick. My fingers curled into fists, but he shook his head. 'Aren't we a little old to be trading punches?' His eyes narrowed. 'Or do you fancy a playground tussle?' He bunched his hands and, bouncing lightly on the balls of his feet, mimicked a boxer's shuffle. The question mark in his eyes was so provocative it's a miracle I didn't take him down then and there. 'Come on, Lee,' he said. 'You know you never bested me.'

No, but I gave him a bloody nose or two.

He wiped a palm on the seat of his pants and pretended to spit into it. 'Friends,' he offered. Aagh! He'd always known how to push my buttons. His smile was impish, as if relishing the inner struggle between sensible grown-up Lee and the classroom hot head. Teeth gritted, I swiped my hand against his, and he tucked it into the crook of his arm and led me to a seat. 'Why stand when we can sit?'

I leant back into the chair, grateful after a full day of teaching to take the weight off my feet.

'Hungry?' he asked as I nabbed a couple of canapes from a passing waitress and stuffed them into my mouth.

I swallowed. 'Haven't eaten since breakfast. My stomach thinks my throat's been cut.'

With a brusque, 'Wait here,' he rose and pushed his way through the buffet table throng, returning a few minutes later with a plate stacked with doll's house sandwiches and a selection of pastries and mini-quiches hardly big enough to satisfy a starving gnat. 'Best I could do,' he said.

I grabbed the plate greedily.

'Thank you.' He declined an offer to share and went off in search of drinks. 'Something non-alcoholic for me,' I called after him, but he couldn't have heard, or else chose to ignore me, because he returned with two champagne flutes.

'Can't vouch for the quality,' he said.

I hesitated. 'I shouldn't—'

'Go on. Get it down you,' he urged. 'Might make this ghastly event slightly more tolerable.'

It was asking a lot of a small glass of supermarket own-brand fizz.

'Bleurgh!' Declan sounded as if he regretted swallowing his glassful in a single swig. He brushed the back of his hand against his lips. 'Whoever ordered this muck deserves to be shot.' I gestured towards Peter, still schmoozing the TV producer.

'That's your man.'

Declan's face twisted. 'Has he always been a penny-pincher?'

I shrugged. 'Don't know about always. He hasn't been with the university long, but he's a great believer in watching the bottom line.' In fact, it was one of his hobbyhorses as those of us with budget responsibilities were discovering.

Declan considered his glass. 'Maybe a second one will taste better. You want another?' He didn't wait for an answer but loped off again.

'I really shouldn't,' I repeated when he returned with refills, but accepted it anyway, thinking, it's only a small one.

We sat in semi-companionable harmony. 'About the Meyer woman—'

'Not your type.'

'Oh, I don't know,' he said, glancing towards Teri, who, having lost interest in me and Declan, had drifted over to the French windows and was staring into the blackness. Her drooping shoulders suggested she was bored out of her skull. Declan grinned. 'Think she's planning to do a runner?' I'd have said it was a certainty but for the autocue reading media tart who'd joined her in admiring the scenery. Instantly, Teri sprang into dazzle-mode, and from Dan's body language – flat palm pressed against the window frame, legs wide, body half-turned towards her – he'd fallen, hook, line, and sinker.

Chapter 3

Teri

I'd wandered over to the window thinking I'd stare out of it until a polite length of time elapsed and I could leave.

But then I became aware of Dan's reflection in the glass and of him standing behind me.

'You know, I really do more than just read autocue,' he said, adding, 'no, I spend a lot of time in make-up getting tarted up.' That glimmer of a smile. So smug, yet so sexy.

'Look, I'm sorry about earlier,' I said.

'No problem. As I said, people are always making assumptions. It goes with the job. If my viewers see me on holiday or on a day off, they say things like, "You're going to have to run if you're to read the news tonight." Ha ha.'

He looked at his watch. 'Ah,' he said. 'Talking of that, I have to dash. I'm reading the late bulletin. But, hey, why don't you and some of your colleagues come down to the studio in the next couple of weeks and see the programme go out live?'

He grinned as though visiting the TV studios would be the highlight of my year. It would be for Lee and Stella, but the highlight for me would be seeing Dan again. 'That would be lovely,' I said.

'Let me put my secretary's number in your phone. Her name's Doreen – she'll sort out the details.'

I leant in as he concentrated on tapping the keypad and caught a whiff of aftershave – bergamot. Warm and sexy.

He handed back my phone and kissed me on the cheek before striding off.

Chapter 4

Lee

Teri's face as she watched Dan exit the room had the triumphant glint of a cat planning a little light entertainment with a freshly caught field mouse.

Declan whistled. 'What a player.'

'Takes one to know one,' I snapped.

He touched his forehead in a mock salute. 'Can't wait for you to introduce us.'

'You're not her type.'

He snorted. 'And Dan is?' His tone was disbelieving, as if he couldn't imagine a scenario where any woman offered a choice between him and the television presenter would opt for the other fella. He had a point. I might have issues with Declan, but there was no denying his almost feral attractiveness. Unfortunately, Teri would undoubtedly prefer the show-biz attractions of a TV celebrity over those of a jobbing print journo.

Declan's eyes twinkled. He's always been good at reading me. 'Ah, Lee. You don't know what you're missing.'

'And I've no desire to find out.' I sounded prim, even to myself, and Declan, unsurprisingly, guffawed.

'Don't ever change, Lee,' he said. 'You're delightful just as you are.'

Which was about as backhanded a compliment as they come.

'Thank you,' I murmured, and Declan, tearing his gaze from Teri, turned, startled. 'Eh?'

Well, no woman likes it when the guy who's just told her she's 'delightful' starts ogling someone else, so I decided to put him in his place.

'How's Marnie?' I asked. 'And the children?'

He waved airily. 'She's fine. The kids too.'

'So your interest in Teri…'

'Purely professional.'

Oh, yeah. Tell that to the fairies.

'You can't afford her,' I said.

'You don't need money to have fun on a date.' His smirk was almost a mirror image of the one Teri was wearing a minute ago.

'She'll chew you up and spit you out,' I warned, but he wasn't listening. His eyes were fastened on Teri, who, with a welcoming finger waggle, was sashaying towards us. Declan murmured appreciatively but Mike Orme, Peter's deputy, whose timing is as lamentable as his nasty hand-knitted tanks tops, waylaid her.

Declan hooted with laughter. 'Don't tell me that old frog fancies his chances?'

I thought not. It was far more likely he was extolling the virtues of the latest university initiative: *Your Success Starts Here.* Teri's stance – one high-heeled foot tap-tapping the floor and the defensive angle of her wine goblet – suggested it wouldn't be long before she told him where to post his slogan. Probably somewhere he wouldn't like.

Declan threw the remains of his fizz down his throat and stood. 'I'll give you a call,' he said.

'It's okay. I'm good.'

No doubt, I should have gone and circulated, but except for Declan – and possibly Teri's conquest, Him-From-Off-The-Telly – the guests assembled by Peter had less charisma than a thumbprint. So, I stayed put, and pondered the problem I'd been presented with this morning.

'Still here?'

I jumped. Declan was back. 'I don't suppose you have your friend's phone number?'

A daft question, which got the response it deserved. 'I do, but I don't think I should give it to you.'

He frowned. 'Why not?'

'Because…' I spluttered.

'Oh,' he said, comprehending. 'Because I'm married?'

Actually, I didn't give a fig about that. Keeping Declan on the marital straight-and-narrow was Marnie's job, not mine.

Declan raised a hand in surrender. 'Okay, I'll respect your scruples. I'll get her number elsewhere.'

I supposed he would, but…

'And don't keep opening and closing your mouth like that,' Declan chided. 'You resemble a demented goldfish.' And with that, he patted my cheek and walked away. If looks could kill, he wouldn't have made it to the door.

Instead, he was barely halfway across the room before he wheeled and came and sat on his haunches in front of me. 'Forgot to say I was sorry to hear about your granddaddy. He was a nice chap.'

I winked away a tear. It was only a matter of weeks since the funeral, and I was still feeling raw.

Declan cleared his throat and stared at the parquet flooring as I ran a pinky finger under my lashes. He coughed again and thumped my shoulder. 'I'd really better go,' he said, 'or Marnie'll be wondering what I'm up to.'

I'm not sure if he was being ironic.

His words though had stirred a tidal wave of emotions. My stomach slithered to the floor, and I licked my lips, mouth dryer than a Saharan door mat, head pummelled with vivid pictures of probably the worst day of my life. The day I did the stupidest thing in the world and which I'd regretted long before dawn broke on the morning after the night before.

Regret which had doubled, tripled, and quadrupled this morning.

Chapter 5

Teri

Lee was still in conversation with the mystery man, so I stepped in her direction only to find Mike Orme barring my path. Here was a man for whom sombre and formal were not part of the sartorial lexicon. He wore what I soon discovered to be his usual attire of smooth-knit tank top over a white shirt and dark blue trousers.

'Ah, Teri,' he slurred. He'd had too much of the free booze.

'Glad I caught you,' he said, reaching out to place a hand on my arm but, in doing so, slopping red wine down his front. I couldn't help noticing the jumper was pilling quite badly. 'I just wanted to make sure you're okay with the new university initiative…?' he began. '*Your Success Starts Here*,' he added, grinning triumphantly.

I wanted to ask which numbcluck came up with that one, but decided it was probably him and probably diplomatic to just smile sweetly.

'Very good, Mike,' I said. 'I'll try to work it into one of my Rochester lectures.'

'Oh yes… Rochester,' he said. 'Er, I notice you're planning on keeping Rochester in for all levels of students? Do you… er… feel he's still appropriate for…?'

'Sorry, Mike. Got to go. Can we talk about this later?'

Deciding Lee and the mystery bloke could wait, I dashed out to my car, found my mobile, looked up the *Ridings Today* number, rang, and asked for Doreen.

And that's how I found myself two nights later sitting in the gallery of Studio One watching the live transmission of *Ridings Today*, with Dan Caine coolly and smoothly – having been made up like a media tart – reading the news from the autocue.

Chapter 6

Teri

I'd been met at the studio reception by a tarty-looking, middle-aged woman in her mid-fifties, with bright red hair piled high and held in place by a large, tortoiseshell comb. She wore a tight, black skirt (cheap fabric) and a frothy, white blouse (nylon) that exposed an amount of suntanned but crepe-y cleavage. This, I assumed – correctly – was Doreen. I'd spoken to her on the phone to arrange my visit and guessed she and Dan were quite good mates, so I decided to be nice to her. She introduced herself as D'reen and led me to a long, narrow waiting room with the words *Green Room* painted on the door. Once inside, she motioned for me to sit on a brown leather, two-seater sofa on one side of the room, the other one opposite having been taken up by a young man of about sixteen who was sprawled on it, legs wide open in that way men do when they're dominating space. D'reen tottered over to a small table at the top end of the room on which were squatting two large urns.

'Tea… coffee… if you want it.'

'I thought there'd be champagne at least,' I said, grinning at the sprawled young man.

'No, darling,' she said. 'This is *Ridings Today,* not bloody *Newsnight.*' She screeched with laughter and teetered off.

Clutching my plastic container of what turned out to be disgusting coffee, I glanced across at the young man opposite. He was lying back on the sofa with his bum hanging off the edge, his groin slightly uplifted in a tabletop position, and his legs spread wide, exposing the bump of his penis against the cloth of his white tracksuit trousers. His feet, wide apart now, were clad in box-new white trainers.

'Are you just visiting to see how the programme works?' I asked, thinking he was probably on work experience from school.

'Nah, I'm on it,' he said.

'Oh. Why?' I asked. 'Have you got a skateboarding duck?'

He looked at me oddly. 'Nah, luv. I'm a footballer.'

Something began to dawn.

'You're not…?' But before I had time to finish the question, the Green Room door opened, and Dan Caine walked in. He saw me first and smiled.

'Agh. Don't drink the coffee. Great you could come. Nice to see you. Are the others here too?'

And just as I was about to explain, he turned to the footballer. 'Ah. Hi, Shayne. How are you?' And before Shayne had time to shuffle into a more upright position and respond, Dan added, 'We won't be long. They'll come and get you in about ten minutes, if that's okay. I'll ask you a couple of questions about how the season's going. Any injuries. The latest girlfriend. And then a bit about the book. Okay? Great. Lovely. Well done.' And he was gone.

Dan explained later that what with research, rehearsals, and checking the autocue, there never was much time to have a pre-programme chat with guests. 'And anyway, with someone like Shayne, you're not going to get much by way of stimulating conversation. It's not as though I have to do deep research on an eighteen-year-old footballer who's got someone else to write his autobiography.'

'You mean he didn't…?'

'Heavens, no. The boy can't read, let alone write his own name.' Dan laughed.

A bit like some of my students, I thought.

Eventually, in came a girl wearing headphones with a mic attached. She said they were ready for Shayne and he dragged himself upright from the sofa, turned and said, 'See ya,' to me and lolloped off.

A few minutes later, D'reen poked her head round the door. 'D'you want to come into the gallery?'

I followed her into a long, thin, semi-dark area. To my right was a low mixing desk of switches, buttons, and levers and above, a bank of video monitors each showing a different aspect of the studio floor or a freeze frame of some video to be screened later. D'reen motioned for me to sit on a short row of seats on the left, and I lowered myself next to a plumply faced man who was leaning forward to talk to the director seated behind the mixing console. The director had headphones hooked over the back of his head with one earpiece over his right ear and the other on his left cheek. The better, I supposed, to be able to hear what was being said both in the gallery and on the studio floor.

The plumply faced man glanced at me and smiled.

'Hello, I'm Richard Walker,' he said, offering his hand. It was gloomy and I couldn't see properly yet, but I made out his hair, which had been gelled into a little peak at the top of his forehead. Very boyish, but not a good look on a man his age.

'I'm Teri…' But I didn't have time to finish because the director, who'd obviously heard something through his headphones, shouted 'Aw… shit!' and Richard Walker smiled in apology and leapt up to move closer to him to see what the fuss was about. D'reen, who'd plonked herself down on my right, pointed out who everyone was: the director, the PA, the sound controller, the vision mixer, and the autocue operator.

Then, the director shouted to everyone and no one in particular, 'We'll have to go without it,' and I assumed some top-of-the-news report had failed to arrive and they were going to have to lead on a skating duck story.

The transmission went by in a mad confusion of shouted instructions.

'Roll ident… coming to Camera 1 in 30 seconds. Camera 2 ready with the close shot. Fifteen seconds to the interview. Take Camera 3. Have we got the item…? Where's the fucking item? Ten seconds to caption… no, that isn't Chief Superintendent bloody Fisher, it's the bloody victim's mother. Where's the right caption? Aagh. Too late, she's gone… Next caption in five seconds. NO! That's the wrong fucking caption, AGAIN. Camera 3… Camera 3? What the fuck are you doing? I don't want a shot up his nostrils – back off… Ten seconds to the break… wind it up, Dan… wind it up…'

Not entirely sure which of the monitors on the bank above the gallery desk to watch, I plumped for whichever featured Dan. He was hearing all the instructions, all the swearing, all the panic through his earpiece, but you wouldn't think it to see him at work. He was so cool.

'It must be confusing,' I said when we met back in the Green Room after he'd washed the make-up off his face.

'It's all part of the job,' he said. 'Goes with reading the autocue.'

He had an after-programme post-mortem to attend that evening, but suggested we have a meal together at the end of the week and I could tell him what I thought of his performance. We agreed he'd pick me up on Friday.

'Anywhere you'd like to go?' he asked.

'Where do you telly types normally eat?'

'Well, I like L'homme-vert,' he said. 'Let's treat ourselves and go there. I'll book,' he added.

I wasn't sure if I should be treating myself at L'homme-vert, one of the priciest places in Yorkshire. I didn't mind spending, but my allowance from Dad was late arriving that month, and I wasn't sure if my lecturer's salary would cover the cost. I looked around for Shayne, who likely earned more in a week than I earned in a year, wondering if he might sub me. Dan must have seen the look on my face.

'Don't worry,' he said. 'It's my birthday on Friday, so it'll be my treat.'

Chapter 7

Lee

You've got to admire Teri's chutzpah. If I'd been caught going behind my best friend's back and deliberately not telling her about a backstage TV studio tour to which she'd specifically been invited, I'd have floundered in a morass of 'umming' and 'erring' and abject apologies. Teri, however, takes the moral high ground. 'I thought it would be a marvelous opportunity to interrogate the language of the news media.' She spoke with the sort of confident authority that brooked no denial. Stella Lastings, who'd joined us for coffee in the Senior Common Room, blinked, and Teri rushed to clarify. 'I'm developing a new linguistics learning unit on the ways in which language tolerates and creates multiple synonymy.' Stella, a historian rather than a linguist, blinked again so Teri added further explanation. 'It's to do with the way different words fulfil the same linguistic function.'

I'm not sure Stella felt any the wiser. Personally, I was impressed with Teri's mastery of the grammar of whichever lexicon she'd mined for her linguistical mumbo-jumbo.

'Very erudite,' I murmured, and Teri's gaze flickered in my direction.

'I did wonder about asking if you'd like to come along too,' she said.

'You did?'

Teri stared me down. 'But I didn't think it would be your cup of tea.'

'No?'

Teri glowered. She hates it when anyone questions her good intentions. Fortunately, Stella Lastings isn't fluent in Teri-speak, so she took the semi-apology at face value. 'Well, of course, I wouldn't have passed up on the opportunity to spend an evening in the company of Mr Dan Caine.' She simpered ever so slightly, and the expression on Teri's face shifted from annoyance to irritation. Stella, seemingly oblivious to the toe-curling effect she was having, continued, 'Mind you, I think I'd have preferred something more intimate.' She chuckled and Teri rolled her eyes. Stella leant forward, and, voice dripping with suggestion, begged, 'Now, spill the beans. What happened when the cameras stopped rolling?' Teri flinched.

'There's nothing really to tell—'

Stella wagged a finger. 'No, no, no. Two attractive people like you?'

Ignoring Teri's almost comical look of appeal, I rose. 'I'm afraid, I'll have to catch-up later. Things to do and stuff.'

'Wait,' Teri implored. 'I need to talk to you about…' She paused, unable to think of anything of sufficiently pressing importance to deflect Stella's leery attention.

I gave her a malicious grin. 'About the new linguistics unit?' I suggested. 'Looking forward to it.'

'Oh, thanks,' I said, laughing. 'You mean I'd get the job because I'm the only one around doing any research?'

'Something like that,' she said.

Frankly, if she thought that was all I had to offer I wondered why she'd mentioned the job in the first place, but, since I'm a great believer in letting bygones be bygones, I said nothing, and, of course, I got the job. But then, was it ever in doubt?

Chapter 9

Lee

One of the core tenets of Peter Heron's management philosophy is that good managers don't hide themselves away in ivory towers. He tells us this at almost every departmental meeting and uses it as his justification for what he calls 'walking the floor' and which the rest of us define as 'trying to catch us out'. I'd also question what constitutes an ivory tower since, if I ever get the chance to work in one, I'd certainly want a reception lobby, private bathroom, smoked glass tinted windows, and plush carpeted floors. I'd probably pass on marble busts of Julius Caesar and Plato, though.

It's hard to know what benefits Peter reaps from his prowling but there's been one positive effect, Teri and I know the location of every ladies' washroom on the campus and use them as a refuge as often as necessary.

'Gosh,' Teri said, on one occasion when we found ourselves hiding at the same time. 'This reminds me of when we first met at sixth-form college and we used to creep into the bogs for a crafty fag.'

'You were smoking,' I pointed out. 'I was—'

'Aiding and abetting,' Teri supplied.

Of course, in those days Crofty, the school janitor, had no scruples about invading the allegedly female only zone to check for miscreants. Peter, on the other hand, simply lurked outside until necessity forced escapees to break ground. Like now…

'Hello, Lee,' he said.

Damn and blast. 'Peter. What can I do for you?' I've learnt to take the initiative. It wrong foots him if he's on the grumble.

'I've spent the morning with HR.'

Bet that'd been fun.

'Staff development and review time.'

I frowned. 'Already?' The annual review process usually began after Easter and dragged on until the start of the autumn semester – which was only just drawing to a close.

Peter nodded. 'New starters only. The people who didn't join us in time to take part in the opportunity to reflect and engage and set targets.'

Which, all credit to Peter, was putting an incredibly positive spin on what I'd always regarded as a box ticking exercise, designed by managerial flunkies to irritate the hell out of people like me trying to get some real work done.

'So,' he continued, 'HR will be emailing you a timetable later today, and I'd like everything wrapped up before Christmas.' He nodded briskly. 'Any questions?'

Yes, loads, but he was already striding back down the corridor. He paused just before turning the corner. 'And when you sit down with Ms

Meyer, don't forget to ask her about the AEE bursary. Things have gone very quiet on that front.'

Chapter 10

Teri

It's not often I feel a shred of fellow feeling with Peter, but the chagrin he's suffering over the lack of positive vibes from the *Ridings Today* producer is not dissimilar to my feelings about my failed bursary application. After three months without hearing anything, and prompted by Lee, I rang the AEE only to be told the money had been awarded to someone else two months previously and had I not been told? The stupid pricks apparently missed my email telling them I'd transferred to the University of Central Yorkshire and had written to me at Mid-Wharfevale instead. I was sure I'd emailed them when I changed jobs.

It was galling. But I took comfort from the knowledge that the cock-up had been theirs and not mine – unlike Peter, whose failure boils down to his inability to 'sell' himself and his proposal.

Also, unlike Peter, I don't keep rabbiting on about my disappointment. 'I don't think the producer understood the concept of what I was suggesting, which was to negotiate the intellectual motif of the modern novel through the salon of the twenty-first century digital medium,' he told Lee and I in the Senior Common Room.

'He simply didn't understand the nature of the modern-day academic logographer. He kept talking about reality television and *Harry Potter*,' Peter said. 'And have you heard of a footballer called Shayne Brickham? Plays for Wakefield, apparently, and he's the next best hope for English football and, he's written his autobiography. For goodness' sake! He's only eighteen. What the hell has he got to say?' He paused, then went on, 'However, all is not lost. The producer was just the start. I'm having lunch with the MD of *Ridings Today*. Then we'll find out what's what – and it won't be silver balls, Brickham.'

It's to be hoped what's what is everything Peter hopes it will be, since I don't think I can take much more of his moaning. Of course, I'm in a much stronger position than he is since there's bound to be another bursary somewhere along the way, while, though he refuses to admit it, his television boat has well and truly sailed.

Meanwhile, I have my dinner date with Dan to prepare for.

Chapter 11

Lee

Sometimes I think Teri has the brain of a cheese sandwich – without the butter.

'Oh no,' she said, stirring droplets of cold water into her black coffee. 'Peter Heron isn't going to sack me because of a trifling administrative error.'

She sipped her drink and added a soupçon more water. 'What?' Her eyebrows arched. 'Why are you staring at me like that?'

'Administrative error?'

'It's the only explanation.' She leant forward, lips pursed. 'I know everybody at the university thinks very highly of the AEE…' Her tone implied she didn't share this opinion. 'But I had a few queries about the application process and the flunky they've got doing the admin, Deidre-Somebody-Or-Other, was absolutely hopeless.'

She was referring to Deirdre O'Connell, senior director, and founder member of the research body, who's renowned for her efficiency and attention to detail.

I shook my head. 'That doesn't sound like Deirdre.'

Teri shrugged. 'Proof's in the pudding. I left several messages, and she never got back to me once.'

It was my turn to purse my lips. Could Teri be right? Had there been an AEE mix-up? It'd temper Peter's fury at the loss of a very generous bursary if he could lay the blame at Deirdre's door. There's no love lost between them – he's the sort of man who's uncomfortable around forthright, opinionated females, and she's not known for suffering fools gladly.

Or even at all.

Teri was counting off on her fingers. 'I had several questions about presentation. What typeface? Font size? Line spacing and—'

I raised a hand.

These were the sort of low-level trivia that would all have been outlined in the application form small print.

Teri stiffened. 'I'm serious. These things matter. I know you don't care about appearances…'

Her eyes drifted to my purple leather ankle boots with their black laces and rubber soles. 'But we don't all think like you.'

Evidently not.

'So, what happens now?' she asked.

I stirred my coffee and wondered, not for the first time, why Teri always ignored my requests for a 'weak Earl Grey tea, lemon, no milk', and brought a café au lait instead.

I raised the cup to my mouth, inhaled the sour lactose aroma and lowered it untouched.

'Just one question: what *exactly* did Deirdre say that made you think the bursary was a done deal?'

She frowned. 'Well—'

'Well?'

Nothing, it transpired.

Chapter 12

Teri

I suppose I should feel guilty about not inviting Lee and Stella Lastings to the TV studios. But if I had, would Dan have asked me out?

The thought of wearing a new little black dress to L'homme-vert with gorgeous Dan Caine put aside any qualms – and any disappointment about the wretched bursary.

On Friday, the doorbell rang on the dot at 7.30 p.m.

And then… my life crumbled.

I'd rushed in from work, waxed, plucked, pedicured, manicured, and dressed. I was ready. And so was Dan, but not for L'homme-vert judging by his T-shirt, chinos, and trainers.

'Ah,' he said, eyeing me up, and down. 'You look great… but… didn't you get my message?'

I looked at the hall table where I throw my keys and phone, and my mobile was showing a message sign. Must have arrived while I was in the shower.

'Change of plan,' Dan said. 'We're going bowling.'

I stared at him.

'My daughter, Victoria, wanted to help celebrate my birthday,' Dan said. 'But she doesn't like L'homme-vert… wanted to do something a bit more active. Hope you don't mind. Won't take you long to change, will it?'

When I reached his car, having put on jeans and a sweatshirt, there was what looked like a teenage girl with long blonde hair sitting in the front passenger seat.

Questions raced through my mind. Not least, is he married? Does he have any more bloody children?

Dan motioned the girl to get out and into the back. She didn't budge.

'It's okay,' I trilled. 'I'll get in the back.'

The girl didn't look round.

'This is Victoria,' Dan said, climbing into the driver's seat.

'Oh. Hi, Toria,' I said, pulling myself upright by clutching the back of her headrest and heaving.

'It's VIC… toria,' she said, not turning round, but bouncing slightly with the force of my pull.

'Not Toria, Vicky, or Vickers?' I asked.

She gave a theatrical shrug, as though my pulling on her headrest had unsettled her entire equilibrium.

My attempt at conversation proceeded along these lines for the rest of the evening although the noise of the bowling alley – with the clattering of falling pins, the loud piped music, and the cheering of teams when one of them made a strike – meant any conversation was difficult.

I'd had a go at ten-pin bowling before, but thought it might be a good move to pretend I hadn't, which allowed Dan to help me.

Letting him help involved him moving up close behind and putting his arms around me so he could manoeuvre his hands over mine. I only had to lean back slightly to feel the strength in his chest as he braced himself to hold me. I glanced out of the corner of my eye to see Victoria gazing heavenwards.

I hoisted the ball into position and set off towards the lane.

Above the din, I thought I heard Victoria mutter, 'Oh, for God's sake.' Then I swung my arm back and then forwards, like a pendulum, releasing the ball. It went spinning onto the lane where it bounced once and shot into the gutter.

'Oh. Bad luck!' Victoria said, looking as though she was enjoying herself for the first time.

My game didn't improve, but I enjoyed Dan's personal coaching. When he disappeared off to the loo, play was temporarily suspended, and I sat down beside Victoria.

'Have you got any brothers and sisters?' I asked.

'No.'

Phew.

'Do you like bowling?'

'It's something to do,' she said, shrugging dismissively. 'You don't mind if I want to spend time with my daddy, do you?'

I was beginning to get a sense of something.

Over the course of the evening, I learnt more about Dan. He'd been married but divorced his wife, Sara, two years ago when Victoria was thirteen. Since then, she'd lived with her mother and spent weekends with her father.

I didn't hear from Dan over the next couple of days despite texting to thank him for a 'fabulous' evening's bowling. So I assumed he was with the wretched girl and didn't have time for a new love interest. His loss.

Chapter 13

Lee

Agreeing to meet Teri for lunch on Sunday was a mistake. I'd thought it'd be easier in the relaxed surroundings of the King's Hotel to explain how the lost bursary might impact on her long-term future with the University of Central Yorkshire. But, no, Teri's head was still ten-pin bowling with Dan Caine – and daughter – and every barbed taunt and sly grin from the Devil child had to be explored in minute and excruciating detail. Inevitably, my mind started wandering.

'You're looking peaky,' Teri interrupted her monologue to observe.

'I didn't sleep very well last night,' I mumbled. Or the night before or the night before or… In fact, not since the morning of Peter's network event when it became clear my period wasn't just late but on a nine-month sabbatical.

'Oh dear,' Teri murmured, pulling her tote onto her knee and rummaging in its depths. 'Ta da!' she exclaimed, pressing a small bottle of something green and greasy into my hands. 'Lavender and eucalyptus oil. Works a treat. Calming and soothing. I use it all the time.'

'And it calms and soothes you?' The passionate vitriol with which she'd been dissecting the character and motivation of the Devil's daughter suggested a stronger dose was required.

'Of course,' she said. 'A couple of drops on your temples, and behind your ears at bedtime and you'll sleep like a log. Now' – she returned to the main topic of conversation – 'What would you have done if your date had turned up with a sulky teenager in tow?'

In Teri's place, I'd have questioned his sanity. Or his origins. Only someone from another planet could look at Teri in her designer shoes and Harvey Nick's garb and think she'd be a sneakers and bowling alley kind of woman.

'I'm still trying to get my head around the fact that you didn't tell him to sling his hook,' I said.

'I thought about it,' she admitted.

But, presumably, didn't, because, though no more than ordinarily good looking, Dan was swathed in a media sheen that spoke of power and privilege and celebrity – a natural métier for the daughter of a millionaire father and a society mother. Neither of whom, by the way, cared for Teri, or each other, as much as they cared for themselves.

'So, what next?'

I'd expected her to say that Dan had re-booked at L'homme-vert – it would have been the decent thing to do – but, no, she was as slippery as a watermelon seed on that one. Which meant nothing had been arranged, and he hadn't telephoned, and she was terrified he wouldn't.

Sometimes men are more flippin' trouble than they're worth. Mike Orme, Peter Heron's number two, is a case in point. Just because we got a trifle convivial at Granddaddy's funeral, he's convinced we're on the High Road to bosom-buddyhood and is constantly suggesting after-work drinks. Mate – I'd rather shave my eyeballs.

Chapter 14

Teri

Lee wasn't as supportive as I thought she could have been. 'Tricky age,' she said when I told her about Victoria's manoeuvrings.

Lee's always played it patiently and reasonably when I've felt strongly about something. When we first met at sixth-form college, she was the first girl to show me any friendship. To be honest, she was the only girl to show me any friendship. I'd come from out of town – North Yorkshire – where we'd lived in a massive country house and I suppose the other girls were jealous. Lee was a quiet thing, a bit plump and mousy, but I pulled her out of her shell. I encouraged her to cut her hair, buy new clothes, and come out with me looking for boys (shame it doesn't work as well now we're older).

We had fun, but there was always that patient reasonableness holding Lee back; as if she was ever so slightly disapproving whenever I suggested doing something exciting or daring.

Her Catholic upbringing, I suppose.

Although her dad is the Harper of Harper's Homes Property Development and her parents have a five-bedroom place in the Alderwood area with a couple of Mercs outside, Lee's never really shed her Irish-Catholic mentality; that chip on her shoulder about being an 'outsider'.

Thinking about what she'd just said, I replied, 'Any age is tricky where children are concerned.'

The truth is, I've never liked children; never wanted any myself. I'm not one of those yummy mummies who feel the maternal pull to be surrounded by designer-clad munchkins. I think children get in the way of your career; they're selfish, costly, and not worth the effort.

Lee'd laughed. 'Typical. A woman who hates kids ends up with a man who has a clingy, possessive teenager.'

'Excuse me. We've had one date – if you can call it a date. We're not exactly ending up together. Anyway, Dan tells me the brat'll be off to university soon, so she'll be off his hands for good.'

Lee looked at me in that way she does when she knows what I'm saying is doubtful but she hasn't the heart to point it out. 'You'd feel differently if you had children of your own. You'd understand,' she said.

What was there to understand? If I'd had kids, they wouldn't be as greedy and self-centred as Victoria. I glared at the phone, stubbornly refusing to ring him. Perhaps it was for the best. If I were to have a relationship with Dan, I'd have a fight on my hands. It'd be like something out of a cheap movie: spoilt daughter making life misery for Daddy's new girlfriend because she wants her parents to get back together and play happy families.

Damn you, phone, I thought. RING!

Chapter 15

Lee

Sunday's attempt to get Teri to consider next steps on the research road was more successful than I'd realised. Because, when I popped into her office mid-afternoon on Monday, her first words were to ask if 'just for now' I'd keep schtum about the lost bursary. 'Of course, I'll have to tell Peter eventually,' she said. 'But I've got a few other research irons in the fire, so I'll hold off until they come through.'

Under questioning, she eventually conceded she hadn't actually submitted any further applications 'but was going to, just as soon as she had a moment'.

Hell's bells and buckets of tripe! Didn't she realise the pickle she was in? Judging by the furrows creasing her brow, the answer was 'no'. So I sat down and explained the terms and conditions of her contract, which was time-limited, and conditional on acquisition of the AEE grant. Without it, Peter could legitimately dispense with her services without fear of comeback.

'Oh!' There was a long pause. Presumably she was processing the information, and then she found a straw to clutch. 'But you said the temporary contract was for two years, so that means' – she counted on her fingers – 'I've got around twenty months to find an alternative income stream.'

Possibly. Always assuming, of course, she could find it, and that Peter could be persuaded to give her time to do so. Stranger things have happened.

Teri drained the coffee, which had been catching cold on her desk. It appeared to fuel her thought processes, because her eyes suddenly sparkled. 'Perhaps I can persuade Pops to invest in a research bursary.' Her eyes glowed. 'The Terence Minghella Meyer award.'

It had a nice ring to it, but it was hard to share Teri's faith in her father's altruism. 'Pops will come up good,' she asserted, digging in her tote for her mobile.

Unfortunately, her dad wasted no time in bursting her 'airy-fairy Terence Minghella Meyer bubble'. There'd be no money from him.

'Pops…' Teri protested, but he'd already ended the conversation, and when she redialled his number, it was engaged.

She hurled the phone into her bag. 'So,' she said. 'What do you suggest now?'

I hesitated.

Suggestion number one – quit – went down like a lead balloon. 'No,' she said. 'I'm not going to be forced out because Deirdre O'Connell said one thing and meant another.'

I sighed. Life was too short to try to convince her she was the one who'd got things wrong. Instead, I outlined a possible lifeline – an invitation to join my online learning research group. She was less than underwhelmed. 'It'd be too weird.'

How? Why?

'You being my boss.'

Poor innocent, I thought. As the department's head of teaching and learning, I was already her boss. But best not to over-egg the point, since she'd had a lot to take in already.

She sat in silence, tap-tapping a fingernail against the empty coffee mug. 'I'll do it,' she said, slapping the desktop with a flat palm. 'It'll show the lot of them – Deirdre, Peter, and Pops – there's more to me than they think.' She stared moodily out of the window, absently reaching out a hand towards the ringing landline. 'Hello,' she barked. Then a smile lit her face. 'Hello,' she said again, her voice caressing the phone. No prizes for guessing the identity of the caller or that she'd be a lost cause for what remained of the working day. I mouthed, 'Speak later,' and left, wondering just what it'd take to persuade Peter to see the serious academic researcher disguised in high heels and designer dresses.

Always assuming there was one.

Chapter 16

Teri

Dan was full of apologies. He'd lost his mobile in which he'd keyed my number. He'd had to ring me at work; he hoped I didn't mind. Mind? I was absolutely delighted and suggested a drink after work, and we met in a local wine bar after he'd presented that evening's programme. We were just settling down with a nicely chilled bottle of French white when his mobile beeped with a text message.

'Oh,' I said, eyeing it suspiciously. 'You found your mobile?'

'Oh, yes,' Dan replied. 'Funny thing. It was right there on the coffee table where I usually leave it – under a pile of newspapers. I'd obviously not looked properly.'

He looked at the text, smiled, and started to text something back.

'Excuse me a second,' he said, tapping. 'It's Victoria. She wants to know what I'm doing this evening.' He tapped some more, reading out the words as he keyed them in. *Having. Drink. With. Gorgeous. Lady… x*

I liked the 'gorgeous' but I wasn't sure about Dan having to check in with his daughter. And I wasn't sure that mobile phones went missing on their own and then turned up in the same place you left them.

'Was Victoria staying with you this weekend?' I asked.

'Yes, she was. Took her shopping on Saturday and then to a movie she wanted to see. We spent yesterday chilling.'

Yes, all right. That's enough about father-daughter bonding.

We drank our bottle and then another and then took a taxi back to my duplex.

The rest of the night should've been magical.

I opened a bottle of red wine. Dan sat on the sofa and I set two glasses on the coffee table and flopped beside him. We joked about skateboarding ducks, and I punched him playfully on the arm and teased him about being a famous face *off t'telly*. We drank some more. He became serious and leant towards me.

'I hope I'm getting the right impression here…' he said.

'You are.' I breathed.

'Because I don't want you to think I'm taking advantage.'

Oh, take advantage, I thought.

He pulled me to him and kissed me on the mouth, moving his lips slowly, carefully, pulling me in.

'Come with me,' I said, standing and holding out my hand.

We went into the bedroom and somehow became nervous with each other again. We play-fought while helping each other undress, then fell onto the bed. Dan raised himself on to an elbow and leant across and over me.

This is where the lights should have dimmed, and soft music played. But Dan was unable to get an erection.

'I need a fluffer,' he joked.

'A what?'

'A woman who'll come and get things moving… a fluffer. They use fluffers for magazine shoots when they're taking pictures of naked men and they don't want a full erection but need more than a damp squib.'

'Fetch me half a dozen fluffers,' I teased.

We tried again, but to no effect. Dan tentatively suggested he'd had too much to drink and couldn't we just cuddle instead? So we did and fell asleep in each other's arms.

In the morning, Dan awoke with a hard-on, so we started to use it rather than lose it. But as he was getting into his stride, thrusting with determined firmness, small droplets of blood appeared on my naked breasts; one or two and then larger drops. I squirmed.

Dan looked down. 'Oh my God!' he yelped, pulling back sharply and out from between my legs. He leapt off the bed and rushed naked into the bathroom. 'Aagh. I'm bleeding… I'm bleeding.' He was almost hysterical.

I pulled on my dressing gown and stood in the doorway. 'It's only a nosebleed,' I tried to reassure him.

He emerged with a torn twist of toilet paper jammed up each nostril, his face white and his eyes darting from side to side clearly considering whether I was the sort of person who'd call an ambulance or leave him to bleed to death on my bathroom floor. I took in the sight of a naked Dan Caine, head back with mouth open in a silent scream, nose jammed with tissue slowly becoming wet and red, his penis, not so much a damp squib as a limp squid, and looking as sorry, and dejected as its owner looked pale and frightened.

Once the bleeding stopped, Dan was reticent about trying to make love again.

'It must've been first night's nerves,' he said. 'Never happened to me before.'

I wasn't sure if he meant the nosebleed or the sexual no-show.

We tried again the following night, but still Dan couldn't get an erection.

He pulled away from me and sat, head in hands, on the edge of the bed.

'I'm sorry, Teri,' he said. 'I don't know what's wrong.'

I'd never known a man with this problem: what's wrong with him? For a nanosecond, I wondered if there was something I was doing, or not doing, that might be a cause. But I dismissed the idea. Heavens, I thought, I've never had problems with men and sex. I normally click my fingers and they come running, trouser zips at the ready.

Dan took himself off to the GP to make sure he wasn't suffering from an incurable man-disease. 'The doc thinks it's psychological,' he told me later.

'Psychological?' I repeated. 'What, you mean you're mentally scarred or something?'

'Well,' said Dan. 'Could be.'

'By me?'

He reached out. We were sitting on the sofa in my living room, a bottle of white wine on the coffee table in front of us and two filled glasses. But neither of us was drinking. He reached out and put his hand on my arm.

'Not you, Teri. My ex.'

The delightful, maintenance-spending Sara who'd spawned the wretched, interfering little bitch-child Victoria.

In a way, I was pleased to hear the ex-wife was the cause of concern.

In another way, I wondered if I had time and patience for all this; *this* being a situation which was going to need careful handling and what would probably turn out to be expensive sex therapy. And I decided I wasn't going into any sessions in the sex department, as *I* definitely didn't need them.

Dan started to tell me about Sara. She was a class act: a blonde-haired secretary to one of the managing directors of a local radio station where Dan had started out as a reporter. The poor sap had fallen for her charms, which involved large tits, shapely legs, and few brain cells, and she'd fallen pregnant with the Devil child, so they'd married in haste.

Sara urged Dan to leave the radio station and try his hand at TV because she fancied the bright lights and bigger pay packet that telly journalists could provide. She also wanted to pack in her own job and become a woman who lunched.

She turned out to be a grasping, pushy wife and mother who constantly found new ways to spend money: bigger house, softer furnishings, riding lessons, and then a pony for Victoria, far-flung exotic holidays, and the designer wardrobe to meet all occasions for both her and her daughter.

Now, while I don't object to anyone wanting the finer things in life, I didn't like the sound of the manipulation being played out by the Ms Caines.

Dan didn't put it all quite like that; he's far too nice. But I read between the lines and out of the gaps popped a nasty, grasping wife who dominated her husband, laughed at his mistakes, pointed out his weaknesses, and assumed credit for his successes.

Worse, she used sex as her bean counter. They only had it if she was in the mood (which had to be good, and her good moods were linked to being able to look forward to something luxurious and expensive). When Victoria was about ten, they palmed her off on Sara's mother for the night and went off to stay in one of the Denbyside Hotel's most expensive suites to celebrate their anniversary. Dan reasoned that the pampering would put Sara in a good mood – and good mood spelt sex.

Sara fell pregnant with what was to be a little brother or sister for Victoria. But then she lost the baby at eight weeks and refused to have sex again.

'So you've not had sex for…' I was about to say but thought better of doing the maths, as the poor love had had enough humiliation to last him a lifetime.

'Oh, you poor darling,' I crooned, pulling his head down onto my shoulder. He leant against me, nuzzling my neck. I kissed the top of his head, and he moved closer, pressing himself against me. I slid sideways back into the sofa, pulling Dan with me. He kissed me, tentatively at first, and then in a sudden burst of passion he seemed to come alive and kissed me so fiercely and passionately I knew we might not need those therapy sessions.

Sure enough and urgently, he started clawing at my shirt, managing to dislodge two buttons and thrusting his hand inside to fondle my left breast while I reached between his legs.

Okay, I thought, feeling the confidence stirring inside Dan's trousers, cancel the fluffer.

Chapter 17

Lee

If Teri has a fault – what do I mean if? – it's a tendency to overshare. I've got this far through life without knowing a single thing about fluffers and would have been content to spend the rest in happy ignorance. Same goes for Dan's erectile dysfunction issues and nose bleeds. 'Really, Teri,' I said, holding up a hand in an attempt to silence her. 'Too much information.'

She raised her eyebrows. 'Don't you think it's good we're working through our problems?'

'Of course, but could you skip some of the finer details?'

Her eyes narrowed. 'You're jealous.'

'Of what?'

'Me and Dan.'

'What on Earth, makes you think—'

'I saw the way you were flirting with him at Peter's event.' Her voice had the slightest of wobbles. 'I bet you wish it was you in his bed.'

For a nanosecond, I wondered if she was right, since there'd definitely been an initial attraction. But, no, Teri's description of a stark-naked Dan, chest streaked with blood, and two plugs of toilet tissue wedged up his nostrils, was indelibly etched on my memory. I'd never look at him in quite the same way again.

'No.'

'No?' She sounded incredulous.

'No,' I repeated. 'Nice bloke, but not my type.'

Her eyes widened. 'But—'

'Yes, yes,' I interrupted, hoping to forestall another litany of Dan's wonderfulness.

She pursed her lips, head cocked slightly to one side as if trying to work something out. She sighed. 'I just don't understand you. If you're not attracted to someone like Dan…' She halted, as if searching for the words to describe the full extent of his magnificence.

Apparently, the task was beyond her because she changed tack. 'So, what sort of bloke *do* you like?'

Good question, and one I'd never really resolved, in spite of – or, perhaps, because of – the efforts Teri'd made over the years to hook me up with what she considered suitable candidates. Perhaps that was it: the chaps *I* liked weren't the ones Teri thought I *ought* to like – in other words, the polished men-of-the-world types she preferred. Considering how long we'd known each other, what did that say about how she saw me? I frowned, not quite sure where my musings were leading. Teri coughed. 'Er, are you going to answer my question?' No, because if I told her what I'd just been thinking she'd take offence and the alternative answer – almost anyone but the chap who'd knocked me up – made my stomach heave. 'Got to go,' I blurted before heading for the nearest washroom with a turn of speed that would've done credit to an Olympic sprinter.

'Wait,' Teri cried. 'Just tell me it isn't the newspaperman, because, honestly, Lee, you're just not the sort to get involved with a married man.'

Too late, I'd already done it.

Chapter 18

Teri

After our romantic tangle on the sofa, I was confident things could only get better between Dan and me. He had a lot of baggage, but now it was out in the open, we could move forward.

After what I came to think of as the confessional therapy session (I could've charged Dan for curing him), he and I spent the next couple of nights together 'just to cement progress' as Dan put it. Having found a new spring in his step, he didn't want anything to trip him up. He was on a roll and I was rolling with him.

I should've been more alert. Things had been quiet on the Victoria front. I was basking in a highly charged and passionate relationship with a handsome man but had forgotten to listen to that quiet little voice at the back of my brain saying, *Where's the kid gone?*

We'd been seeing each other for exactly a fortnight, and I decided to celebrate – not with an expensive meal at a high-end restaurant (I'm aware that's what the delightful Sara would've done) – but by cooking Dan a meal, lighting the candles, lowering the lights, and letting nature take its course.

All was going well. Dan arrived straight from the programme. He still had traces of make-up on his face.

The meal went well. The candles burnt softly. We took our brandies to the sofa and settled back. Then Dan's mobile rang. I murmured for him to leave it, but he said it might be important and moved perhaps a little too swiftly to answer it.

'Ah, hello, darling. You're back,' he said. Darling? Back?

'What? Tonight?' he continued. 'Well… well, yes, okay, then. I'm with Teri at the moment, but I'm sure she won't mind.'

Turns out Victoria had been to a health spa with Mummy, and they'd just got back, and Victoria was missing Daddy and would Daddy pop round to see her and say 'nighty-night'.

'You don't mind, do you?' he asked.

****

'What on Earth did you say?' Lee asked the next day.

'Well, I could hardly say I did mind,' I told her. 'I couldn't stop him from going to see his kid.'

'There's going to have to be some big compromises if you're going to keep seeing Dan,' Lee said, looking at me in that concerned way she has.

'I can do compromise,' I said. 'And I'll win – watch me.'

But Victoria and Dan didn't do compromise, and by the time I realised that it was too late. I'd fallen for Dan and convinced myself I could wean him away from the clingy kid. But as Lee so often pointed out, I didn't have kids, so didn't understand the pull of the little beggars. And nor did I appreciate that as well as loving his kid, Dan loved his work.

It was two against one.

But then I'm nothing if not up for a fight. I was determined; Dan and I were going to be an exclusive item.

When he invited me to the Royal Television Society annual awards dinner, I knew I'd cracked it. He wouldn't take someone to a work's bash he wasn't serious about.

Chapter 19

Lee

Peter's voice could have taught icicles a thing or two about being chilly. 'And you think inviting Ms Meyer to join your research group is a good idea?'

Yes, I did. She might have rubbed a few staff members up the wrong way, but it was standing room only in her lectures – something that couldn't be said for many of our colleagues. 'She had a positive effect on last semester's student engagement survey,' I said.

Peter's lips compressed as if it'd kill him to acknowledge the justice of this observation.

'I've spoken to Deirdre,' I said, interrupting the relentless drumming of his fingertips.

'And?'

'She said Teri's application had potential.'

'Really?'

'Oh, yes. She said Teri's synopsis showed real scholarly intent.'

No need to add that she'd described the accompanying literature review as weak and the methodology as sloppy, since, knowing Teri, she'd have been so convinced the AEE grant was in the bag she'd have cut a few corners. And there'd be no corner-cutting on my watch.

'And you want her on your team because—'

I chose to misunderstand. Peter's easier to deal with when he's feeling rattled. 'Deirdre?'

He frowned. 'Deirdre? Don't be ridiculous.'

'You think I'm ridiculous?'

He winced. 'No. No. No. Not at all.'

'So?'

His tongue slithered across his bottom lip. 'I just—'

I waited while Peter took a long breath and tried again. 'Ms Meyer is not always respectful of university protocol.'

'She struggles with the red tape,' I offered. 'The university's systems and procedures aren't always intuitive.'

In fact, they're usually in triplicate, and often impenetrable.

'Hmmm.' Peter, who'd joined the university with a mission to 'look under the bonnet and more effectively operationalise the day-to-day running of the business', had had his own battles with the 'this-is-the-way-we've-always-done-things' brigade.

Still, the sense of fellowship didn't necessarily make Teri more endearing. 'Her teaching style is not what you might call conventional,' he grumbled.

Yes, and that's why students loved her, and also why I was determined to get her this research gig so Peter had no excuse to let her go. Peter, in his starched shirts, sharp suits and polished brogues was convention personified, and when he 'dropped in' on one of her early lectures, he'd been as uncomfortable as a fox in high heels. I'd been there too – it's part of my job to work with newbie lecturers to develop their teaching – but Peter just likes to show who's boss. He calls it 'rallying the troops'. I call it being a douche.

Teri'd strolled into the lecture theatre and, lolling against the front-of-stage lectern, asked the assembled first-year students what they knew about war hero poet John Wilmot? The students exchanged puzzled glances.

'Was he a Battle of Britain fighter pilot?' ventured one.

'Did he serve in the trenches in World War One?' suggested another.

'No, no,' Teri'd said. 'He was a sailor and the war he fought in was a much smaller affair than either of those.'

More blank faces as the students tried to figure out which conflict she might mean. Teri, helpfully, told them a little more about the poet's troubled upbringing with a soldier father and a puritanically religious mother, his dad's death when he was still a boy, and his imprisonment, aged eighteen, after he abducted a fourteen-year-old girl. 'When he was released, he joined the navy, and fought in several important battles.'

Even blanker faces. Teri added more detail, speaking animatedly about Wilmot's political career, as one of the youngest members of the House of Lords, his liaisons with various celebrities, and the problems with alcohol which frequently landed him in trouble with the authorities. 'He once went into hiding, posing as a fertility doctor, after he became involved in a drunken brawl with a night patrol in which one of his friends died,' Teri'd concluded.

Sharp intakes of breath and more expressions of surprise from the students. Eventually, one of them raised a hand. 'I don't think I've seen anything about him on the TV or radio,' he said. Several other students nodded.

Teri had feigned surprise. 'Of course not. He died more than three-hundred-and-fifty-years ago.'

There was a babble of chatter from the students. She'd described Wilmot so vividly they'd thought he was still alive. She had them hooked. Peter, though, was less impressed.

'Bit of a drama queen, too,' he'd commented at the time.

Today, I agreed, yes, her style was different. 'But students find her classes challenging and thought-provoking.' I paused and shot him a sly glance. 'There's no danger of anyone falling asleep when Teri's centre-stage.' A statement that could be taken a number of ways, but Peter 'harrumphed', perhaps remembering his inaugural address to the department.

We'd been herded into the Joseph Priestley lecture theatre to hear him outline his 'vision' for our collective future, promising that, henceforth, we'd enjoy a more 'dynamic symbiotic engagement that would produce a greater cross-pollination of thinking, and though we might have to punch a few puppies along the way, it'd result in an improved ideation that would allow us to better action our key deliverables'.

Which, roughly translated, meant: 'You lot need a kick up the backside if this university is to survive and prosper in a rapidly changing higher education landscape.'

And the unspoken addendum read: 'Furthermore, since my five-figure annual bonus depends on improving the bottom line, I'll kick as hard, and as often as necessary to get us where we need to be.'

Of course, since such plain speaking was beyond Peter's vocabulary, he'd droned on, and on, seemingly oblivious to the simmering resentment of his audience who were fidgeting and twitching, thinking of the emails demanding a response, the exam papers waiting to be marked, and the spreadsheets needing to be completed. And then the inevitable happened. Zzzzz! Zzzzz! A loud, guttural snore cut through the hot air. Peter had blinked, mouth flapping like a startled goldfish, as Stella, sitting at the back of the room, succumbed to the heat, and the stuffy atmosphere and the incomprehensible drivel.

Peter, avoiding my eyes, 'harrumphed' again and straightened the papers on his desk. 'She's a novice researcher,' he said. 'You'd have to carry her all the way.' He paused. 'Perhaps I should have a word with Deirdre myself?'

I shrugged. 'She'll only tell you the same as I have.' I hesitated. Probably best to come clean about the negative comments regarding the methodology and the literature review. 'She said Teri needed to give a bit more thought to her sources and how she'd structure the project.' Peter grunted. 'But,' I continued. 'I'll work with her to develop her understanding of the level of detail that's required.'

'Okay. Okay.' Peter stood and ushered me to the door. 'Have it your way. I just hope you don't live to regret it.'

I *didn't* think I would. Teri'd thrown her heart and soul into her teaching, and she'd *seemed* committed to branching out into research. So what could go wrong?

Chapter 20

Teri

I took the day off to get myself ready. I should've been running Level 1 tutorials to go through some work I'd left them the week before. I call it homework, but that academic arse Peter Heron calls it 'ongoing lecture-orientated discussion'. However, half the little beggars have been sloping off early for Christmas so I don't suppose many of them would be turning up for tutorials. And those who do turn up won't have done the prepared work and couldn't take part in a 'lecture-orientated discussion' if it lay on the floor in front of them and shouted 'take me'.

So what was a girl to do? Sit in her office all day with a few sweaty Level 1s or get herself ready for a big night?

I chose the latter so that when Dan called for me, I was looking the million dollars I so obviously am.

We arrived at the Denbyside Hotel and the doorman said, 'Evening, Mr Caine.' Giving him ever such a slight bow. 'Enjoyed your show last night.'

'Thank you,' Dan said and strode further into the foyer. 'It's not a show,' he hissed to me. 'It's a bloody news programme.'

'Dan!' Some screechy female yelled from the opposite end of the foyer – a girl of about twenty-three, in the shortest, tightest, yellow freak of a frock. She tottered over; her arms outstretched to embrace Dan in a bright yellow cloud hug. 'Who are you with?' she asked him, not even looking at me. I suppose the dazzle from all that yellow had made her have some sort of retinal explosion, and she couldn't see me behind the glare.

'Er, this is…' Dan began to introduce me, but screechy female simply undid the hug and hooked her arm in his, dragging him to the heavily carpeted flight of steps leading up from the foyer into the ballroom.

Dan didn't even look behind him to see where I was. Screechy was obviously giving him some good gossip because he threw back his head and laughed. I followed at a sedate pace.

And so it was for the rest of the evening: lots of producers, directors, autocue cuties, and gallery assistants pouting and parading, and guffawing at the in-telly jokes and congratulating each other on whichever little programme they'd just made. Dan was so busy talking skateboarding ducks he hardly said a word to me all night. Throughout the meal, people would come over and put their arm round his shoulder or kiss him and shriek about something that had happened in telly-land. At one stage, between the strangely coloured, shrimpy-looking starter, and the barely cooked, rubbery duck, I jokingly asked if telly was always like this and Dan looked at me quizzically and said what did I mean?

'Well, all this kissing and shrieking and patting yourselves on the back,' I said. He looked hurt and was just about to say something when the yellow frock suddenly appeared and screeched, 'Dan, darling. Do us a big favour. Can you present the Sports Programme of the Year award?'

'Why? Who's supposed to be doing it?'

'That prick footballer, Shayne Brickham, but he's not turned up.'

Oh, my friend Shayne.

Dan didn't need any encouragement. He was on his feet and pushing his chair back.

'Hey, you're not going to leave me?' I asked, but he didn't hear. Screecher grabbed his arm (again) and tugged him away, presumably to read up on sports because, as far as I know, the only athletic thing Dan knew anything about was ten-pin bowling.

There was an appreciative roar from the audience when Dan appeared on stage to present the award to some boys and girls who worked on the sports desk of *Ridings Today* and, to be honest, he did it very smoothly; but then he's a television professional. There was much obligatory back slapping between Dan and the boys, and kissing between Dan and the girls, and then kissing between the boys and the girls. The photographer got them all to line up with Dan in the middle, handing over a garish little glass sliver, which I suppose was meant to be the award. Then there was more shrieking and kissing and Dan stepped off the stage where screecher was waiting, ablaze in yellow, to lead him away to another table full of scantily clad screechers.

I stared gloomily into my glass of what was now slightly warmish white wine. I knocked it back and reached for the bottle standing in its little glass cooler in the middle of the table.

'Here, let me help,' said a man standing behind me. He leant over, forcing me gently but ungainly forwards into the table as he reached for the bottle, grabbed it by the neck, slipped into Dan's vacant seat and started pouring wine into my glass. I was about to say, 'What the hell…?' when some instinct stopped me, and I looked closer. I vaguely recognised him. He was a plumply faced man with dark hair gelled into a little duck's arse on the top of his head which, frankly, is a ridiculous look on any man over the age of twenty-five, and even more odd-looking on someone in his late forties.

Hot breath, sticky with stale red wine, wafted over me as he said, 'You're with Dan, aren't you?' And before I could reply he went on. 'You're Teri from the university?'

'Yes, how did you…?'

He introduced himself as Richard Walker, managing director of *Ridings Today* – and Dan's boss. Thank goodness for that instinct of mine. Yes, Mr Walker had been in the studios the night I went to watch the programme go out. Mr Boss Man was not my type. I don't go for duck-arsed plump guys, so I was hoping this one wasn't going to give the old come on. And, in fact, he wasn't.

'I'm glad I've caught you,' he said. 'You'll know Peter Heron…?'

'Oh yes,' I replied, wondering what was coming next. 'He's dean of my faculty – English and Media.'

'Ah, yes. So he probably knows his stuff,' Duck's Arse said. Something stirred in my memory banks. 'You probably know he's being considered to present our new Friday night book programme?'

Ah, that was it! Peter Heron, the would-be television literary star.

'Oh, I knew he was angling, but I didn't know he was seriously being considered,' I said. Duck's Arse eyed me closely.

'You seem doubtful?' he said.

Now, I must confess, it was the wine; it was Dan leaving me on my own; it was the screechy female in the yellow frock; it was the arrogant, back-slapping television types; it was this plump man with the ridiculous hair. But, most of all, it was the thought of Peter Heron, made up, and coiffed, talking the late-night talk with amateur authors, boring bloggers, and bloody book club members that conspired to make me say what I said next.

'Between you and me,' I began, leaning towards that slightly reddening plump face and trying to avoid looking at the sticky little tuft of gelled hair. 'I wouldn't touch the old imposter with a bargepole, let alone a bookmark. He's never read anything in his life apart from Post-it Note-sized psychology sound bites on delivering best bloody practice in the corporate environment.'

Chapter 21

Lee

Peter Heron was wrong about Teri. Admittedly, she threw herself into the arms of Dan Caine with more energy and passion than she did my research project, but all things considered, she wasn't the dead weight Peter'd predicted – at least, not once she'd established that 'no, I wouldn't be looking over her shoulder every two minutes' and that she was 'most definitely not my underling'.

'So you're satisfied with her performance,' Peter asked after collaring me in the Senior Common Room.

Not as satisfied as Dan, perhaps, but… 'Yes,' I said.

Peter rubbed his hands together. 'And you work well together?'

Where was this leading? 'Yes.'

His hand rubbing was picking up speed. 'Good,' he said. 'Because I'm pulling together some personnel to work on a new team diagnostic survey and we'd greatly benefit from your input.' He indicated the settee behind us. 'Sit down. Let me explain.'

Team diagnostic survey? Sighing, I sat, pulling my face into what hopefully would pass for an expression of interest.

After ten minutes of Peter obfuscation, the only concrete piece of information I'd garnered was that Teri and I needed to report to his office at 5 p.m. for a 'thought shower' involving ourselves, Peter, Stella Lastings, and Mike Orme.

Great! It'd take some persuading to get Teri into an after-hours meet-up with three of her least favourite colleagues.

'It'll just be another one of his talking shops,' she said. 'He'll talk and we'll have to listen.'

'Yes, but—' I stopped, because she had a point, although that wasn't really the point. Rumours were flying around about a planned 'efficiency programme' that would almost certainly result in 'structural downsizing' and Teri, more than most people, needed to curry Brownie points with Peter if she was to avoid joining the ranks of the downsized.

'Nobody will notice I'm not there,' she said.

'They're not blind! And…' I raised my fingers. One. Two. Three. Four. 'They can count.'

Teri waved a dismissive hand. 'Just tell them I've got a prior engagement and that you'll fill me in on anything important.'

'Do you want a career or don't you?'

She stared, and I waited, fully expecting she'd say the university could go hang, and she didn't need the tin pot salary we paid her, because she could manage nicely on Daddy's monthly allowance. Thank you very much.

She didn't. Which was surprising. 'Okay, okay,' she said. 'But I bet Peter'll have nothing important to say. And it'll be as dull as dishwater.'

She was wrong on the first count, at least.

Chapter 22

Teri

I hate Christmas. As a child, I spent the jolly festivities on my own playing with my expensive toys – a new dolls' house, a pink bike, or whatever. Charlie would be in his room reading the manuals he'd asked for: *Animal Husbandry for the Amateur*, *Allotment Management for the Self-Starter* and, oddly, *Fashion through the Ages.* Strange lad, Charlie, but I suppose it hinted at what was about to come. Dad usually took himself off for a walk and ended up in the pub, only to come home to the delights of my mother's burnt offerings, she having spent too much time on the cooking sherry and not enough tending the turkey. They would row, Dad would head back to the pub, Mum would burst into tears and, pausing only to pick up a bottle of brandy, rush to her bedroom, slam the door, and lay, sobbing quietly on the bed until falling into an alcoholic stupor. I did go up once and rub her back, telling her to 'shush, it'll be all right' but she simply buried her head deeper into her pillow and ignored me. I remember taking the bottle of brandy back downstairs and emptying the rest of the contents down the sink, but then got a massive telling off for wasting expensive drink. So I decided leaving her to her own devices was probably for the best.

Charlie and I would later sit together on the sofa watching the festive telly programmes while stuffing ourselves with cold, burnt turkey sandwiches.

But this Christmas was going to be different. I had Dan in my life, and I would be spending the holiday with him. We'd only known each other a few weeks, but what weeks they'd been. I could honestly say I've never felt this way about a man before.

I started googling exotic festive breaks and eventually narrowed the choice down to either a Caribbean cruise or a trip on the Eastern and Oriental Express.

Lee was impressed but concerned (her default position, generally). 'Won't it cost a fortune?' she asked.

'Well, yes,' I said. 'But I'll give Dad a ring and get him to send me a bit extra this month – tell him it's his Christmas present to me. Anyway, it's my first Christmas with Dan and I want it to be special.'

The trouble was, although Dan wanted Christmas to be special, he wanted it to be special for his daughter as well. When I broached the subject of going away together, he loved the idea.

'Oh, that'll be great. We'll be together like a real family,' he said.

A real family?

'Yes. You, me, and Victoria.'

'Oh. I wasn't thinking of taking Victoria.' I tried not to sound horrified. 'It will be just you and me. Think how lovely and romantic it will be.'

'Oh, but it's my turn to have Victoria for Christmas. She was with her mother last year.'

I tried to persuade him; I even suggested he gave the Devil child some money so she could go off for the holidays with some little playmate of hers, but Dan was having none of it; he was spending Christmas with the fruit of his loins.

So we rowed, and I told him to do what he liked. We made it up later, but I couldn't change his mind and so we agreed we'd do our own thing for the festivities.

Chapter 23

Lee

Peter's meeting was the first stage in his long-planned mission to 'weed out the lazy asses' who, he said, 'were holding us back'.

Strange, therefore, that he'd invited Teri to join the team diagnostic working party. 'I thought she'd welcome the opportunity to become part of the wider picture,' he'd said when I queried the invitation. Heaven knows what he meant by the 'wider picture' but I didn't like the wolfish grin on his face. He knew as well as I did that part of Teri's popularity with students lay in her maverick disregard for rules and regulations. *They* didn't care that she refused point blank to attend meetings to discuss subjects as diverse as the utilisation of effective learning spaces or the importance of feedback sandwiches. But Peter did. So, what game was he playing?

Peter, I thought, *are you being a tool?*

He must've sensed my scepticism.

'Don't you think she'll benefit from the experience?' His voice was as oily as a snakeskin salesman. 'I'm sure she'll add an interesting dimension to our discussions,' I'd murmured, and Peter'd smiled approvingly. 'Ah, yes,' Ms Harper,' he said. 'Always so discreet.' His tone suggested benevolent adult giving a bright child a pat on the back. 'Your loyalty to your friend is admirable but…' He paused. 'Just why *are* you friends? You're chalk, and she's cheese.'

The emphasis on the last word suggested something particularly over-ripe and pongy rather than a run-of-the-mill cheddar.

I shrugged. 'Oh, we go way back,' I'd said. 'And I don't really have time right now.'

Nor the inclination to explain the origins of our complicated, mutual inter-dependency, and the gratitude I'd felt when brittle, bolshy Teri squared up to the posh bullies at our sixth-form college who were making life hell for gawky, bookish, unsophisticated me.

Teri always says we became friends because I was kind enough to offer the hand of friendship, but why wouldn't I want to be friends with someone who went out on a limb for me?

Besides, we were both, in our different ways, outsiders. Teri's home life was chaotic. Her mother was a dipsomaniac, her father a cruel bully, and her brother was depressive. Quite a contrast to my loving, sheltered Irish-Catholic-Mass-every-Sunday-and-family-prayers-at-bedtime background.

Our friendship shouldn't have worked – still shouldn't work – yet somehow it does.

And, thankfully, Teri was also making being an academic work.

Except…

'Having a career is killing my social life,' she wailed as, with Peter on the prowl, we kicked our heels in the ladies' facilities at the end of our corridor. 'If I'm not at work, Dan's at work. And if I'm not at work and he's not at work, he's hobnobbing with other telly types. Or worse, cosying up with his blasted daughter.'

Ah, yes. Teri was struggling to cope with Dan's twin passions – his job and his daughter, both of which consumed time and attention that, in Teri's opinion, could more usefully be devoted to Teri herself.

And now Christmas was on the horizon.

'I had such plans,' she grumbled. 'Somewhere romantic and intimate and—'

'Enough,' I said, dashing into a vacant stall, so my lunchtime sandwich could part company with my stomach. 'Tummy bug,' I said, rinsing my hands afterwards.

Teri raised an eyebrow.

'If you say so,' she said, somewhat sceptically, I thought.

For a horrible moment it seemed as if she might pursue the matter, but, of course, she'd got other things on her mind. Like re-applying her lipstick and quizzing me on why Dan would prefer to spend Christmas with the Devil child rather than with her?

I couldn't begin to guess, but that didn't stop Teri from examining an endless number of possible theories, which always came back to the same irrefutable point: the Devil child had bewitched him.

'So where will you go for Christmas?'

She pouted into the mirror and applied an extra lick of fire engine red.

'Dunno.' She shrugged. 'Eating a ready meal for one?'

I had a better idea. I was home alone for the holidays, too. Mammy'd decided she couldn't face Christmas at home without

Granddaddy so she'd booked herself and Daddy onto a Canary Islands cruise, and my sister Fliss, who'd have been my backstop, would be eating mince pies and Brussels sprouts in Wales with her husband Euan's family.

'Come to mine,' I said.

Chapter 24

Lee

I was still in my pyjamas when Teri arrived mid-afternoon on Christmas Eve.

'Not dressed yet?' she said, eyeing my PJs as if they were the most dubious outfit on Earth. Without waiting for an answer, she deposited a cool box and a loaded wine carrier on the kitchen floor.

'I'll bring the rest of my stuff in later, but just wanted to get a head start on prepping for tomorrow's dinner.' She glanced around, as if assessing which work surface most nearly met her exacting demands.

'Okay,' she said, pulling a leather pouch from the tote still hooked over her arm. 'Chopping boards?' she queried, digging into her bag again and yanking out a chef's white tunic. While she slipped it over her posh frock and buttoned up, I opened a drawer.

'Help yourself,' I said, pointing. She nodded, unwrapped the pouch, and laid out her knives. In a few minutes she was peeling, chopping, and slicing.

I watched fascinated.

I'd become so used to seeing Teri in her neatly tailored dresses and stiletto heels that I'd almost forgotten she'd begun her working life cheffing on cruise ships and luxury yachts.

'Shoo,' she said, waving what looked like a meat cleaver. 'Get dressed.' Actually, I was already on my way out the door, retching, and heaving as the smell of onions and sprouts filled the room.

When I came back downstairs half an hour later, Teri was leaning against the kitchen sink, sipping a glass of bubbly.

'You still got that tummy bug?' she asked. 'You really ought to see a doctor.'

I took the champagne flute she was offering. 'I shouldn't really be drinking.'

'Why?'

'Because…' Words failed.

Eyes narrowing, she downed her glass, and poured a refill. 'So,' she said. 'What is it you aren't telling me?'

Where to begin?

****

Teri was determined to get to the bottom of things. 'What are you going to do?'

I didn't answer, largely because my head was hanging over the rim of the bathroom loo and – eurgh! Teri choked back a gulp.

'Is there anything I can do?' she asked from the safety of the landing. I heaved and retched again.

'No,' I managed eventually.

'Who's the daddy?' she asked.

'You don't want to know.'

She advanced to the door. 'You mean, you don't want to tell.'

No, I just didn't want to admit to doing IT with Mike Orme.

Teri folded her arms and propped herself against the wall. 'I don't understand why you didn't tell me you were seeing someone.'

'Because I'm not,' I mumbled.

'What!'

I exhaled slowly, feeling just a teeny bit less wobbly. I rose cautiously, brushed my teeth, and splashed some water on my face. 'Sorry, about that. It comes on suddenly.'

Teri said nothing, her face twisted in an expression of concentration. I lowered my eyes. Didn't take a genius to know she was remembering an incident in the Senior Common Room a few days earlier.

I'd been queuing at the food bar when Stella Lastings, who's got a voice that carries, started quizzing Teri about the source of my tummy bug. Her inference was clear, and Teri, who always seems to think I can't fight my own battles, leapt to my defence, and raising her pitch to match Stella's, wasted no time in telling her I wasn't in a relationship and would never dream of having a one-night stand.

Which hardly needed saying since it'd take a special kind of woman to dream about sleeping with a balding, middle-aged man, who teamed hand-knitted tank tops with paisley ties, chain store slacks, and leather loafers.

I'd been having nightmares about it ever since.

Nevertheless, Teri'd been very convincing, and Stella let the matter drop, but Mike, who'd been sitting nearby, lost grip of the mug in his hand, slopping coffee over the table, his trousers, and Teri's tote.

Which didn't go down well.

'Mike Orme,' she said now. 'You slept with Mike Orme.'

It was a statement, and not a question.

Chapter 25

Teri

Okay, so I'd rather have spent Christmas with Dan, walking hand-in-hand along a white sandy beach and making love on warm, star-filled nights, but Lee and I made the best of it and I think it did her good having me there.

I'd guessed there was something up; Lee had been 'off' for a while and when I realised she hadn't touched a drop of her drink, it dawned on me there was something more going on. A lot more. Lee had been putting on weight recently; she looked pale; she wasn't drinking.

'You're pregnant,' I declared.

I was right. But a one-night stand with tank top Orme – how on Earth could she?

She told me about the shock and then the hopes she'd had when she found she was pregnant, and the pressure she was under from Mr Misery to get rid of the thing.

'I think Mike's right,' I said, resting my hand on her arm.

I'm not sure the mummy manuals allow for the amount of wine we drank, but in the morning, I found Lee chucking up again. I sorted her out. I made her shower, put on clean clothes, and eat some unbuttered toast. Don't ask me why, but unbuttered toast is the best thing for a hangover, so I assumed it would be okay for morning sickness too.

She was feeling better by the time we'd settled ourselves in front of the little Christmas tree in her lounge. It was a real one – complete with pine needles. I can't see the point – they make such a mess. I always made do with a little fibre optic thing. But Lee is a traditional girl and had decorated hers with silver and red baubles. It looked quite tasteful – for her.

She plucked a present from under the tree and handed it to me saying, 'Here you are. I hope you like it. I've got the receipt so you can change it if you want to… but I thought it was your colour.' People are generally nervous about buying me things because I have such specific taste.

More in hope than expectation, I ripped open the present. My heart sank even as I pulled at a pseudo-silk scarf decorated in a swirly pattern in shades of orange and gold. Orange and gold! For me! I sometimes wonder whether Lee knows me at all.

I reached under the tree and pulled out a box beautifully wrapped in red tissue paper. Lee opened it nervously. I'd bought her some expensive truffle serum in the hope she'd use it rather than that cheap hand cream she slathers everywhere.

'Oh,' she said, her expression doubtful. 'I'll keep it for best.'

'Put some on now,' I insisted, taking the bottle from her and undoing the top. 'And then, let's do the Christmas thing and go to church.'

I thought it would help Lee to spend a bit of time thinking good Catholic thoughts – and coming to her senses about this wretched pregnancy.

It was all rather nice – candles, gentle music, soft intonations. I didn't understand the ritual of it all, but it felt peaceful and welcoming. Most of the congregation was made up of older folk and small knots of families. One such family group shuffled into the pew in front of us. I took no notice of the two women and kids, but there was something very familiar about the bloke: light brown, floppy hair that curled cutely over the top of his collar, and a neat, tight bum from what I could see. When he turned round to wink at Lee (wink at Lee!) it dawned. He was the good-looking newspaperman from Peter Heron's soiree who was all but having it off with Chrissie. I nudged Lee to intimate '*look who's here…*' when she hissed, 'Hands off. He's married.' Cheeky cow – that hadn't stopped her having it off with tank top man.

When it came to the kiss of peace, I made sure I kissed everyone – including the newspaperman – and I was pleased to note he made a special beeline for me.

Chapter 26

Lee

Teri, who didn't go to church from one Christmas to the next, insisted on accompanying me to the 11 a.m. High Mass 'because I was in too fragile a state to go on my own'. I don't know what she thought I'd do if left to my own devices – prostrate myself on the altar and demand forgiveness for the wickedness that'd landed me with child? – but I knew she should have stayed at home as soon as she started dipping her fingers in the font at the back of the church.

'Don't!' I hissed, and grabbing her arm, forced her up the aisle.

'Teach me how to curtsey,' she whispered as we squeezed into a pew.

'It's not a curtsey,' I said. 'It's called genuflecting.'

'It looks like a curtsey,' she insisted.

'Well, it isn't.'

'Is!'

Confirmation that she really wasn't suited to church arrived with Declan, who, despite being accompanied by his wife and kids, *and* his mother still managed to shoot a speculative look of admiration at Teri as they filed into the row in front. She smiled slightly before demurely dropping her eyes to the hymn book on her lap.

I jabbed an elbow into her ribs. 'Stop it!' I ordered, scrambling us both to our feet, as the choir launched into the opening verse of *Adeste Fidelias*, and the priest swept into church splashing holy water on the congregation as he progressed.

'Hell's bells,' Teri squealed, wiping her eyes. 'What in heaven's name was that?'

Declan peeked over his shoulder, winked, and raised a quizzical eyebrow. I shook my head and glowered, and Teri stifled a giggle.

Fair play, though, she made an effort to blend in, and apart from a semi-sotto voce complaint that the priest was a 'windbag' all went swimmingly until the kiss of peace.

'What's this?' she queried as our neighbours shook hands and brushed cheeks. Once she got the hang of it, she embraced it with enthusiasm – as did Declan, who, grinning broadly, gripped Teri's hands in his and pulled her in so he could brush his lips against both her cheeks. Teri returned the kiss with interest and left her fingers resting in his just a shade longer than necessary.

'Don't,' I said. 'He's trouble.'

'Oh,' she said, smiling. 'So am I.'

Now what was that supposed to mean?

Chapter 27

Teri

I'm not a monster. But the truth is I don't like children. I can't bear the sight of pregnant women flaunting their enormous bellies and then, later, flaunting their tedious offspring. You can hardly go into a coffee shop, library, or gallery without there being a tribe of mumsies with their four-by-four chariots and assorted children taking up space, making too much noise, and leaving a sticky mess.

But that wasn't the reason I was so against Lee having this kid of hers. I didn't believe that gormless Orme would do the right thing, leave his wife, and support Lee in playing happy families. Nor did I think Lee would cope bringing up a kid on her own. Let's face it, her good Catholic mammy would excommunicate her for having a child out of wedlock, and Daddy Harper would probably disown her and kick her out of the house he built for her.

But the real reason was that Lee would be throwing away so much of what she'd worked for. Even I could appreciate how much she'd been through to get to where she was professionally. Once she'd taken the maternity leave of however many years women get nowadays, she'd want to come back part time and we all know women have to be full-time and full-on to get anywhere, even in our poxy university.

On top of all this, I wasn't convinced Lee really did want this child. I popped over to see her every day after Christmas and each time she'd been upset and dithery about what to do. I had to juggle my visits with seeing Dan, who'd come over to my duplex on Boxing Day, suitably repentant, and stayed. I didn't want to tell him about what was going on and came up with the excuse that Lee and I were working on a research project and needed to finish it before the start of term. He bought it and seemed quite happy when I left him in the apartment on his own for a couple of hours. I had to ask him not to keep putting his feet on the coffee table.

I decided action was needed so as soon as life opened up after New Year's Eve (which Dan and I spent blissfully together with a bottle of champagne). I went to see my GP and asked how you went about getting an abortion. She went through the ghastly options. I thought the best solution was to book Lee into a private clinic so she wouldn't need to go to her own GP (probably a good Catholic doctor who'd looked after the Harpers since they first came to live here and might take a judgmental approach towards Lee's predicament).

Lee objected, but when I told her I'd booked her assessment appointment for the second week of January, she seemed relieved. 'Don't worry,' I told her. 'It's all paid for. Daddy has sent me a bit extra this month.' This was a lie. Daddy hadn't even sent my usual monthly allowance, but I put the clinic's bill on my credit card and hoped for the best.

After her assessment it was recommended she have a medical abortion because she was less than ten weeks pregnant. It meant taking two tablets – one at the clinic and the second one at home the next day.

I drove her in for the first pill thinking it was a shame she wasn't staying in overnight to make the most of the clinic's facilities, but I snaffled a couple of glossy mags left in the waiting room thinking they'd cheer us up later.

When we were back at her house I insisted on staying for a couple of days. I still hadn't told Dan about the abortion. I simply told him we were having some girly time, and he smiled, and said how nice.

'But I'll miss you,' he said as he prepared to go back to his own flat.

'I'll miss you too,' I told him and realised it was true. I was getting used to having him around.

I stayed at Lee's for almost a week. She had an official sick note and had told Chrissie in admin she had a tummy bug, which is pretty close to the truth. I pulled a sickie to look after her. 'You got a tummy bug, too?' Chrissie asked.

Lee was very quiet most of the time; no fun at all. But, given the circumstances, I suppose she wouldn't want to be cracking jokes.

I went back to my flat at the weekend and found on the doorstep the biggest bouquet of flowers. 'Miss you, need you, love you' was all the card said. Dan!

I rang him straight away – and within half an hour he was ringing my doorbell. No doubt whatever he had planned for the rest of the weekend had involved spending money on his only child, but, to his credit, he cancelled all arrangements, and devoted himself to me.

And he did *devoting* in the most amazing way. On Monday morning as he was dressing to go to the *Ridings Today* studios, and I was getting ready for uni, he said, 'You know, Teri. I hate having to leave you.'

'Well, you don't have to,' I said.

'No, I mean… this,' he said. 'Leaving you here in your flat, while I go back to mine.'

'What are you suggesting?' I asked.

'Let's get married.'

Chapter 28

Lee

Teri arranged everything – found a private clinic, booked appointments, accompanied me through seemingly endless interviews with business-like nurses and medics, held my hand when I needed it and, afterwards, hugged me, and wiped away my tears. And she never uttered a single word of criticism or condemnation – just offered a loving, efficient practicality that was surprisingly soothing. She was a star and, if she wasn't there in the middle of the night when I woke and sobbed myself back to sleep, it was hardly her fault.

Chapter 29

Teri

Dan's proposal took me completely by surprise. Yes, I thought we might move in together, eventually. But marriage? I told Dan I'd need to think about it. Oddly, for someone like me who'd always loved 'em and left 'em, the idea of having Dan as a permanent fixture in my life grew on me. Rapidly. By the end of the day, I'd made up my mind. Dan was kind, generous, and patient and, best of all, he loved me. And, let's face it, who else would take me on?

I told him yes, but under the condition we got married as soon as possible, as I didn't want time to change my mind.

I'd had visions of a tropical beach wedding: just Dan and me and a couple of stranger witnesses. Me in a floaty outfit and bare feet, Dan in one of his classic pale suits. Both of us watching the sun set over a pale turquoise sea. No family, no guests, no cake, no fuss, and definitely no Victoria.

Dan agreed – to the tropical beach wedding – but when he heard of my suggested guest list (or lack of it) said, 'But I couldn't get married without my little girl being there.'

And as I hadn't wanted to give his little girl the satisfaction of a two-week tropical beach holiday (with the minor matter of our wedding tucked in the middle of it), I suggested we have a register office wedding at which she could be present and then Dan and I would leave for a tropical beach honeymoon. He'd bought the idea, although it took some persuading not to invite his colleagues.

'They'll all be expecting a big party,' he reasoned. But I didn't want a load of screechy, flashy television types whooping it up and drinking themselves stupid at my expense. I persuaded Dan I wanted it to be just the two of us, intimate and private, in fact, I managed a little tear as I told him the thought of a 'big bash' actually frightened me and he stroked my face and kissed my cheek by way of reassurance. 'It's your day,' he said, 'and you must have what you want.'

What I did want was life to be about just Dan and me. I'd finally found someone I loved and who genuinely loved me, and I didn't want anyone coming along and ruining it.

Lee asked later whether I wanted any of my family at the wedding. Hardly. My father had all but given up on the factory, leaving it in the hands of Edward Pranks and communicating only by email from his cottage in rural France, and from which he never stirred himself. It wasn't even worth the effort of phoning him.

I didn't really understand the arrangements with the factory. Good old Edward started out as Dad's driver, became his personal assistant, then became manager at the mill – and now runs the whole caboodle. Don't ask me about the financial side. All I know is Dad takes money out of the business to keep him in red wine and gourmet cheeses while sending me (and my older brother, Charlie) the odd cheque when he remembers. My mother, who was always very fond of the cooking sherry but not to living permanently in France, turned to drink in a more determined way once Dad was no longer there to check the bottles outside the scullery door. She was now boozing it up in a one-bedroom apartment among the ex-pats in Lanzarote. I rang to tell her I was getting married and she – dramatically effusive – said, 'That's wonderful, darling. But I can't possibly come. I couldn't stand the airport… the flight… and where would I stay? Oh no, it's all too much.'

I didn't push it.

She arranged for a bunch of pink carnations to be delivered. If there is one flower I hate it's a carnation. I put the bunch straight in the bin.

Charlie was supposed to take over the steel business when Dad left but he'd had a run in with Edward Pranks and took himself off to manage a smallholding in Suffolk from where I received the occasional Christmas card from him and his partner, Denis, but little else in terms of sibling support. I rang him too, to tell him about the wedding, and he made some excuse about how he and Denis couldn't get away as they'd just bought four new goats and didn't want to leave them until they'd settled in.

'Goats?' I queried.

'Make lovely cheese, sweetie,' Charlie said.

I told Lee she'd have to be mother of the bride, matron of honour, and chief bridesmaid.

'Wouldn't you want Victoria as a bridesmaid?' she asked.

'Bugger that,' I replied.

On being told her father was to marry again, Victoria had gone out, and got thoroughly blathered, knocking back vodka shots in the local park with a group of girlie friends.

I suggested to Dan that she was a little young to be drinking like that.

'She's so pleased for the old man,' Dan said, recounting how he'd gone to pick her up and she'd told him she was celebrating his news.

More likely drowning her sorrows.

'I think we should give Victoria a wedding present,' Dan announced.

'But it's our wedding,' I explained.

'I know. But in a spirit of the occasion,' he replied. 'I'd like to give her some money.'

He was always giving her money: for clothes, for drinks (she wouldn't have been able to buy all that vodka herself), for days out, for holidays. For simply being. I pointed out he was generous enough already.

'Oh, the odd ten quid here and there.' He smiled in agreement. 'No, I was thinking of something a bit more. An amount she could use to buy something really nice so she feels part of the celebrations.'

'But you've already given her money to buy an outfit and, by the way, a new dress does not have to cost £650. Not at ASOS anyway.'

I could hardly contain my anger when I later told Lee. He'd given her £5,000.

'She behaves so badly and he gives her money,' I cried.

'But she is his daughter, and he feels bad about divorcing her mother and leaving her.'

'He's hardly left her,' I said. 'She's with him every bloody weekend.'

'I know,' Lee said.

But even she couldn't think of anything more comforting to say.

Chapter 30

Lee

Life goes on. Or, at least, Teri's did. Mine felt like a walking wake. Which was unfortunate because I'd been roped in for maid of honour duties for what Teri was billing as 'wedding of the year' and a smile was non-negotiable. It was tough going though, because, having swapped a tropical beach ceremony for a utilitarian service in a dingy register office, Teri'd turned into Bridezilla.

'Nowhere else available at short notice,' she'd said when I queried the choice of venue.

'But why the rush?' I asked. 'You've got the rest of your lives to plan the perfect nuptials.'

'You'd understand if you'd ever been properly in love.'

Fortunately, my teeth snapped shut before my lips could ask: 'But are you properly in love?'

Seemed to me, proper love would've been a bit more accepting of Dan's faults and foibles. 'Does the Devil child have to spend every weekend with us?' she'd ask, launching into a long tirade. *Why does she need so many new clothes? And why is he always buying her presents? And what about the money he pays his ex-wife?* 'Maintenance, it's called. But what does she do with the money?'

A rhetorical question since she didn't pause for breath long enough for me to venture an opinion.

'Fritters it away. That's what she does. She's forever at the hairdresser's or the spa or having luxury breaks with the demon daughter.'

Don't know how Teri knew all this since she and the ex-wife were little more than nodding acquaintances.

But she had more to get off her chest. 'I thought maintenance was supposed to maintain the kid – not the freaking mother.'

All this might have been easier for Teri to bear if Dan'd been more respectful of house rules. Like not putting his feet on the coffee table, not eating take away chicken tikka masala in the living room or leaving used cereal bowls in the sink instead of placing them in their designated place in the dishwasher. 'How many times do I need to tell him they go in the top rack on the left-hand side?' she'd ask me.

I don't know, as many times as it takes for him to get it right?

And, though, in the early days she'd been happy to spend nights in cuddled up on the sofa, now she moaned that Dan'd turned into a couch potato. 'I can't remember the last time we went out to dinner.'

I could. They'd been to the opening of a new French restaurant last weekend. She'd started with fricassée de champignons, followed by confit duck leg, Dan'd had fritôt de brie and boeuf bourguignon and they'd shared a bottle of Chablis and a Sancerre and finished with coffee and brandies. I know all this because she'd told me so – at length.

'I wouldn't mind…' Clearly she did. 'But, if we're going to spend our evenings in front of the television, I'd like to sit down and watch a film without Dan feeling the need to cuddle up.'

Useless to point out that cuddling up was what people in love did. 'What do you know about it?' she retorted. So, I left well alone, and kept my fingers crossed this was just pre-nuptial nerves. That the wedding would be fine and they'd live happily ever after.

Chapter 31

Teri

The Town Hall is a giant Victorian edifice that dominates Market Row, the main road that sweeps through the centre of the city. The exterior of the building is in need of a sandblast, dark and dirty as it is from the constant traffic grinding past the monumental flight of steps that lead up to the ten-column Corinthian colonnade through which visitors move to reach the building's heavy wooden doors. The entrance opens into a domed vestibule where, by crossing the Minton encaustic tiles laid in a geometric pattern on the foyer floor, access can be gained to the 8,000-seat concert hall, the council chamber, the magistrates' court, the ladies' and gents' lavatories (tiled in elaborately bright red and lit by miniature 'Odeon' fittings), and the register office.

Lee and I – late, having had a last-minute gin to steady our nerves – dashed in. But we needn't have rushed. Dan wasn't there.

'Hah. We should have driven round the block,' Lee said, trying to cover her nervousness.

'Where is he?' I hissed. Then suddenly, he, too, ran in panting for breath.

'Sorry… sorry,' he said. 'Victoria…'

He didn't need to explain. Behind him, hardly rushing, was the sullen little cow sporting a look of indifference. Clearly, she'd decided to change the colour of her lip gloss before venturing out for the occasion of her father's wedding, her make-up being of more importance than her father's nuptials.

Chapter 32

Lee

I didn't for one moment believe Victoria was quite the complete Devil child Teri made her out to be, but it was definitely unfortunate, to say the least, that she was responsible for making Dan late for his wedding. Poor girl, gasped Dan, she'd been feeling poorly, and almost fainted just before they left the house. They'd had to wait twenty minutes until she felt a little better.

Teri was frankly disbelieving and looked as if she'd like to throttle the child. But the registrar didn't give her time. Instead, she said, now everyone had arrived we might as well get on with things. Which we did and Dan Caine and Teri Meyer duly became husband and wife. It was telling, though, that Teri and I arrived only a matter of minutes before Dan and Victoria. Teri had downed a couple of stiff gins straight after breakfast and a couple more as she dressed and did her hair and make-up. And another one before getting into the taxi. 'Just to steady my nerves,' she said. Steady her nerves? She didn't have a nervous bone in her body.

Chapter 33

Teri

Because Dan had moved out of the marital des res and into a rented flat when his marriage broke up, it seemed sensible he should give that up and move in with me until we could buy something expensive and luxurious together; something that reflected his status as a highly paid television presenter. But when I showed him brochures for beautiful five-bedroom executive homes on landscaped and gated estates that Lee's dad, Mr Harper Homes, had produced, he said he couldn't afford that sort of thing.

'Why ever not?' I demanded. 'I'm on a decent enough salary at the university – and I have my allowance when Dad remembers to send it – and you're on megabucks.'

He shook his head. 'Don't forget, I'm still paying the mortgage on my old house – and maintenance for Sara and Victoria.'

'But why should you be paying for Sara? And why can't she pay her own mortgage?'

'You know she doesn't work, Teri,' Dan said.

It was true: he'd told me that after losing the baby, Sara had become not just frigid, but depressed. Whatever it was, the former secretary lost the will to work. Tapping away on a computer spreadsheet in a nice little office in town had been too much for the fragrant Sara. Better accept as much cash as possible from her ex and take herself off for nice, restful spa breaks.

'You should tell your ex-wife to get off her backside and get a job,' I said.

'Ah, if only I could,' replied Dan. 'But don't forget, Victoria still lives at the house.'

Ah yes. Victoria. She liked to spend weekends with her daddy and if her daddy was living with me, how would that work?

When I got the job at the university, I'd bought my two-bedroom duplex, or rather Edward Pranks had supplied enough dosh for the deposit and my allowance helped pay the mortgage on what wasn't exactly a vast expanse but was a carefully decorated and expensively furnished cream and vanilla bachelor girl pad.

'But what about Victoria?' had been Dan's first question when we contemplated his moving in.

'What about her?' I asked.

'Well, she likes to spend weekends with me so she'll need a bedroom for when she stays.'

How did I feel about having the Devil child staying in my flat? I'd rather pull my glossily painted toenails out.

Chapter 34

Teri

'Are you listening to me?' I asked, knowing full well he wasn't. He'd rushed in from work and pecked me on the cheek, but his eyes were on the pile of envelopes on the kitchen table.

He was always distracted when he came home at night. He claimed it was the adrenalin from that night's programme; he was still on a high from the effects of live television. He couldn't concentrate on anything until everything was in order, and the only way to get things in order was to go through his evening ritual.

We'd only been married a few weeks, and I was already getting a tad irritated by this. Even though I usually uncorked a bottle of wine and placed two glasses on the kitchen table, Dan would first have a soft drink to line his stomach, he said. Lime juice was the flavour of the moment and he'd reach into the fridge for the bottle of cordial, unscrew the top, place the top on the counter near the fridge, move over to the opposite side of the kitchen and the cupboard where the tumblers were kept, get himself one, pour the juice into the glass, put the bottle down on the counter, move to the sink to top the cordial up with water (splashing the work surfaces on either side, which I then had to mop up), take a big slug and go, 'Aah, that's better.' Every evening!

I'd stopped trying to tell him to pick up the bottle, walk across to get the top, screw the top back on, and put the bloody thing back in the fridge because he would say, 'Yes, okay,' in a distracted way but never did as I asked. He'd be too busy glugging back the juice – and making something of a noise while doing it too. All the while, his eyes would be on the pile of post on the table.

I then had to go over, get the bottle of juice from the counter, walk over to where the top had been abandoned, screw it back on, and put the bottle back in the fridge, shutting the door with a heavier force than was entirely necessary.

He then would examine the first envelope. No ripping of the envelope for him; he liked to savour the process, especially if a particular letter was handwritten, and he received a fair few handwritten missives addressed to him care of the *Ridings Today* studio and either left for him in his pigeonhole or redirected here. Most of these delicately scrawled notelets were from middle-aged, menopausal, empty nesters who had nothing better to do with their sad little lives than voluntary good deeds at the local church and fantasising about the chances of a good-looking television presenter falling for them once they'd written to him telling him how much they liked the suit he was wearing on Monday night's programme. Some of them enclosed little presents: a scarf he might like, a silk hanky embroidered with his initials to wear in his top jacket pocket, some ginger biscuits they'd made themselves, or worst of all, pictures of themselves in natty little bikinis 'having fun in the surf'.

He loved those handwritten letters. He'd look at the writing on the envelope, trying to work out who it might be from, then he'd turn the thing this way and that as though the process would shed some light on proceedings. If he was in a particularly self-tantalising mood, he'd put the envelope back on the table, unopened, while he looked through the rest of the post, saving the cream until last, as it were. Each letter got its own due veneration; even a gas bill was examined in detail even though we paid by direct debit. He would put all his concentration into whatever missive he held in his hand.

'Anything interesting?' I'd asked.

'Mmm?' he'd replied.

That 'Mmm?' was so irritating. He would be reading the paper, for instance, and I would say something and, without looking up, he would say 'Mmm?' and carry on reading!

'Are you listening to me?' I would say, raising my voice. He'd lower the paper and give me a distracted look.

'Er, what?'

'Oh, go back to your paper,' I'd say – and so he would! And when he'd finished reading the paper, he'd simply lay it down on the coffee table in front of him, generally open – open! – but certainly out of page order so when I came to read it the sport section was somehow at the front while the interesting lifestyle bits were at the back.

And books. He couldn't put his books back neatly on the bedside table. Oh no. He had to leave them open but face down on the floor next to the chair in which he'd been sitting reading. He wouldn't even put a bookmark in. 'You'll break the spine,' I told him when he pushed the book down to better flatten it against the pale oak floorboards.

'Books are meant to be read and used.' He laughed. 'You're so anal, Teri.'

'I'm not anal,' I said. 'I just like things to be nice.'

'Well, everything in this flat is very nice,' he said. 'And you're nice, too. Come here and let me show you how nice I think you are…'

I was tempted. It would be so easy to slip into his lap and feel his arms wrap around my waist. But I was irritated. I can't relax when the flat is a mess; when things are out of order.

'I haven't got time,' I said. 'I must clean this place up.'

If anyone was anal, it was him, and his lime juice and letter-opening ritual. Once the envelopes had been opened and contents read, they were left in no particular order, in an untidy pile on the table, which I'd just laid for our meal. Why couldn't he put the envelopes in the green bin for recycling? Why couldn't he chuck away the circulars and the charity begging letters? Left to his own devices, he'd leave piles of correspondence on the table to grow – torn envelopes and inconsequential letters, discarded now he knew they didn't carry the promise he'd earlier thought they contained, whatever promise that might be.

His annoying little habits were beginning to get to me. I leant against the edge of the kitchen unit, a tea towel slung over my arm midway between drying up that morning's breakfast dishes, left to drain, and moving over to the oven to take out whatever it was I'd been cooking.

Next, he'll ask me if there are any messages.

'Any messages?' he asked, looking at me for perhaps the first time that night and obviously believing it was my role as an unpaid secretary to check the answerphone, even though, since he moved in, most of the calls on the landline were for him. It would be the Claxton WI, or a local Rotary Club wanting him to give a talk – Life as a Famous Television Presenter – or it would be a local library group or animal rescue sanctuary wanting him to become their president. The glamorous life of a TV celebrity.

When these blessed organisations rang and I answered, I said Dan wasn't available and they should ring the studio to talk to Doreen. But invariably it had been Doreen who'd given them this number, and anyway, they said they didn't want to disturb him while he was busy at work, so could I take a message? So, I'm not busy, then?

Why they bothered ringing the landline anyway, when Dan gave his mobile number to anyone, willy-nilly, I just don't know. And why he gave his mobile number out, I don't know either. He hated to miss a call; I suppose. Even when the phone rang and there was no one there when we answered, it clearly being a try-on by some call centre in Delhi, Dan would press 1471 to get the number and ring it back. 'Don't do that, you idiot,' I yelled at him.

'But it might be something important,' he replied.

'Yes, the call centre cashing in on you ringing a premium number.'

So, you'll understand when I say how annoying it was while we were out together, Dan would be constantly checking his mobile.

'Sorry about this,' he said, having answered his phone as we walked around the local lake, hand-in-hand, on a rare day off together.

He'd turn away to concentrate more closely on the call eventually flicking his hand in my direction in the hope I'd interpret it as a sign to get a pen and paper out of my bag so he could make a note. It was always either the studio – could he do a last-minute interview, now, this afternoon? Or some do-good organisation wanting his services. And he always said 'Yes' whatever the request, even if it meant leaving me on our day off to dash into the studios and record some inane, fatuous interview with someone like Shayne Brickham.

Chapter 35

Lee

Back at work, Peter's team diagnostics working party was now 'touching base offline' on a fairly regular basis. At least Peter, Stella, Mike, and I were meeting regularly, Teri rather less so. Peter tutted frequently at her inability to 'diarise' the meeting schedule, which meant she almost always sent last-minute apologies for her non-attendance. 'Perhaps we should simply sunset her involvement in this project,' he suggested after her fourth no-show. I sighed. If only he'd do the same for me?

But that'd mean I wouldn't be able to punctuate his pontifications about 'deep diving' and 'push and pull strategies' and 'getting down among the weeds' with reminders that in 'decomposing to a lower level of granulation' we mustn't lose sight of our 'secret sauce'.

In other words, our primary function as a university was to educate the next generation of thinkers, and not simply to generate profit.

Unfortunately, Peter's not fluent in plain English.

He's good at delegating, though. 'Perhaps you'd like to cascade the situation to Teri,' he suggested.

I didn't 'like' but considered it prudent to avoid providing Teri with an opportunity to tell Peter what she thought about his efforts to 'sharpen the point of the pencil'. She laughed when I passed on the news.

'I suppose it means I'll be first for transitioning when the downsizing begins,' she said, mimicking Peter's management-speak. She shrugged. 'Who cares?'

Well, she ought, but Peter and his obsession with 'looking under the departmental bonnet' was just another in a long line of irritants. She was irritated with Dan because he was untidy; with Victoria, because she was always underfoot; and with the ex-wife for siphoning off a share of Dan's income, which Teri considered belonged to her. 'She's always treating herself to new clothes,' she raged, thumping her chest, 'while I'm still wearing this old rag.'

Since the rag in question was practically brand-new and carried a designer label, and price tag to match, it was hard to sympathise.

'And Dan,' she said, launching into a new rant. 'He pays more attention to a piece of junk mail than he does to me.'

I found that hard to believe.

'Do you know how long he spent studying an envelope this morning?' she demanded.

I gawked.

She nodded. 'Turning it over and over between his fingers, trying to work out who'd sent it.'

Yes, I could see how that might niggle but… 'I suppose everyone's picked up a letter and wondered who'd sent it.'

'But they don't spend ten minutes staring at it!' she screamed.

No. I'd have simply ripped it open, so why didn't Dan…

'Because it was addressed to *me*,' she bellowed. 'So none of his business.' She was panting heavily. 'And, it had the logo of a Parisian perfume house plastered in large letters across the front. Which,' her voice dripped sarcasm, 'should have been a big clue as to the identity of the sender.'

Oh dear! Although why she was getting into such a tizz about a piece of junk mail was beyond comprehension.

'And when he's not staring at envelopes, he's glued to his mobile phone.'

Talk about the pot calling the kettle black.

'Texting nighty-night to his precious daughter. Or, sending her snaps of what we're eating for dinner. Or, just checking with the office…' Teri drew the back of her hand across her forehead. 'You don't know what I've got to put up with.'

Actually, I did, because she told me ad nauseam. Between her and Peter, and grief over the baby I hadn't known I wanted until it was too late and fighting the temptation to deck Mike, who kept hinting he'd like to take our relationship to a new level – well, I was darn glad I'd accepted my sister's invitation to join her and the family on a spring break. It was the only bright spot in an otherwise gloomy landscape.

Chapter 36

Lee

There were many, many times during the almost interminable drive between Yorkshire and our Norfolk holiday home when I thought I must've been more than several sandwiches short of a picnic to have agreed to tag along with Fliss and her family. Or at the very least I should have insisted on travelling in my own car rather than sitting in the back seat wedged between my toddler niece and her seven-year-old brother. We were barely two junctions down the motorway when Ritchie asked, for the first time, if we were nearly there. No, we weren't. And not likely to be there any time soon since the entire country seemed to be little more than an endless succession of road works – and toilet stops. Either Ritchie needed the loo, or Fee's nappy needed changing.

It was like travelling in a different world.

Eventually, we crossed into East Anglia, and the countryside became gentle and rolling. For a while we followed the coast road before moving slightly inland to our cottage, several times slowing to a crawl as we followed families on bikes making their way along the twisty roads.

'Mum, Mum.' Ritchie bounced up and down. 'Can I get a bike? Mum, Mum, can I?'

Fliss hedged her bets.

'We'll see, darling. They might be too expensive.' Ritchie grimaced. He'd heard that line before.

I nudged him gently and mouthing 'yes', put a finger to my lips and nodded meaningfully towards the front seats. He grinned and nodded back.

So, Ritchie, and I hired a couple of bikes and every day of our little break, we jabbed a pin in a map and set off to explore. We jumped waves on long, flat beaches, ate fish and chips sitting on harbour walls, and consumed industrial quantities of ice cream.

It was perfect. Ritchie's simple pleasure in my company was balm to the soul, and the exercise meant I came home pounds lighter and felt and looked better than in a long time. My clothes felt looser, and, in a rash of enthusiasm, I signed up at the local gym where I made two discoveries. First, that cycling on an exercise bike is nowhere near as much fun as cycling outdoors with the wind on your face, and second, you're never too old to fall for a line from a bloke with a fit body and a face to match.

Chapter 37

Teri

One thing that was really getting to me was the fact Victoria was in almost constant touch with Dan. But the devious little sod never rang the landline at my flat; she preferred to ring her daddy on his mobile or text him.

We'd be enjoying a meal at a local restaurant or a weekend away and 'beep' his mobile would announce a new text. He'd reach into his jacket pocket and retrieve the mobile, look at the message, and smile. I'd never know what it said unless I asked.

'What is it?'

'Oh, just my little girl,' he said.

'Well, what does she want?' I said, cross at the intrusion.

'Oh, nothing… just hoping we're having a nice meal.'

'How does she know we're out having a meal?'

Dan looked at me incredulously. 'Because I told her earlier.'

'When… earlier?' I demanded.

'She popped into the studios for lunch,' he said.

'Well, you never said,' I said.

'There was nothing to tell,' he replied. 'She pops in from time to time if she hasn't got any lessons. It's a nice thing to do.'

Putting aside the idea that a fifteen-year-old would be having lessons all the time throughout the day and probably shouldn't be leaving the school grounds, I retorted: 'You never invite me for lunch at the studios.'

'Well,' Dan said with more impatience in his voice than I thought necessary. 'You don't have a very high opinion of the people I work with. You're always saying how "screechy and needy" they are – your words, not mine. So I just thought you wouldn't want to come to the studios to have lunch with me – or them.'

True, I'd told him often enough I thought the telly types he worked with were a bunch of drama queens and he was a fool for dropping everything when they rang to ask him to go rushing down to the studios to host some last-minute televised debate or stand in for another presenter who was away. 'Teri,' Dan would say, 'it's my job… And I happen to really like all the people that you call "drama queens". They're my friends as well as colleagues.'

Then it dawned on me: Victoria was clearly included in the jolly TV crowd.

'Oh, so she gets invited to telly lunches with you and the team, but I don't?'

'Oh… Teri…' Dan sounded exasperated now.

I desperately needed to talk to Lee. But, of course, she was on holiday, and her mobile was going straight to voicemail. I needed to tell her how the Victoria situation was getting out of hand. It wasn't so much the intrusion, but that most of the time when Victoria contacted her father it was in some way to butter him up for something she wanted. There would be one or two calls and one or two texts and then a clincher. 'Victoria wants…' Dan would tell me as a precursor to whatever it was she'd demanded: new clothes, an expensive watch, a holiday. I told him he was being too generous, but he just smiled, and said how he liked to indulge her. 'She's had a tough time, poor kid,' he said, 'what with the divorce and everything.'

She'd had a tough time? My God, she should try stepping out of the cotton wool blanket her parents wrapped her up in and see what the real world was all about.

Chapter 38

Lee

'Hey,' a voice interrupted my thinking, and a strong, bronzed hand placed a cardboard flask in the cup-holder on the handlebars of my exercise bike. 'You seem to be working double hard, so I brought you this.' He gestured towards the drink. 'It'll keep you hydrated.' He smiled, saluted, and walked off. I stared, unable to avoid noticing the broad sweep of his shoulders and tight glutes beneath his gym shorts. He paused, turned, and strode back. 'Don't tell anyone or they'll all expect one.' He grinned, and strolled across the gym floor, stopping as he passed another member to demonstrate the correct position to execute a bent over row – except I didn't know that's what it was called then.

I swept sweaty tendrils of hair off my face and resumed pedalling. 'Hey,' that voice again. 'Here.' He tugged at the bobble holding his blonde hair in a tight ponytail. 'Looks like you need this more than I do.'

Startled, I stammered, 'Thanks, but—'

He shook his head and indicated the drink. 'Give yourself five. You'd be surprised what a difference it'll make to your energy levels.' He waited while I sipped tentatively.

'Oh, that's good,' I exclaimed. He gave a thumbs-up and pushed the hair tie into my hands.

'Get the hair off your neck, it'll help keep you cool.'

It was a master class in the perfect soft-sell – and on my way out, I stopped, and asked the receptionist about the ponytailed trainer.

And that was the start of a beautiful relationship in which David Greenspan blew away the gym cobwebs. He had me running on the treadmill for what felt the entire length of the Great North Road, cycling coast to coast, and rowing from one end of the Leeds-Liverpool canal to the other. And then we moved into the weight room. Forty-five minutes later, I ached in places I didn't even know had muscles.

'Stop grumbling,' David ordered at regular intervals, and I'd swear rudely. Sometimes under my breath – mostly not. 'Potty mouth,' he'd tease. 'You enjoy it really.' I grunted, but there was no denying it was pleasant to have the undivided attention of a good-looking bloke – even if it was only for sixty minutes, three times a week, and it required a regular direct debit payment.

And then about a month into our training relationship he dropped a bombshell. 'Older women, like you, Lee, are so much more attractive than younger ones.' I was spread-eagled on the gym mat, gasping for breath after completing ten push-ups, and his words took a moment to sink in.

'Really?' I asked. Yes, really. And me, in particular.

I struggled to a sitting position and sneaked a peek at his suddenly uncharacteristically serious face. He stuttered slightly. 'I-I-I don't suppose you'd care to come for a drink with me?'

Chapter 39

Teri

When Lee finally came back from her holiday, I recounted the latest row with Dan and told her about Victoria and the intrusive texts.

'Why does she need to do that?' I asked when we got together for coffee in the Senior Common Room. 'Why does she feel she has to hope we have a nice meal… a good weekend? And why do she and Dan meet up so often without telling me?'

'Well, ringing to hope you're having a nice time is a kind thing to do,' Lee said. 'And maybe Dan is a little sensitive to how you feel about Victoria, so he feels awkward about mentioning her. He realises you're jealous.'

'I'm not jealous,' I exploded. 'No, she does it because she wants to interfere and be involved in everything we do.'

'Isn't that a good thing?'

'No. I want there to be things that just Dan and I do. Things that just Dan and I know about. Why can't we go out for a meal or go away for a weekend without him having to tell her?'

'He's her father, Teri. He wants her to feel involved.'

'Well, I wish he didn't. I'd like a private life – one which doesn't involve a selfish brat of a daughter.'

Chapter 40

Lee

There's only one drawback to being a normal-sized mid-thirties woman, dating a pec-toned young man in his early twenties – at some point he's going to want to consummate the relationship, which means exposing three decades-worth of lumps and bumps. Now if I'd had the body confidence of Teri – and spent my entire life eating like a budgie – that wouldn't have been an issue. But I hadn't, and it was.

David was sweetly – irritatingly – patient. 'We'll take things at your pace, Lee,' he said, and my fingers very nearly curled into fists.

Nevertheless, he was undeniably good arm-candy, and there was a great deal of vicarious pleasure in counting the envious stares, and some incredulous ones too, when we walked into a bar together.

Unfortunately, he could also be a terrible killjoy. 'Another glass of wine, Lee? You've had two already.'

Yes, and I'm having a third – and probably a fourth and fifth as well.

And the longer we dated, the more it became clear why he had a six-pack, and I didn't. He eschewed alcohol, chocolate, sweets, crisps, and biscuits; ate hardly any carbohydrates or red meat; and filled up on good proteins – beans and pulses, mostly. And eggs. 'We are what we consume, Lee,' he said. I knew exactly what I'd be if I followed his diet – full of wind.

As relationships went, it was all a bit dull.

However, the same couldn't be said about the rest of my life, because with Peter Heron cracking his 'wind of change' whip and Teri apparently in self-destruct mode, both at home, and work, I'd got about as much drama on my plate as I could handle. Peter, at least, was reasonably consistent in that he had a clear game plan. Teri was so up and down it was hard to know what she wanted – other than to get the 'Devil child' out of her life. Useless to tell her that it wasn't going to happen – she just muttered something about 'teaching Dan a lesson'.

'Don't be an idiot,' I said, thinking it was just an empty threat and then – Peter had another one of his dratted soirees, and I was exchanging pleasantries with Chrissie from admin when she broke off mid-sentence and stared intently across the room where Teri was huddled in a corner, flirting outrageously with Declan.

'Excuse me,' I murmured, looking for somewhere to place my empty glass. 'I need to go—'

'He can't help himself, can he?' Chrissie blinked rapidly. 'He was all over me at last year's pre-Christmas soiree.'

Yes, and she'd been rather obviously all over him too.

'Dumped me like a ton of bricks afterwards.' More rapid blinking.

Good Lord – were those tears in her eyes?

'He'll find Miss High-and-Mighty-Meyer a different kettle of fish,' Chrissie said, rather nastily, I thought.

'Excuse me,' I repeated. 'I need to—'

'You're wasting your time,' Chrissie said. 'I know his type,' she continued.

Which was ridiculous, because if she'd known his type, she wouldn't have got stuck in the broom cupboard with him.

'They think they can have any woman they want.'

Well, if Declan thought that he must have forgotten the church Christmas disco the year before he moved to London. As always, he'd been surrounded by a score of adoring girls – a bunch that did NOT include me. Instead, I was making a soft drink last a phenomenally long time as I chatted with Kelvin Turvey, who despite being a bit of a geek, was clever, and shy and good looking in a long-legged, clumsy sort of way.

Declan, however, had already become one of those guys that, to borrow a Yorkshire phrase, likes to think of himself as the 'cock of the walk' and he'd sauntered over to us, swooning maidens in tow, and tried to pull me to my feet. 'Come on, Lee. Let's dance.'

'No, thanks.' I had two left feet and had no intention of displaying them to Declan. Or anyone else. Sharp intakes of breath from Declan's harem and silence from Declan, who, eyes narrowed, considered us. Eventually, he shrugged. 'Okay,' he said.

It was the first and only time Declan ever asked me to dance. And possibly the first and only time he'd been turned down. But I'd learnt one thing: Declan didn't waste time hankering after what he couldn't have. Especially when there were plenty of other fish in the sea. So, if I could thwart him now, I might just save my friend from making a big mistake.

She didn't want saving, though. When I raised my empty glass and signalled to her to join me for a refill, she shook her head, and frowned. '*Go away*,' those expensively shaped and tinted eyebrows signalled as clearly as if she'd shouted it across the room.

'Don't!' I mouthed back. She stuck her tongue out, and allowed Declan to take her hand in his, and pull her towards the door.

Chapter 41

Teri

Another day, another row with Dan. Generally, we managed to be polite with each other, but each time he mentioned his daughter I'd freeze, and it got so that he hardly dared mention her at all and simply said, 'I'm going out on Monday night…' or something like that and I would know he was meeting her or taking her somewhere. Never mind me. I only live here; I'm only your wife.

He tried occasionally to say something along the lines of 'Look, Teri, we're not leaving you out of things. You are more than welcome to come with us.' But I told him I'd married him and not his daughter, and as far as I was concerned, he could go and play happy families; I had better things to do. He'd sigh as though I was missing some point or making a big mistake. And life got more icily polite.

It nearly blew up when I wanted to book a holiday, but Dan said he couldn't get away from work. I rang D'reen and (innocently) asked her to look at Dan's work diary on the pretext I wanted to find a week when I could spring a surprise holiday on him. The daft cluck believed me and said, yes, he did have a week marked off in July. Idiotically, I thought for a minute he'd marked the week off to surprise me, but no.

When I asked him about it he was first annoyed I'd gone behind his back to D'reen, and then sheepish because he had to confess he wanted to take Victoria away somewhere as she was apparently 'growing up' and probably wouldn't want to go on holiday with the 'old man' in future years. He tried to say he had hoped I would go with them, but for goodness' sake, why on Earth would I want to go anywhere with this man who became cloyingly doting and boring when he was with his insufferable daughter?

I didn't see much of Lee apart from quick chats at uni. Often when I rang on an evening or weekend, she was just about to go to the gym or she'd just come back from the gym. What was it with that girl? I couldn't see any noticeable difference for all this gym business. But I needed to talk to her and on the rare occasions we did get together, I would tell her chapter and verse about what was happening or not happening with me and Dan – and Victoria. She tried to give me advice about 'seeing the other person's point of view' and I asked, what about my point of view? She said, maybe I was being a bit unreasonable, expecting everyone to fall in line and do whatever it was I wanted. 'I don't think it's unreasonable for a wife to want to spend time with her husband,' I said.

'But you do spend time with him,' Lee said.

'But he has so many other commitments. I'm fed up with sharing him.'

'No one can have another person exclusively,' she responded.

'It's so bloody unfair,' I moaned.

'Life's unfair,' she said, taking a sip of her white wine, 'and I'm afraid you have to make compromises.'

So the next row was about Peter Heron's media soiree and whether Dan would accept the invitation to come and be a telly type and thus provide me with some Brownie points, as it would put me in Peter's good books. But no. Darling Victoria had been rehearsing some dance routine and was taking part in a school show and going to see that was more important than helping me.

The row was short, sharp, and explosive. Dan stormed out, got into his BMW and accelerated away while I reached down, grabbed the coffee table with both hands and pulled upwards, overturning it, and sending coffee cups and magazines flying off. Shit, one of the mugs still had coffee in it, and as it hit the floor, the mug, forced under its own centrifugal force, spun round in a tight circle, spilling the cold, brown liquid over my oak flooring.

So I went to the soiree on my own and had probably drunk a little too much because I was actually having fun. I took the piss out of these ridiculous 'media' types who took themselves and their 'digital first', 'crowdsourcing apps' and 'live update threads' so seriously. Especially entertaining was a reporter called Cassie who, intermittently flicking her long, lank hair back from her face, was responding well to my teasing that she must meet a lot of interesting people in her job (as if interviewing Diamond Wedding couples and moaning council tenants could possibly be interesting). She was just expounding on the fact that the most interesting people were not celebrities and royalty but 'ordinary people with extraordinary stories' when a startlingly good-looking man came up behind her, put his finger to his lips to indicate 'shush' to me, then put his hands over her eyes and went 'Boo!' Cassie squealed, ducked down and, under his hands, spun round, and giggled. 'Oh… Declan… you daft sod.' She'd turned pink with delight.

Declan? I knew him from somewhere. That's it: Christmas at Lee's church. The newspaperman sitting in the pew in front of us.

Declan grinned at me. 'Cassie,' he said, 'you're needed. There's a fire at the tyre warehouse on Wellington Road. Can you nip down there and join Jon? A photographer's on the way too.'

'Are you not coming?' Cassie asked, buttoning up her jacket.

'No, I've got things to do here,' he said, looking at me, and winking.

Cassie broke into a run and headed for the exit. 'Ah, these young cubs.' Declan sighed, half turning away from me to watch her skip through the door.

I studied the back of his head: the light brown hair, longish, and floppy, cutely curling over the top of his collar, and I remembered he'd also been at last year's Peter Heron soiree (only that time, he'd been cosying up to Chrissie in quite a purposeful way).

'Don't you want to go with her?' I asked.

He turned back to me. 'Nah. Not much of a fire really, and it'll be out by the time she gets there.'

I looked round the room and saw Lee standing with Chrissie, looking our way. Chrissie was sending daggers. Tough, I thought; you had your chance. Lee had that concerned look on her face and was making some sort of gesture with her hands. Should I beckon her over?

No. This guy was seriously gorgeous and was looking at me in a way that made me feel as though I were the most fascinating object in the room. He introduced himself and when I told him who I was, he said, 'I know.' Ridiculously and girlishly flattered, I asked him if he wanted a drink, indicating the buffet table.

'Yes, but not here,' he said. 'Look, I'm a good friend of Lee's so you know you can trust me, and I know who you are and there's something I'd like to talk about. So can we go somewhere quieter and have a chat?'

****

It was never meant to happen. But to be honest, after the time I'd been having with the Dan situation, it had to happen. I needed some happiness in my life and here it was being offered to me by this gorgeous man.

I knew nothing about Declan other than he was some boss at the local paper and, although he was 'media' he wasn't screechy telly. He seemed more down to earth than these theatrical TV bods with their scripts and autocue dramas. And he was seriously interested in me. I could tell by the way he propelled me out of the soiree room. I looked back over my shoulder to indicate to Lee I was going, and I could see her mouth opening as if to shout after me but I flapped my arm in the hope she'd understand the semaphore for '*everything's okay, I know what I'm doing*'. She started to move towards us, but I spotted Peter Heron heading her way with Richard Walker – Duck's Arse – in tow. *Good old Peter*, I thought.

I left my car at the university because even I recognised I'd had too much to drink, and travelled with Declan in his rather battered, silver grey VW Golf. As I was climbing in, I noticed a sticker on the windscreen. *Evening Leader Leads* it said. 'Leads where?' I joked.

'Huh, very funny,' he said, obviously having heard that one before.

We headed up Wellington Road where black smoke pumped out of the roof of a warehouse and I spotted young Cassie, notebook, and pen poised, standing on the pavement talking to one of the firemen. 'Atta girl,' Declan said, grinning.

He knew a little basement bistro on Parker Place, and we ducked down some stone steps into the bar where he ordered a bottle of white wine, and we settled into a corner on some not very comfortable cushions dotted along a bench placed uncomfortably low beside an old wine barrel doing service as a table.

'Well,' I said, taking a drink. 'Was this just a ruse to get me here, or do you really need to talk to me about something?'

'Would I lie to you?' he joked. 'What it is, is that I wanted to meet your old man.'

Part of me was disappointed; I thought it was me he'd wanted to get to know. The other part was shocked. Why did he want to meet my father?

Declan read the look on my face and said, 'We've started a new business supplement in *The Leader* and we're featuring some of the county's most important industrialists. I know your dad is more-or-less retired, but he'd make a really interesting profile.'

I felt used and let down; my anger rising. 'Oh, for God's sake, why couldn't you just ring the factory?'

'Because,' he said, 'I wanted to get to know you and this seemed a good way of getting you on your own.' I started to stand, but he put a hand on my arm and pulled me gently back down. 'Honestly, believe me. I did ring the factory but the bugger in charge wouldn't tell me anything but by then I'd seen you at that do at the uni last November and I wanted to get to know you. I have to say, it was our friend Lee who stopped me.'

'You were more than happy with one of the admin girls at that event, if I remember rightly,' I reminded him, thinking of the way he had Chrissie pinned up against a wall.

He grinned again. 'Yes, but I'd rather have been with you.'

Why should I believe him? He was a journalist, for goodness' sake. He'd sell his granny for a good story.

'Look,' I said, relenting a little. 'Dad has very little to do with the factory now. He's semi-retired and perfectly happy living in deepest France where he doesn't like to be disturbed. And he certainly wouldn't appreciate any publicity. In fact, if you spoke to him, he'd probably tell you to shove off in not very polite terms.'

Declan looked a little crestfallen, but not altogether surprised. 'Gotta confess,' he said. 'I did speak to him.'

'What…?'

'I'm a journalist. I have my sources,' he said. 'I found out where your old man was living and went to see him.'

'You actually went down there?'

'It has been heard of for people to go to France.' He laughed.

'What did he say?'

'Ah, he told me to shove off and not in very polite terms.'

'So you did get me here under false pretences,' I said.

'I did.' He laughed, and then he leant forward and kissed me.

I pursed my lips tightly and pushed him back. 'What are you doing?' I demanded.

'Something I've been wanting to do for months,' he said, pulling me towards him, and kissing me again.

This time I didn't push him away but, in between kisses, I managed to tell him I was married.

'I know,' he said.

I told him we shouldn't be doing this.

'I know,' he said.

I explained I couldn't take him back to my flat.

'I know,' he said – clearly disappointed. 'And we can't go back to my place,' he said and stupidly, I knew better than to question why not. 'We could get a room…?' he suggested.

'At this time of night,' I said, looking at my watch. It was gone 11.30 p.m. 'They'd know we were only after one thing,' I said.

'I know. We are,' Declan replied.

'No,' I said. 'This is ridiculous. I'm going to call a taxi and go home.'

He looked at me like a little boy lost, but then he nodded, gave me one last quick kiss on the forehead and stood up, pulling me to my feet. 'You're right. I'll wait with you till the taxi comes.'

I have to confess I was surprised he gave up so easily but, true to his word, he waited with me on the pavement outside the bistro until the cab arrived, saw me into it, and waved me off cheerily.

As we pulled away up Wellington Road, the smoke still drifted heavenwards from the warehouse and the stench of burning rubber hung in the air. But there was no sign of Cassie who'd probably tweeted everything she'd seen and heard, and long since filled in *The Leader's* website templates with a story that captured the whole drama of hundreds of tyres going up in flames.

My mobile beeped. I looked down and saw a missed call, a voicemail, and two texts. The missed call and the voicemail were from Lee.

What are you doing? Are you mad? Ring me the instant you get this message.

The first text was also from Lee: *Ring me NOW*.

The second text was from an unknown number: *Safe journey home. I think I'm in love.*

My phone popped a request: *Save this number to your contacts*? I pressed the '*yes*' button and keyed Declan's name.

Lee was incandescent when I saw her at uni the next day. She hadn't dared ring me at home in case Dan answered, and had been on tenterhooks all night.

'You don't want to get involved with Declan,' she said. 'You're married to Dan, Teri. What are you thinking?'

'Look, Lee. It was all innocent. He wanted to talk about my father for some business supplement. I told him Dad would never do it and he accepted that, and he was the perfect gentleman and we had a drink and I got a taxi home.'

Lee looked at me as though she didn't believe a word. I didn't tell her about the kissing or the mobile phone message or the fact Declan had sent twelve further texts during the night along the lines of, *Yup, definitely in love…*

Chapter 42

Lee

One unexpected consequence of my relationship with David was his increasing frustration with life as a personal trainer. 'You're a very inspiring person, Lee,' he said once over drinks in a chic wine bar. I was only half-listening – something that happened a lot in David's company. The things that rocked his boat – hip hop music, street fashion, weightlifting – barely even floated mine.

'You make me feel I'm capable of achieving anything I want.'

Eek! That made me sit up. Where was this leading?

To a First Class Honours degree.

'I love being a trainer and helping people achieve their fitness goals but—' He shrugged. 'Ladies who lunch can be very shallow.'

'So, why university?'

'You, Lee.' He laughed. 'You make it sound so interesting.'

Really?

He struggled to explain. 'I don't really know… except I've always thought I should read more.'

'But you don't have to go to university to read books.'

'No, but which books should I read? I need a bit of direction.'

'You could join a book group.'

'No.' His chin jutted. 'I've made up my mind.'

I hesitated, wondering how to break it to him about entry qualifications and tuition fees and a whole host of other stuff – But he'd already done his homework and he'd spoken to somebody in our Admissions team, who'd confirmed he'd got the right number of points, and, had advised him to apply through the Clearing system when the exam results came out the week after next. He reckoned he could work his gym hours around his classes so he'd be okay for money and just needed to sort out references – 'I was hoping you'd be able to help there,' he said – and, though, strictly speaking, it was slightly unethical because of our personal relationship – I agreed. Fast forward a month-and-a-half and freshers' week found him strolling ten minutes late into Peter Heron's induction lecture and parking himself in an empty aisle seat near the front of the auditorium.

No apology, no blush of embarrassment, no self-conscious attempt to assume an interested, listening expression. He simply sat down, crossed his legs, right ankle resting comfortably on his left knee, and leant back in his seat, hands clasped behind his head. A picture of raw, young, fresh sexuality.

I felt a pang of regret – we'd both agreed it wasn't a good idea to continue a relationship. 'I don't want to compromise your professionalism,' he'd said. Which was very gentlemanly of him, but also a huge relief. It'd be nice to pour a glass of wine without having to listen to him tut-tut. But, nevertheless, he was very – 'Gorgeous,' Teri, who'd also observed his arrival, whispered in my ear.

Chapter 43

Teri

The dozen-or-so texts Declan left on my mobile had to be wiped off, even though I was reluctant to do so. The poor boy was obviously smitten, and it was flattering. But, although Dan wasn't the sort of man to go checking my phone, I didn't want him to see the messages. There was the argument that, yes, he deserved to know someone else fancied me and wanted to be with me, which might bring him to his senses and realise I was not to be messed with. But the counterargument was that I didn't want to hurt Dan by him thinking I was being unfaithful. After all, I wasn't being unfaithful. Quite the opposite. I'd always been loyal to Dan, despite the various temptations that offered themselves.

Take, for instance, David Greenspan, in my Level 1 English in the Time of Charles II. Older than the usual student, he'd just arrived at uni: totally gorgeous. Shaggy blond hair, six-pack in a tight T-shirt, and long, lean limbs in designer-ripped jeans. And quick and clever as well. Who wouldn't be tempted? I was, but I had to consider Dan.

And now Declan was on the scene.

Was I planning to be unfaithful with him? I knew I shouldn't, but he was an extremely gorgeous man, and what made him even more gorgeous was the fact he found me gorgeous, too.

I didn't respond to any of the texts, thinking Declan would get the message, go away, and leave me to mend whatever was left of my broken marriage. Dan and I hardly spoke now. I was cold and frosty most of the time and he was out and about most of the time, either with his daughter or, more often, with his television mates working in programme proposals. He did manage to tell me, over one particularly polite Monday night dinner where we found ourselves at home together at the same time, heating up a Marks & Spencer ready meal for two, that he was working on a documentary that would mean him going away for a week's filming in Scotland. He'd be meeting and interviewing former Yorkshire folk who'd moved north of the border.

With something of an effort that I saw and appreciated, Dan suggested I go with him. 'We'll be filming all over the place, including the Western Isles, it's beautiful up there… And you could go exploring, walking…'

It was a good try, typical of nice old Dan. But surely he knew me better than to think I could bear to spend my spare time up in the Highlands eating haggis and battling midges. I was civil in my reply. 'It's good of you, but I'd be bored rigid. No, you go off with your mates and have a good time filming.'

'It won't be a holiday, Teri,' he said, 'it's work.'

'Even more reason why I shouldn't go with you,' I said. 'That way you don't need to worry about me and what I'm doing when you're supposed to be working.'

Dan tried to interest me further by showing me a map of Scotland with places highlighted in red he'd be visiting, but other than noting the names and numbers of the various hotels in which they'd be staying, I left it at that. 'I can ring you on your mobile if I need to get in touch,' I told him.

'We'll be in places where there's no mobile signal,' he said.

'Phew.' I managed a weak laugh. 'In that case, I'm glad I'm not coming.'

We left it at that, and he set off for Scotland a couple of weeks later in a large, white estate car with Bill, the cameraman, Patsy, the researcher-producer, and a boot-load of television recording equipment.

The large, white estate car had probably barely reached Newcastle on the A1 when I texted Declan.

Chapter 44

Teri

I knew I shouldn't be doing this, but he continued to text me, although the number of messages dropped to one at a time (rather than a dozen) and the frequency to just once a day. His last one read: *Not giving up.*

My message back simply said, *Good.*

We met for a drink that night after he'd 'put the paper to bed'.

'Do people really say that in a newspaper?' I asked him as we sat in the Parker Place basement bistro, considering it to be 'our' place, no doubt.

'No, not really. Now everything's digital and on websites, the news is never safely tucked up and done with for the night,' he said. 'If something happened now – say this bistro burnt down – I'd be able to get a story on the website within seconds whatever time of the day or night.'

'Well, let's hope it doesn't burn down then, and you can have another drink,' I said.

'It might not be burning down,' Declan said, 'but it sure is hot in here. It must be you.'

I'd never been called hot stuff before, well, not to my face, and talking of bed – while the newspaper wasn't safely tucked up – we eventually were. We'd hardly had time to down the first glass of wine before Declan was kissing me, running his hands lightly over my silk shirt, and suggesting we get a room.

'We don't need to,' I said, thinking how Dan would, by now, be safely over the border and considering kilt patterns in the Edinburgh evening mist.

I knew I shouldn't be doing this, especially after talking again to Lee about Declan. She half believed my story about him only wanting to talk to me about my father, but I couldn't resist questioning her some more about him. Turns out they'd been at school together and she knew – or semi-knew – his wife.

'Oh,' I said, feeling momentarily deflated. 'He's married?'

'Yes, Teri,' she said. 'You must have realised that?'

'No, he seems such a happy type. Young, free, and single… not the married sort at all. I mean, look at the way he was sniffing and licking Chrissie.'

'Ugh, you're disgusting, Teri,' she said. 'And another thing. He's got kids.'

That should have been the red alert. But… There was something about Declan I couldn't resist. Surely it would do no harm to have a drink with him.

But once I saw him again, sitting in the basement bistro in the semidarkness, waiting for me to arrive, thoughts of wives and kids went out of my head.

We drove back separately to my duplex; me getting there first, so I was able to check my hair and make-up, undo a few buttons of my shirt, and be standing, welcoming, in the hallway when he rang the buzzer. He came in and, without taking his eyes off me, gently nudged the door closed behind him with his foot while reaching for me and pulling me into his chest, nuzzling his face down into the side of my neck. I've read in cheap novels how women melt into their men's arms, but, honestly, I melted. There was nothing I could do; I wanted this man. I've known lust before; hell, I've known love before, but nothing like this. I wanted to consume him; lap up every part of him; be part of him. Quite simply, I couldn't keep my hands off. He pulled me down onto the white oak floorboards and with an urgency that had us both scrabbling, pulling, and tearing clothes off each other. We were kissing, pulling, and rubbing, sighing, snarling, and then came together right there in the hallway. At one point, he kicked out with his foot against the reclaimed wood hall dresser, but I was too distracted, too happy, to say, 'Be careful. That's antique.'

When we finished and lay there, half naked, and panting, neither of us spoke for a few minutes. I lay in Declan's arms, and we both stared at the ceiling.

'Nice place you have here,' he said eventually, laughing. 'Er, does it have a bedroom, or should we stay here?'

We spent that night together – well… we spent the rest of that night and the early morning hours together, making love three times more before Declan finally said he had to go. He pulled on his clothes and as he fastened his watch, I looked at the bedside clock: 3.30 a.m. I wasn't going to ask where he was going, who he was going back to, what he would say when he got back. I didn't want to know. He leant over to kiss me goodbye. 'I'll let myself out,' he said. 'You need your rest, you've been a busy girl.' That twinkly eyed look again. 'Tell you what,' he added. 'Take tomorrow off – let's go somewhere.'

I should've been in uni the next morning, but what the hell? It was only Level 1 tutorials. They could catch-up and, having composed a general 'send to all' text to the students saying I was ill, I waited for Declan to return.

The rest of the week followed a pattern. Declan said he'd taken some much-owed time off work and I rang Chrissie to say I was really ill and wouldn't be coming in for a few days and could she look at my timetable and let all my students know to save me the bother of having to get out of my sickbed to text them every day? She grumpily agreed.

Declan came to the flat each morning and, surprisingly, we didn't fall back into bed. Instead, we went off for a walk round the park, for a picnic by a lake, to visit a local stately home, to have lunch in a museum café. We drove up into the Dales and I took photos on my camera of the limestone pavements at Malham. Declan wouldn't have his picture taken. 'Can't stand having my photo taken, so don't even try,' he warned me, and got quite cross when I tried to take a surreptitious selfie of the two of us.

Wherever we went, we wandered hand-in-hand, or arm in arm, stopping at gates to kiss, leaning over coffee pots to kiss, buying gallery tickets only to walk away from the booth to kiss, looking at paintings in an exhibition and kissing; constantly stroking, rubbing, and pulling at each other. 'I can't keep my hands off you,' he said.

'Don't even try,' I told him.

We bought food and returned to my apartment to cook dinner, which we ate together listening to CDs Declan had in his car – unusual choices given they were classical rather than pop. They included Elgar's *Cello Concerto* and Faure's *Requiem*, which made me sad, and surprisingly tearful.

'Hey… hey,' he said, when he realised, I was crying. 'What's wrong?'

'It's the music. It's just so beautiful,' I told him. 'And I'm so happy. I don't want this to end.'

And then, only then, when we'd had dinner, listened to music, did we go to bed and make love – sometimes gentle and soft, sometimes passionate and wild. And Declan stayed with me all night.

It was probably Day 3 when I told myself again that I shouldn't be doing this – at least, not without having some questions answered. I could hardly believe it myself that I managed not to ask until then, but a huge part of me didn't want to know or accept what the answers would be.

Declan said, yes, he'd been married to Marnie for nearly twenty-five years.

'What…?' I was genuinely stunned he'd been married for so long.

'We were sixteen,' he said. 'First boyfriend and girlfriend and, of course, she got pregnant, and everyone was saying we were too young and that it would never work, so we got married to prove 'em all wrong.'

'And the baby?'

'Ah,' Declan said. 'She had a miscarriage when we got back from honeymoon. But by then we were married, and I could hardly bugger off and leave her. I thought it was the right thing to do to stand by her. I'd just started at the paper as a junior reporter, so I was busy, and time went on and well… suddenly twenty-five years go by.'

'But you've got other kids?' I said.

'Yeah, we thought, after the miscarriage that she couldn't get pregnant, but God knows what happened. Pow! She started pushing them out like peas. Well, not peas, exactly, but a lad, who's now fourteen, and two girls, one ten, and the other eight months.

'Well, you can't be an unhappily married man if you're still having kids together?' I said.

'That's the point,' Declan said, looking at me seriously. 'I'm not an unhappily married man. I won't lie to you, Teri, there was nothing wrong with my marriage. I wasn't looking to leave. I wasn't looking to find anyone else. But then I met you.'

And it was a good line. The only problem was, I believed it. Oh, I knew I shouldn't be doing this, but it had been a glorious few days of long lunches, relaxed walks, and time that drifted. Declan talked some more about his family. He told his wife he was away on a week's assignment for the paper. Strangely, he didn't seem to feel guilty about this. He didn't exactly say what she didn't know wouldn't hurt her, but he was almost casual in the knowledge he was getting away with being unfaithful to his wife of twenty-five years as if, by some gross self-delusion, after that length of time, he deserved an affair.

'I love her,' he insisted. 'But I love you.' And that was his excuse and his reasoning.

I felt incredibly sad as we made love on the final night, the night before Dan was due back and the night before Declan was supposed to return from his 'work trip'.

I cried as Declan lay over me, as though this was the last time we'd ever be together.

'Hey,' he said, pausing, and looking down at me, lying on the bed beneath him. 'What's up?'

'Oh, I don't know… it's just that… well, life's going to go back to normal again, isn't it?'

'Afraid so,' he said matter-of-factly.

Only for me, it didn't go back to quite the normal I'd known.

Chapter 45

Lee:

I deserve a medal as big as a dustbin lid as recompense for yet another coffee break ruined by Teri's incessant whining about Dan and her yearning for Declan.

'I know I shouldn't be falling in love with him,' she said.

'Don't,' I said.

'You can't just not fall in love with someone,' she said.

'Yes, you can, especially when the "someone" is already married.'

'It didn't stop you,' she said, glaring.

'I wasn't in love.'

'That's even worse,' she said.

Possibly, but Mike had hit on me at Granddaddy's funeral when I was vulnerable.

'I'm vulnerable too,' Teri said, pulling her mouth down in a forlorn attempt to look sad.

'Nobody's died,' I said.

'My marriage is dead.'

Drama queen. 'The ink's barely dry on your marriage certificate. It hasn't had time to die.'

'Lee,' she said, 'you're turning into a sour old maid.'

Well! There was no way of answering that one – not politely anyway – so, muttering something about 'going to the gym' I left her to it, and swapped her love travails for those of David, who having briefly flirted with a cougar – me – was now dating a sugar plum princess aka hairdresser Becky. 'It's love,' he confided as I plodded on the treadmill. How sweet. And dreary, because his every other sentence began 'Becky this…' or 'Becky that…' Once, midway through a set of bent over rows, he whipped out his mobile, and held up a succession of photographs taken during a weekend break in Scarborough. The temptation to point out that boring clients to death was a sure way to kill business was almost overwhelming. But all those hours of listening to Teri paid off, and I bit my tongue, said nice things about Becky – 'so pretty' – and admired the east coast scenery.

And, when, a couple of days later, I bumped into the pair of them at the supermarket, I even managed a whole minute of polite conversation, which, since Becky was clearly several curlers short of a perm, took some doing. 'She's nothing like you, Lee,' David confided next time we met at the gym – which may have been a compliment. Or, there again, might not. 'I think she could be the one,' he added, clouding the compliment issue even further.

But she wasn't the one, because she dumped him some time later in favour of a bodyguard with better-defined pecs and a bright red Mini Cooper with a Union Jack roof.

And that's when David and I finally ended up in bed.

Chapter 46

Teri

Dan arrived home full of tales about the Yorkshire folk managing to survive in deepest Scotland – running fish and chip shops, selling whittled walking sticks, and rebuilding dry stone walls. He'd found it all fascinating. But his cheery persona only irritated me. He was too nice; he saw good and interest in everyone, while I could only be cynical about them.

Over the next few weeks Declan and I managed sneaky lunches together, and we sometimes met for a drink after I finished work, but he could never stay long. He had to either get back to the paper or go home to his wife, and we certainly had no chance to get a room and make love.

And that was really frustrating. I never knew how much I missed sex until I wasn't having any with Declan. Dan tried once or twice to get amorous, but I brushed him off. I couldn't stand his wretched fumbling. If I couldn't have Declan, I didn't want anyone.

Dan withdrew into his cool, polite shell, and we had a final, glorious row as Christmas approached.

I remembered the argument this time last year and now, my first Christmas as Dan's wife, and what does he want to do? Spend the freaking festive season with his freaking daughter. Again.

'But you had her last year,' I said. 'I thought it was your ex-wife's turn to have the precious child.'

He sighed in exasperation. His reasoning was that, as I'd been so hostile lately and clearly didn't want to be with him, he might as well spend Christmas with Victoria. 'And where exactly will you go?' I asked, telling him he needn't think about having jolly crackers and fun and games in my flat. He blew the wind out of me: he was going to his former marital home (for which he was still paying the mortgage, obviously). Sara was going away with a new boyfriend to some tropical island, leaving Victoria on her own. Made sense for Dan to bunk down over there. I told him if that was what he was going to do, he could pack his things and move over there permanently. So he packed his things and, because Sara didn't want him moving in there and then, he moved into a hotel until he could find a flat, which he then moved into. And I started divorce proceedings.

And told Declan I was free.

Chapter 47

Teri

I thought Declan would want to celebrate, and certainly the night after Dan moved out, Declan came round to the duplex and we made riotous love, laughing, and yelping in delight, right there in the hallway minutes after he stepped over the threshold.

'God, I've missed you,' I said as we both struggled to our feet.

'Me too,' he said, pulling on his jeans, and flattening his hair down with his hands. We were still in the hallway and I pulled at his arm to lead him into the living room. 'Ah,' he said. 'I can't stop. Sorry, love. There's a big story on and I've got to get back to the office.'

'But I thought…' But whatever I thought, he didn't want to know, and with a quick peck on the cheek and a friendly slap on my behind, he was gone.

We saw each other when we could; I appreciated Declan had a senior post at the paper and he was a busy man and on-call much of the time – and he also had a family – so he couldn't just drop everything and come when I wanted him to, and when we were together, he'd often have to dash off to cope with something at the office or at home. Being the 'other woman' took some getting used to.

****

Declan and I were having a meal together at my flat one evening after he'd told the office he was leaving early and persuaded Marnie he was working late, and he suddenly looked up and around, and said, 'This is a fabulous place you have here,' as though he was seeing it for the first time. 'I mean, how great to have a place like this… and the freedom.'

I took it as a hint that his marriage, his wife and his kids were oppressing him and said, 'Well, you know you're welcome to move in.'

He looked thoughtful for a moment, considering, as though the idea of moving in with me had never occurred to him, and then he shook his head. 'No, I mean the freedom to move, without anyone else around telling you what to do,' he said. 'I'd love a place where I could just be on my own, to do whatever I wanted to do, whenever I wanted to do it. I've never had that.' He looked wistful.

I refused to feel deflated and persisted; it made sense. He could leave his wife and move in with me. We loved each other; we were good together.

Even I could see I was pressurising him and was annoyed at having to do it. What was wrong with the man? It was bad enough my having to persuade Lee that what Declan and I had was wonderful – in the face of her continuing and strong disapproval – without my having to persuade Declan too.

'Look, Declan,' I said. 'I don't like being the other woman. I'm not willing to play second fiddle. I love you and you love me. You've got to decide what you want to do.' I wasn't exactly saying it's Marnie or me. But that's what I meant.

It took a few days. I nagged him. I pleaded with him. I even cried. And eventually he said, 'Okay. Okay. I'll leave. But I'm not moving in with you – yet. Do it gradually. Let Marnie get used to the idea. I'll get a flat – how will that be?'

That will be just fine, I thought. But then he said he wouldn't do anything about it until after Christmas. He wanted to spend Christmas with his wife and kids.

Chapter 48

Teri

The flat was on the top floor of a three-storey Victorian terrace in a not-all-that-smart part of town.

Leyland Road could've looked better if the residents had bothered about the peeling paintwork on the doors and window frames, or the general neglect in the front gardens, or the number of cars that had seen better days parked on the road. But they didn't and the overall effect was of a tired and run-down place. It was probably because of the students; they'd commandeered the area – not just Leyland Road, but all the terraces around there. Owners of what had once been smart, large Victorian houses had rented the odd room to a student and then, finding there was money to be made, either let off the whole house or sold up to a landlord. The net effect was the same: elegant, old, stone houses taken over by as many students as could be safely – and sometimes not so safely – squeezed in between health and safety regulations and crammed into poky little bedsits.

I shouldn't grumble, given that most of the students attended the university where I taught. They had to live somewhere. But I hated the idea when Declan decided to move there.

'It's cheap,' he said. And when your wife throws you out – and demands maintenance for her and the kids – cheap is good. Look on it as shabby chic.' He laughed.

He had, as he'd wanted, spent Christmas with Marnie, and the kids but, as he told me later, they'd had a furious row the day after Boxing Day. Marnie had been cleaning up after the festivities and found Declan's mobile under the bed (where he left it having used it to send me a night-time text before we both went to sleep). Of course, she'd turned it on (she knew his password: 0000. The daft boy never changed it from the factory setting). She found dozens and dozens of texts to and from me. At least I'd had the sense to delete my messages, although once Dan left there was no need, and I treasured the little bings and beeps that came through announcing another missive about how much Declan loved/missed/needed me.

Declan told me the row and resultant 'talking' went on for days. The kids were sent to stay with their grandmother, Declan's mother, away from the raised voices, accusations, and tears, while he and Marnie thrashed among the dying embers of their marriage wondering if they could or should throw something on the mess to reignite it. In the end, Marnie, from what Declan told me, said Declan 'must give up that whore' and Declan defended my honour and said he couldn't so Marnie said he'd have to leave, and he packed a bag and went off to stay with one of his walking mates. Within a couple of days, he'd seen the flat in Leyland Road and signed the lease.

He hadn't let me help him move in, and I'm rather glad. It would hardly have been the right thing to be sitting in the removal van as he loaded whatever his wife had allowed him to take from the marital home. Nor did I much want to see the reaction of his children. It would've been messy, noisy, and sad. Even someone like me wouldn't want to see that.

He said I could go round later that evening once he'd got sorted. As it turned out, he hadn't needed a particularly large removal van and there was very little to sort. Marnie hadn't allowed him to leave with much other than a single bed; some sheets; a duvet and towels; a CD player – for the collection of CDs he kept in his car; a portable TV; one badly beaten, brown leather chair – which must've once partnered an elegant Chesterfield sofa; two suitcases full of clothes; a cardboard box containing an assortment of mismatched crockery, cutlery, and pans; a pile of books and maps; a rucksack; and his walking boots.

'Welcome to the happy home,' he said as he waved me in.

All the depressing features of a rented attic flat were there. Any ideas I might've had that it could be a romantic hideaway gave way in the face of the white Artexing on the walls, the frayed carpet, and the general air of gloom. 'I bet the bath is yellow plastic,' I said.

'Mustard,' he yelped. 'It'll be all right – for now,' he said, holding out his arms, pulling me to him.

'Let's go back to my flat,' I suggested.

'No,' he said, nibbling my ear, pulling me closer. 'I've made the bed. Let's christen this place.'

Chapter 49

Teri

There'd been moments during the night when I honestly believed I could get used to sleeping with him in a single bed. We made love riotously and passionately – he, almost angrily, trying to drown out the hurt and anger of what had just happened to him, I suppose.

But by morning, after we woke, and had sleepy sex, hardly able to speak to each other, I longed to have space to move.

'You'll have to get a double bed,' I said.

'Why,' he replied, leaning over, holding himself above me, but close, so his bare chest just hovered over my breasts. 'Don't you like being so close to me?'

'Go get me some breakfast.'

'I'll have to go to the corner shop – it means leaving you,' he said.

'Go then,' I said.

I listened as his feet thumped down the stairs, and then his mobile rang. Where was it? His jacket was slung over the back of the leather chair in the room; the mobile was in one of the pockets. I answered it without thinking. It was Marnie.

'Is he there?' she asked. No 'hello' or 'may I speak to Declan, please?' Just 'is he there?'

'No, he's er…' I said and before I could finish, she put the phone down.

What had I expected? Did I expect her to be cheery and make polite conversation? I stole her husband. He left her for me. She wasn't going to ring up and pretend we were friends, was she? She wasn't going to waste her time being nice. But nor did she waste her time being nasty. She didn't scream at me on the phone accusing me of being a scheming, conniving cow who couldn't give a damn about a man's wife or his children; she didn't ask me if I was satisfied now I'd played my little tricks. She didn't ask if I realised what I'd done and how I could live with myself. She didn't ask so much as a How Dare You? Hey, I felt like saying, play the game. I'm waiting for you to make me feel even more guilt than I do now, so I can have a good wallow in it. But Marnie wasn't playing the game. Was she being subtle? Was she making me wait? Would there come a time when she wouldn't be able to resist shouting at me, telling me how much she hated me? I hoped so. The 'you're a thieving, lying bitch' approach would be easier than this short, sharp 'Is he there?' routine.

Chapter 50

Lee

Teri's turbulent love life was having a more and more detrimental effect on her work – and it hadn't gone unnoticed. The student rep on the staff-student committee complained she was regularly late for classes, took 'forever' to reply to emails, and hadn't updated her module information on the university's virtual learning site since the beginning of the academic year. 'And,' the rep concluded, 'she frequently interrupts lessons to take personal phone calls.'

'She's having a difficult time at home,' I said. 'It's possible the calls are related to her…' I paused, searching for an appropriately ambiguous word. 'Difficulties,' I offered eventually.

The rep snorted. 'Oh, yes, difficulties. That'd account for the simpering and the kissy-kissy mouth when she hangs up.'

Chrissie from admin added her mite. 'She's late with her module assessment details, she still hasn't completed last year's module review forms, and her semester marks are overdue.'

Mike Orme said she'd refused to take part in a peer assessment review, had failed to complete a fire safety webinar, and had missed an important workshop on strategic learning.

Stella Lastings didn't have any specific work-related complaints. 'But she's frequently rude and overbearing.' Which, considering some of the things she could have said, was a remarkably restrained character analysis.

All in all, I was the only person who didn't put the boot in.

Fortunately, Peter was embroiled in a work-planning dispute that was holding up progress on his 'root and branch' overhaul of the department. Otherwise, Teri would've been out on her ear faster than a bullet out of a gun.

I tried giving her a hint, but she kept bringing the conversation back to Declan, who was *maddening, and irresistible and…* I put the phone in a drawer and went to make a cup of tea and when I came back, she'd rung off.

For the next week or so she gave me the cold shoulder, which meant no more invitations to join her for an after-work drink, no more shared breaks in the Senior Common Room and no more rhapsodies about Declan or moans about Marnie. Which suited me fine. It was January again and coming up to the anniversary of my termination and I'd got as much grief as I could handle.

Eventually, she broke the silence – it was after midnight and I was in bed although, despite several glasses of wine, sleep was proving elusive. I groaned when I recognised the caller ID.

There was barely time to say 'hello' before Teri launched into her spiel… the passionate sex… the narrow bed… the craving for space… and finally Marnie. Little half sobs, interspersed with faintly decorous sniffs punctuated her account. 'I know I've hurt her, and I'd understand if she screamed and shouted at me but' – stifled sob – 'and it would be so much easier if we could just get all the anger out into the open' – tiny sniff – 'what does she think she's achieving by ignoring me like this?'

Seems Marnie was giving her the cold shoulder.

She had, it seemed, spent the whole day mulling over all possible permutations of why Marnie should be 'treating me like this'.

Perhaps she was fighting to keep her husband? Which seemed incomprehensible, given Declan was an incorrigible love rat. But some women have funny ideas about the sanctity of marriage.

'Am I a bad person?' Teri blurted out.

'No.' Well, not always, anyway.

'Is it so wrong to love Declan?'

There was no answer to that question.

'Things will work out, won't they?'

How should I know? But hadn't she learnt anything from Dan? Wives and kids can't be wiped off the face of the Earth simply by wishing them away.

'I can't give him up, I can't, I can't.'

Which was ridiculous. She could if she wanted, but she didn't want.

She sighed, a long, slow exhalation of breath.

'We'll chat tomorrow,' she said.

Please, no, I thought, ending the call and, switching the phone to silent mode, crept downstairs, pulled a bottle of wine from the fridge and a wineglass from the cupboard. Perhaps if I drank enough, remembering wouldn't hurt quite so much. Some hope.

Chapter 51

Teri

Declan is unlike any other man I've ever met.

Lee always said I can twist men around my little finger and to an extent, she's right. But with Declan, well, that wasn't the case. I couldn't take him for granted. He was definitely his own man, liked his own space (especially now he was living in a flat on his own), didn't suffer fools gladly, was matter of fact to the point of being almost blunt, and if he didn't want to do something, he wouldn't do it.

For instance, many's the time I suggested we go out for a drink or meet for a meal and he was tied up at work and, rather than passing the job on to a deputy or someone like young Cassie, he stayed at the office to do it himself. 'Sorry, big story on…' Was the most common excuse I heard.

Having thought when he moved into Leyland Road, I'd be seeing him practically every day, we only saw each other probably twice a week. It was even difficult to see him at weekends when I'd have expected we could spend the whole of Saturday and Sunday, plus nights together. 'Stories still have to be written on a weekend, love,' he'd say if on duty at the paper. Or, 'I've got to have my own life,' he'd say if planning to go up into the Dales or to the Lakes with his walking pals, or, 'I've got to see the kids' if Marnie allowed him visiting rights to take them to the park or whatever. I didn't offer to go with them. Been there and done the kid-sitting business.

So, all in all, there was precious little time left for me.

He still texted me, but the messages were never quite as frequent or, frankly, as loving as they had been.

Then, one Friday evening leaving work, I was feeling particularly sorry for myself as I knew I'd be going back to my empty duplex and there was no chance of Declan coming round because this was his weekend to see the kids. What was the point of having gone through my split from Dan and played the 'other woman' with Declan if I was still on my own? Aren't I supposed to be getting more out of this? So I rang Declan.

'Oh, I'm glad you called,' he said, which cheered me up, because I reckoned it meant he'd cancelled his babysitting duties for a night of lovemaking with me. 'Can you email me over a recipe for a casserole?'

'What…?'

'Yeah, I'm doing a casserole… for the kids' tea… got most of the ingredients, but don't know exactly how to put it all together…'

'Do you want me to come over and make it for you?' I asked.

'No, no. The kids have been horribly fractious today. Wouldn't want to inflict them on you.'

'Today? You mean you've had them all day?'

'Yeah, I took the day off and they bunked off school. We've been up to Malham. Great day for it but they're not great walkers.' He laughed. I didn't. He could take days off for his kids, but not for me. I was about to tell him what I thought of his child-bonding antics, but he interrupted me to say he was rushing. 'Just wing the recipe over as soon as poss please, love. See you.'

I kept the recipe simple. We don't want the poor darlings choking on tough meat, do we? I was too angry to cook for myself, so opened a bottle of white wine, and poured a generous glass. It must've been about 9 p.m., and several glasses later, when I rang Declan to hope the casserole worked out and he was having a lovely evening. His phone was switched off, which was unusual given he had the kids with him, and Marnie was in the habit of ringing every couple of hours to make sure he hadn't poisoned them or something.

Then I did something bad. I don't know what it was that made me do it, but some niggling little doubt was scratching away at my wine-fuddled brain.

Once, when Marnie had rung on Declan's phone, I'd made a note of her number. I don't know why. But now I rang it.

She answered, and I said, 'Er, hello, Marnie. It's Teri. Sorry to bother you, but I've got some of your son's books here. Declan must have accidentally left them. And I wondered if he would need them for school on Monday?' Where had that come from?

'Oh… er…' said Marnie, obviously considering whether to slam down the phone without speaking as part of the silent treatment she'd given me before. But, because this was about her precious first born, she obviously thought better of it. 'Hang on,' she said, and I heard her ask someone, 'Do you need the books that your dad left at Teri's?'

And that someone replied, 'No, I've got all my stuff in my bag.'

'Oh, is he there? Your son, I mean? I thought the kids were with Declan tonight?'

'No,' said Marnie. 'They're all here.' Her tone suddenly took a snidely cheerful note as she added, 'So he's told you he's with our children tonight, has he? Well, well…' And it was me who slammed the phone down.

****

Clearly, I had to challenge Declan and when he came round to my flat the following Monday evening, I was ready with the lie that I'd popped out to Tesco and bumped into Marnie and she had the children with her, and I thought they were with him and Marnie insinuated that Declan had lied to me. Hearing all this, Declan laughed and said Marnie was a devious woman and I wasn't to read anything into anything she said or did and that she should've told me a big story had broken and he'd had to hand the kids back and return to the newsroom.

Which was a good excuse and well executed given that Declan had to think fast on his feet but by then he was pulling me to him, nibbling my cheek, my ear, stroking my back and asking how I could ever doubt him and his love for me and he was kissing me and, well, one thing led to another and what could I do but give in to him?

Chapter 52

Teri

Why did I do it? Have I no self-respect?

Declan had been distant the last few days – last few days? He'd been distant for weeks. I put it down to his missing his children. Well, he should've thought about that before taking up with me. I know that sounds harsh, but it takes two to tango and I genuinely wouldn't have been interested in a married man if he hadn't been so interested in me.

Declan was having problems with his son who, after Declan left, had adopted the role of head of household and resented his father's visits, which he saw as an intrusion. In truth, the kid was probably badly hurt. He sounded a bright boy, academic from what I made out from the very little Declan told me when he was in the mood to talk about such things – which he often wasn't. 'Can't be doing with all that emoting shit,' he'd say.

His eldest daughter, though, was a different matter. She Loves Her Daddy and Her Daddy Loves Her. Declan called her his Little Miss Mouse, for goodness' sake! Coming back from having taken her out one day, he'd stared dreamily at the hoodie he'd let her borrow during a sudden downpour. It hung, drying over the bath in his mustard-coloured bathroom. I'd tried to console myself with the thought that the child was probably an overweight, spoilt brat.

Declan had been happily married for twenty-five years until I 'came along and started playing my little tricks' as he so cruelly told me during one of our rows. I get the guilt. I get the blame. I wasn't aware of playing any tricks. I thought I was just going along with what he wanted.

Anyway, I thought, if he can be distant, so can I. As it happened, I'd planned a trip to Oxfordshire to look at Spelsbury Church that weekend. Originally, I'd asked Declan if he wanted to come too.

'What on Earth for?' he asked.

'Well, it's where Rochester is buried,' I said.

'Don't tell me,' Declan said. 'You're going to look at his grave and get all earnest about your research again.'

'Well, yes, and no. I've been stuck for ages and not done any serious stuff on it for years. It might do me good to wander round places where he had connections.'

'But what good will it do? He's been dead and buried for over three hundred years. Why go this weekend? Stay and connect with me.' I think he almost leered.

'No, if you're not coming, I'm going on my own.'

'Please yourself,' he said and added. 'And bloody Rochester.'

I'd booked a B&B, taken my overnight bag with me to university so I could get straight off on Friday afternoon, and treated myself to a new spiral-bound notebook. At the top of the first page I wrote: *John*

Wilmot, the second Earl of Rochester, buried under a plain stone in the graveyard…

And then I changed my mind. Declan was right. Why was I going on what could amount to nothing more than a wild goose chase in the Oxfordshire countryside when I could be with him? I decided to surprise him. I'd nip to the supermarket and buy a decent bottle of wine and some food, take it round to his flat and we'd have a fabulous picnic in bed. I'd show him distant.

I was late leaving university, thanks to Mike Orme wanting to discuss student support. He could see I was in a hurry to be off, but our associate dean is not one for picking up on hints that his colleagues have a life outside work. And, I suspected, any life he might've had outside work had been severely curtailed by his wife following that very peculiar affair with Lee. I say *peculiar* because I just can't see him doing anything as daring and exciting as making love in a store cupboard. But then, I was surprised to hear he had – and with Lee! No, Mike's a quiet, scholarly man – totally out of place at our university where apart from the odd feeble stab at historical research, like my half-hearted dabbling into the roistering Rochester, nothing of note gets studied in any great detail. Knowing this, and that his colleagues are on the whole well-meaning but lazy, Mike tries to make our lives as miserable as possible by imposing on us as many student mentoring-type activities – outside of actual lectures and tutorials – as he can manage.

Part of me thinks he's quite a sad person, given that he wears a uniform that always involves a variety of tank top. The other part reckons he's a sadist, given his love of administration, much of which he does for Peter Heron.

'Mike, put me down for whatever. I've got to dash,' I said. 'See you Monday.'

I half ran into the car park but as I approached my car, saw it had a flat tyre.

'Shit.' I ran back to the gym where I knew Frank, the porter, would be clearing up after the early evening staff Shanghai Yoga session. He was still a bit off with me over the Stella Lastings rumour I put about. It was when I first started at the uni and heard Stella gossiping about Lee having an affair with someone. I didn't realise at the time it was true – and that it had been with tank top Orme – but I decided on revenge and put it about that Stella had been spotted in the boiler room with Frank and they were doing more than inspecting the plumbing.

For goodness' sake, I thought, can't the man take a joke? Anyway, bless him. After much muttering he lolloped down to the car park like an obedient Labrador and changed the tyre for me.

By the time I got to the supermarket it was busy with those Friday-night-family-goes-shopping-together groups where one kid sits in the trolley – which is always parked to block as much of the aisle as possible – grabbing everything in sight and mewling when its mother tells it to put things back, while Dad and the other kid just dawdle looking bored and getting in the way.

By the time I'd dashed home, had a quick shower, and got back to Leyland Road, it was nearly 8 p.m. and Declan's flat was in darkness. I rang the doorbell, but there was no reply. I rang his mobile, but the voicemail kicked in. I didn't leave a message.

I reasoned with myself that he must've gone for a drink after work and would be back later and so I would return later too, find him relaxed, and happily surprised to find me on his doorstep.

I left it until about 10 p.m., then drove back round to Leyland Road. What a surprise he's going to get, I told myself.

There was a light on in the bedroom of his flat. I pulled in behind a battered-looking red SUV parked right behind Declan's car. I walked towards the door of Number 12 and took a reassuring look back at Declan's silver Golf, with the *Evening Leader Leads* sticker in the windscreen. Looking at the SUV parked behind his, I noticed it too had a poster in the windscreen. And it too read *Evening Leader Leads.* I rang the bell marked 'O'Brien'.

And now, after tying myself up in knots about being the other woman, I found myself standing on Declan's doorstep while, presumably, another other woman was inside possibly enjoying the double bed I made Declan buy during one of our few domesticated outings, this one to Ikea. Declan and I rarely did those domestic things other couples do. We went to the cinema now and then, but he hated the theatre as being 'too much arsing about in make-up' and only listened to opera on his car CD player because he could never sit still long enough to hear the fat lady sing. We occasionally went wandering around a local park, but he preferred to go off for a day's walking on his own. He'd only ever come to the two Peter Heron soirees under protest, and I never got invited to anything going on at the *Evening*

Leader. It might 'lead' somewhere, but it certainly wasn't to any form of social life. Having got the paper out this Friday night, however, Declan had clearly found time to socialise, probably with some tarty little tramp from telesales.

Oh, come on, I told myself. He's been out with a mate – a male mate who owns the SUV – and they've come back for a beer. But why were there no lights on other than in the bedroom? And why, having heard the bell, hadn't Declan stuck his head out of the window as he sometimes did to toss me the keys and save him the bother of coming down three flights of stairs?

Perhaps the car belonged to someone from *The Leader* who just happened to live in Leyland Road? Perhaps Declan was in there on his own. In the bath. In bed, asleep.

I debated ringing the doorbell again. No. If he's in the bath, he won't want to be bothered. Likewise, if he's asleep. I'll just go and call him in the morning. I won't disturb him.

As I walked back past the SUV, I tried hard not to look in the windows. I wished I hadn't seen what looked like a green silk scarf on the front passenger seat, or the lipstick case, or the half-empty bottle of mineral water.

Oh, come on, I told myself again. Okay, it was a woman's car, and obviously someone who worked for *The Leader*, but there was no reason to assume she wasn't someone who lived on Leyland Road.

She was probably a mousy little person who worked in something incredibly dull, like quality assessment control, and probably had no idea there was someone else from *The Leader* who lived on her street.

That, or she didn't work for *The Leader* but had just bought the car from someone who did and hadn't had time to peel off the *Evening Leader Leads* sticker. Feeling better, I drove home.

Chapter 53

Lee

I hate driving through town late at night, especially at weekends when there are too many drunks – many of them our students – stepping off the pavement and into the road without looking. Tonight, when St Patrick's Day had provided the perfect excuse for a pub crawl, was a case in point. The streets were full of people who were so drunk they couldn't walk six paces without getting a foot stuck in a bucket. Or regurgitating the alcohol they'd spent the evening throwing down their throats into the gutter. Wait! I slammed on my brakes, recognising the lanky blond-haired bloke puking up under a lamppost. Two police officers, who'd been standing cross-armed, next to their patrol van, unfolded their arms, and strolled towards him.

'Please,' I said, jumping out of my car and kneeling next to David. 'I know him. I'll see he's all right.'

The older policeman considered, while the younger one helped David to his feet. 'He's not usually a drinker,' I babbled. 'That's why—'

'Take him home, mam,' the senior officer said. 'And make sure you give him a talking to in the morning.'

'But he's not my—' I broke off. Perhaps it was better they thought he was my son.

With a final warning to 'keep a better eye on the boy', the men helped me load him into the car and I headed… where? Taking him home was not an option – no one would ever describe me as house proud, but there was no way on Earth he was going to kip on my sofa. Or in in the spare room. Bad enough the car would need hosing down and fumigating in the morning without having to start on the house as well.

'Take me home, Lee,' he mumbled. 'Take me home.'

Home, it turned out, was a dinky, first-floor flat a couple of doors down from Declan's attic pad. I knew this because Teri'd given me a guided tour a few weeks previously. She was dropping off some knick-knacks, which she said would make the place more homely. Not sure even a pair of scented candles, some brightly coloured cushions, and a couple of pretty vases of dried flowers could be so transformative.

'Of course, Declan still needs to do a bit of work on the place,' she'd said. 'But, for now, we're happy to do shabby chic.'

Which was a posh way of saying tired and tatty.

Declan's VW, with its distinctive yellow and blue *Evening Leader* sticker, was parked outside David's front door. He'd helpfully left just enough room for me to squeeze in between his car and a rather battered red SUV. I stared at the family-sized vehicle. I was sure I'd seen it before but, where?

Manhandling David through his front door and up the stairs to his flat was a job and a half that required a lot of pushing and pulling, and some cussing. He wasn't deliberately uncooperative, he just seemed to have little control over his arms and legs.

There's a good reason why the good Samaritan is an endangered species, I thought, as I dragged him out of his clothes and tucked him into bed, it's too much like hard work.

Oh dear! David had curled himself into a ball and was shedding great, heart-stopping tears. 'Becky's dumped me and I miss her so much,' he cried, between shuddering sobs, and half-sniffs. It was completely unexpected, and he reminded me so much of baby Fee that I cradled him in my arms, 'shushing' and stroking his hair which – ugh! – was matted and rank and dirty. Gradually, he quietened, drifting off to sleep with his head on my chest. And, child-like, he stirred into wakefulness every time I tried to wriggle free. So, I stayed put, and slept as best I could – which wasn't terribly well. Teri might extol the virtues of a narrow bed and a handsome bloke, but I prefer more room and someone who isn't snoring loud enough to wake the dead. Somewhere nearby I heard a car's engine revving noisily and impatiently and, once, someone hammered loudly at a door. Flippin' students, I thought. Why can't they keep normal hours like the rest of us?

Eventually the noise died down and sometime around 6 a.m., David loosened his grip, and I eased myself out of the bed. *Zzzzz! Zzzzz!* An extra loud snore – think: pig having its throat cut – and David jolted awake, no longer drunk but horribly hung-over. 'Dry toast,' I told him as he groaned and whined.

'No bread,' he said.

'What about a strong black coffee instead?'

'No coffee,' he said.

In fact, the cupboard was more-or-less bare. 'What do you live on?' I asked, surveying the empty shelves.

'Been staying at Becky's a lot,' he gulped, 'but she's kicked me out. Said she'd got someone new.' A tear trickled down his cheek. I patted his shoulder. Now was clearly not the right moment for the 'other fish in the sea' conversation. 'Why don't you have a shower and wash your hair and clean your teeth while I go and get some provisions?' I suggested instead.

'No shampoo or shower gel.' He paused. 'Or toothpaste or toothbrush. Left everything at Becky's.'

'Okay,' I said. 'I'll get them too.' I flipped the strap of my body bag over my head. 'Now, before I go shopping, is there anything else you need?'

He stared at the spew-stained jeans and T-shirt lying on the floor. 'Some washing powder.' He sniffed his underarms. 'And deodorant, too. Wait,' he called as I opened the door. 'Can you get some paracetamol? I've got a hell of a headache.'

It was on the way back from the twenty-four-hour mini mart that I remembered where I'd last seen the SUV. Hell's bells! Should I tell Teri?

Chapter 54

Teri

'So what did you do?' Lee asked, putting her teacup down on a table in the Senior Common Room the following Monday morning.

'Well, I just drove home,' I told her.

'But if it was as innocent as you're now suggesting, why didn't you ring his doorbell again and why, for that matter, are you so upset about it?'

The thing I like about Lee is I can tell her anything, and she usually understands. What I don't like is when she starts asking me questions like this, which are full of common sense, but to which there is no answer.

'Did you ring him the next day?'

'Yes.'

'And?'

'There was no reply.'

'When did you ring? He could've popped out for some milk or something.'

'I rang at 7 a.m., half seven, eight, eight-fifteen… nine…'

'I get the picture.' She looked as though she was about to laugh but, seeing my pale face and the dark circles under my eyes, thought better of it. 'Did you speak to him at all over the weekend?'

'Not until last night.'

'And then what?'

'Well, he sounded pleased to hear from me.'

'"Did you tell him you'd been round on Friday… that you'd been trying to get hold of him?'

'Er…'

'You didn't, did you?' She looked aghast. 'Oh, Teri. You should've said something.'

'I know. But I don't want him to think I'm spying on him.'

'You aren't spying on him. You want to know who the nasty little trollop in his bedroom was on Friday night.'

'Oh, I really don't think that…'

'Then why not ask him what he was doing…?'

'Oh, Lee. For goodness' sake!' I said crossly, snapping my arms against my sides in frustration.

But I knew she was right. Why hadn't I told Declan I'd been standing on his doorstep, unable to get an answer on Friday night, and that I'd been ringing him every half hour all day Saturday and most of Sunday too? When he finally picked up the phone on Sunday night, he was cheerful.

'Hey. How'd the weekend go?' he asked.

'Brilliant,' I lied. Why did I do that?

'How was Rochester?'

'Still dead.' I laughed. 'What have you been up to?' I tried to keep my voice light.

'Oh, not much. Had a couple of bevies after work on Friday, came home, early night. Went up to the Lakes on Saturday – on my own – did a bit of climbing. Weather was good, so stayed up there – camped. Just this minute got back.'

I would've believed him, I honestly would. Except that to go climbing and camping in the Lakes, Declan would've taken his car. And his car was parked outside his flat in Leyland Road every time I went round there during the weekend. And I went round at regular two-hour intervals. I parked at the end of the road so I couldn't be seen from Number 12, and I swear that car never moved. And nor did the red SUV parked behind it.

I didn't tell Lee that.

Chapter 55

Lee

I worried endlessly about that blasted SUV, which was still parked outside Declan's flat when I finally went home mid-morning. There was no doubt in my mind that it belonged to Marnie – I'd seen her park it outside church only last Sunday – so its presence on Leyland Road suggested she'd spent the night. I didn't doubt for one minute that Declan was perfectly capable of cheating on Teri, but did sleeping with your estranged wife count as cheating? And what did it mean for Teri? She liked to describe Declan as her significant other, but was she nothing more than a nice bit on the side?

And if Marnie had spent the weekend in the dingy top-floor flat, what had she made of Teri's homely little fixtures and fittings? In Marnie's place, I'd have smashed them to smithereens, which'd certainly raise a few questions next time Teri came calling.

So should I mention the car to Teri? Or leave her to find out of her own accord? And what if I was wrong and there was an innocent explanation? And was it any of my business, anyway?

Aagh! My head was in a spin.

In the end, the perfect solution presented itself: do nothing. And hang around to pick up the pieces as and when necessary.

Chapter 56

Teri

Monday went by in a blur of misery. Why hadn't I been honest with Declan? He would've had a perfectly reasonable explanation. Perhaps he went up to the Lakes with a friend in the friend's car – although he'd said he went on his own. He'd sounded pleased to hear from me on Sunday night, but when I suggested he come round to my house, had said he was knackered and on an early shift at the paper the next day. I offered to cook him a meal after work. He said he was doing a late shift.

'But you're on earlies,' I reminded him.

'Yeah. I'm doing back-to-back shifts. There's a big story on. Double murder over the weekend, and there are police press conferences and re-enactments… and we need everyone in the newsroom. Sorry, love. I'll ring you…'

Level 2 got less than their tuition fees' worth during my lecture on the Moral and Monarchical Panics of the 1600s and in the tutorial that followed it was easier to let them body swerve any suggestion we discuss puritanical stances in favour of the sex, scandal, and hedonistic pleasures of our own dear twenty-first century royal family.

'Life still bloody?' Lee asked when we bumped into each other later in the day.

'Bloodier,' I said.

'Come for a drink after work,' she suggested.

'No, I'm going to catch-up on some sleep,' I told her. 'I didn't get much last night.' What with driving round to Leyland Road every couple of hours, I didn't get any sleep at all.

I had an early night and the following day felt better, went into uni, did a couple of tutorials but otherwise, wasn't too busy. I texted Declan offering to make him a meal, but he texted back saying he had to go to a press conference.

What?!?!?! In the evening?!?!?!

Dble murder… he replied. Funny, I hadn't seen anything about a murder over the weekend on the news, but then, I hardly watch the local news nowadays. I can't risk seeing Dan.

2morrow, then? I asked.

Can't

Thurs???

OK, c u at yours

Why did I feel as though I was just getting crumbs in this relationship? I had to have it out with Declan. There was no way I was letting a man treat me like this. But I love him. I love him. I love him. And that was the bloody problem. For the first time in my life, I'd found a man who meant more to me than I obviously did to him.

And I didn't trust him. All his excuses. All his lies. He was obviously up to something and that something was seeing other women. What else could it be? He could only spend so much time at work or with his kids. There were far too many nights now when he claimed to be 'too tired' to come round or busy 'seeing someone about a story'.

On the Thursday, I'd cooked cassoulet and opened a bottle of expensive red wine, and before the poor boy had a chance to swallow the first mouthful I started.

'Look, Declan, I'm not nagging…'

'Which means you're about to,' he said, adding, 'Women always do that. I'm not nagging but… Okay, what do you want?' His tone was harsh, and it startled me.

'I was only going to say that I love you and want to spend more time with you…'

He sighed and shook his head. 'For God's sake, Teri. I'm busy at work, I've got three fucking kids to feed, I've got an ex-wife who's constantly on my back for one thing or another, and now I've got a girlfriend who wants to have me at her beck and call all the time. Don't any of you fucking well see… I need some space.'

'I'm sorry, Declan,' I said as softly as I could. 'Look, I promise not to keep on at you. It's just I want to see you…'

'You're seeing me now and you're ruining it with your bloody nagging.' He slammed his glass down on the coffee table, allowing some of the red wine to splash on the white wood, and stood up. I stood up too and reached out to try to hold his arms, but he shrugged me off, reached for his jacket, and stormed out.

I cried. I really cried. What on Earth was wrong with me? Why did I feel like this? Angrily I walked into the kitchen, saw the cassoulet dish, and scraped the food into the bin with bad tempered, heavy strokes. I threw the dish into a bowl of soapy water so that suds flicked up and around the sink, spattering the lazulite blue and yellow tiles. I went back into the living room where I picked up my glass of wine and downed it in one. For a moment I felt breathless and dizzy, and then the doorbell buzzed. I went into the hallway and opened the door ready to tell whoever it was to 'fuck off'. Declan stood there with a sheepish look on his face, his eyes twinkling behind an ever so slightly mischievous smile.

'Oh, hell, Teri. I'm so sorry.' And he stepped forward, took hold of my arms and pulled me to him and then onto the floor.

Again, we found ourselves having urgent, breathless sex, which ended with us giggling as we lay in each other's arms looking up at the ceiling.

'Nice place you've got here,' Declan said. 'Can I have something to eat now?'

'Afraid not. I just chucked it out,' I told him.

'Ah, well, we'll have to live on love tonight. Not as many calories.'

Oh, how I love him.

He stayed all night, and I revelled in having him with me. I was careful with everything I said. I didn't want to annoy him again. I asked what he was doing at the weekend.

'Off to the Lakes,' he said.

'Can I come?' I asked.

'What…? Teri, you've never walked further than round the local park. You couldn't get up one of those fells.'

'I can if you take me,' I said, imagining the two of us hand-in-hand, climbing a remote hill, and making love on the summit as the sun went down.

He was thoughtful for a moment. Then he said, 'Right, lass. We're taking you up a mountain.'

Chapter 57

Teri

I was beginning to regret my insistence on going for a 'day's walking' with Declan. But he'd been so incredulous and, I have to say, mocking, when I asked him to take me to the Lakes, I thought I'd better put my request into action.

Declan had laughed as he sought reassurance. 'Are you absolutely, positively, completely sure you want to come?'

'Yes.'

'It'll be cold, wet, and hard work. They're hills, you know, not pedestrianised shopping areas.'

It was just so good to see him in such a good mood, and he was obviously looking forward to spending time with me on the Lakeland Fells.

He'd even come to the camping and clothing shop with me to buy boots and a waterproof jacket – a nasty plastic thing with toggles and zips and a hood with an elasticated edge to keep it tight against my face if it rained. What a sight. He said I could borrow one of his old rucksacks to stop me buying a lovely soft leather version in tan. 'One drop of rain and that thing'll be ruined,' he said, spluttering over the

£250 price tag. And I had to agree his breathable nylon version was probably more cost-effective and serviceable. I drew the line at buying a zip-up fleece, which came in either bottle green or the most peculiar shade of orangey-red. I'd seen too many pensioners wearing those shapeless things to think of ever wearing one myself. I told Declan I'd take one of my old cashmere sweaters for if it got cold.

I've met many men in my life and, although it might sound conceited, I've never had to do the chasing. Men have always been keen to take me out for dinner, join me at the theatre, come on holiday with me, cancel something else they'd planned so they could be with me, laugh at my jokes… Declan was different. I didn't repeat my stalking exercise because I had my pride, but I was gradually beginning to realise that while this was a relationship of mutual lust for both of us, it was not one of mutual love and longing – it was only me doing the loving and longing, and that's an unusual place for me to be. But the more Declan seemed to push me away, the more I wanted him. Oh God. What happened to the girl who could love 'em and leave 'em?

I thought this trip to the Lake District would seal something between us.

Chapter 58

Lee

I owe a debt of gratitude to the newspaper travel writer, whose name I forget, who penned a piece on a cooking and walking holiday in Tuscany. Whoever she was, she made it sound good fun – much more entertaining than Fliss's suggestion that I join her and the family in a rented cottage in North Wales. I've nothing against either the Principality or its people, but it's undeniably wetter, and colder than Italy, so I lied and said I couldn't get annual leave on the scheduled dates and booked the walking and cooking trip instead. Goodness knows why the write up stuck in my memory, but the holiday was well-priced, the single room supplement was reasonable, and I'd never been to Italy before.

Teri hooted with laughter. 'Cooking. You?'

It would've been insulting if her incredulity wasn't well deserved.

'You wouldn't catch me holidaying with a bunch of strangers,' she added. 'And you won't have anything in common. They'll all be energetic, outdoor types with weather-beaten complexions and hand-knitted socks and woollies.'

Talk about stereotyping.

'And most of them will be teetotal, and drink green tea, and be tucked up in bed by half-past nine,' she predicted. 'Or else, sad little spinsters who'll stop every two minutes to admire the view and take photographs of obscure alpine plants.'

'I'm not going to the Alps.'

'Whatever… you get the picture.'

I did, horribly, and I'd have cancelled, and forfeited the deposit if she hadn't already suggested it. I didn't want to give her the satisfaction.

Chapter 59

Teri

Rather than clearing as the weather forecast promised, the mist had grown thicker by the time we got to the Lake District. Seen just a short time ago from the approach road 2,000 feet below, the fluffy white clouds appeared like cotton, lightly suspended above the fell top; wispy things.

'It'll shift,' Declan said, hardly looking up at the mist in his haste to lace his boots. I could only take his word for it. I shoved my feet into my new walking boots and bent down to lace the damn things up. They were so stiff.

'You should've broken them in,' Declan said.

Broken them in? They're boots. I'd had dozens of pairs of boots that hadn't needed breaking in. Mind you, they were generally made of the softest leather and felt more like slippers. These were great hulking things like oversized, clompy trainers.

Declan's rucksack felt uneven and bulky on my back even though I hadn't put much in it apart from a bottle of sparkling spring water and a prawn sandwich I'd grabbed from M&S. Oh and a dinky little beret in case my hair got wet, and some lip salve, a tube of hand cream, and my moisturiser.

We set off. Or rather Declan leapt off, and I trailed behind. We were on an incline immediately, and all I could see was uphill.

'Are we going right up there?' I asked.

'Yup. Right to the top,' Declan said in a slightly impatient tone. His mood had chilled since our shopping expedition and he'd been quiet on the drive up to the Lakes, turning the radio on so we could listen to music rather than talk. 'Look, you can stay in the car and read the paper if you don't want to come,' he said as I looked at the looming hillside.

'No. I'm coming,' I said.

I couldn't see the top because of the mist. So that wasn't terribly reassuring.

Oddly, I got into my stride. Thanks to a bit of power walking round the park I was semi-fit, but I couldn't catch-up with Declan; he took off like a bat out of hell. Walking in the hills was something he liked to do alone – or with his climbing buddies – and he'd warned I'd slow him down, and if I did, he wouldn't wait for me. I hesitated to admit that despite the earlier jokes when I'd asked if I could come with him; he didn't particularly want to be with me today.

Declan was moving faster up ahead and there was now a fair distance between us. I was soon aware the only sounds were the bleating of sheep back down the hill, behind and below, and my own heavy breathing.

The rough grass gave way in parts to chewed mud and then occasional stretches of snow where I had to kick my toes in to stop slithering. Snow! In April. But then we were climbing quite high and, I realised, the mist was getting thicker and wetter.

I stopped and yanked the rucksack off my back, found my natty little beret and put it on, and then took the bottle and had a swig of water which exploded in my mouth. Fizzy water was a mistake; it felt dry and powdery on my tongue. I rammed the bottle back in the rucksack and looked up, expecting to see Declan, hands on hips, waiting impatiently for me. But he'd disappeared into the mist.

Uneasy that he'd got so far ahead, I tried to move faster, but my boots, which had been rubbing, were now making my heels and toes feel quite sore. The hillside was getting steeper and the mist thicker, and soon I could see just a couple of yards in front. I was aware of white cobwebs of damp mist forming on the sleeve of my jacket. I placed my feet heavily, trudging slower, and slower, aware of how cold, and tired I was getting. I hooked my thumbs through the shoulder straps of the rucksack to ease it off my back, as though that would somehow lighten the load and make walking easier.

Suddenly the ground levelled off, and I guessed I'd reached the top, although I couldn't really see given the mist was now like a thick, white blanket. Well, I'd got there, but I didn't have a clue as to how I was going to get down. Suddenly scared, I looked around wildly, hoping for the reassuring bulk of another human figure. But everywhere I looked was whiteness, and all was quiet, and still.

'DECLAN!' I shouted. Over 2,000 feet up a mountain and, as far as I knew, completely alone, but the noise felt embarrassingly loud, and if I hadn't been so frightened, I would've felt stupid. What does one do, stranded in a white-out on top of a mountain? I didn't want to walk on, as I wasn't sure where I was going. If I turned round, could I retrace my steps well enough to find a path going back down? Declan warned me about people wandering off the wrong side of a mountain and descending into a completely different valley to the one in which they'd started. 'If you did that,' Declan said, 'You'd have a long walk back – there aren't any buses in these hills.'

It was too cold and wet to sit and simply wait in the hope the selfish bastard would return and find me. Maybe other walkers would appear and help me down? But what other idiots would there be climbing misty, mud-sodden mountains in this weather? My feet hurt. My hands were cold. The cashmere sweater was useless. I'd have given anything for a warm, comfy fleece right then. Against my better judgment, I sank down on the wet grass and hugged my knees, more for comfort than anything else. Perhaps I'd get hypothermia and die, and the search and rescue party would eventually find my body and put up a plaque: *She came to the hills and the hills spat at her…*

****

'What on Earth did you do…?' Lee asked, wide eyed in astonishment when we met for coffee in the Senior Common Room. 'Well, I yelled for Declan again, – but no reply, again. Then I had a brainwave. I had my mobile with me, so I got it out, although my hands were so cold I could hardly key in his number.'

'But you wouldn't have got a signal up a mountain,' Lee said.

'You're absolutely right,' I agreed. 'So I just started screaming. Really loudly.'

'And Declan appeared?'

'No. A rather nice couple from Lytham St. Anne's emerged, coming up out of the mist like a pair of shining angels. God, who are these people who enjoy labouring up mountains in the mist? Anyway, Eric and Diane – that's the couple – realised I was in a bad way and abandoned their summit attempt to help guide me down. It seems I'd not reached the top but something they called a false summit. There were bags more to go, which was presumably where Declan had gone. Anyway, they had maps, and compasses and, best of all, some Kendal Mint Cake, and a flask of coffee, so they gave me something to eat and drink and it was all very jolly, and we got down safe and sound, and they left me in a nice little tea shop near where we'd left the car.'

'Yes, but what about Declan?'

'Well, Diane wanted Eric to go back up the mountain to see if he could find Declan coming down. I think Diane wanted to stay with me having a cup of tea in the warm. But Eric persuaded her to go with him and, bless them, they found Declan about halfway up, going frantic, looking for me. They told him where I was and all three of them came down together. I thought we'd all have some nice, toasted teacakes but Declan was in a bloody foul mood and demanded – demanded – we head off home straight away.'

'Is he still mad at you?' asked Lee.

'Mad with me? Why on Earth should he be mad with me? I'm the one who was abandoned and left to die a miserable death on a sodden hillside in the middle of bloody nowhere. If Diane and Eric – love them – hadn't come along, I'd still be up there – probably dead.'

I told Lee Declan hardly spoke on the way home. He dropped me at my flat and said he wouldn't come in. I didn't hear from him the following day – Sunday – and nor did I bother texting or ringing him. 'I thought I'd make him suffer,' I said.

Lee gave me one of her funny, close scrutiny looks.

'Anyway,' I said. 'I hope my experience hasn't put you off your little walking holiday?'

Chapter 60

Lee

My heart was in my brand-new walking boots, which I'd been advised to wear for travelling to save the luggage allowance.

'Chill,' Teri said as she dropped me off at Leeds-Bradford airport for a connecting flight to Heathrow.

Chill? Where had she got that from? It was the sort of thing Declan might say, although she didn't seem to mention him as much these days and I didn't like to ask because the last time I had (innocently) enquired, how's Declan? she turned a bit icy, so I was playing it safe and not mentioning him either.

'You'll enjoy it once you get there,' she promised. 'I know you will. And don't forget to look out for Dan.'

Dan?

'I hear he's holidaying in Tuscany this year. It's popular with media types.'

Just what I needed to cheer me up – a gaggle of luvvies. However, things began to look up at Heathrow, thanks to a funny little chap who accosted me as we queued to go through passport control.

'You're rambling, aren't you?'

Eh?

He pointed at my pristine boots. 'Is this your first rambling trip?' He didn't wait for an answer before continuing, 'This will be my twenty-fifth rambling holiday and I've loved every single one of them.'

Passports checked, he gestured to a seat in the departure lounge. 'I like to play a little game,' he confided.

A game? Here?

'I try to spot other ramblers,' he said.

Pardon?

'Look, that lady over there.' He pointed to a grey-haired woman wearing a waterproof anorak and grey trousers. 'You can tell she's an experienced walker. Look at her boots, well-worn, and polished. No blisters for her.'

I stared at my feet. 'Oh dear! I should have bought some plasters.'

'Don't worry,' said the bloke, pulling a first aid kit from his rucksack. 'I always bring plenty.' He handed me a blister pack. 'Put these in your pocket and see if you can spot any of our future companions.'

So, until we were herded into our seats, one at the front, and one at the back of the aircraft, we amused ourselves by trying to identify potential members of our walking group, and, at the other end, collected our baggage, and headed for the arrivals hall, scanning the crowds for the holiday rep-cum-tour and walking guide. Myrtle was a tall, very English, jolly hockey-sticks gal. I'd bet good money she'd been head girl or captain of games at her expensive boarding school. My airport friend winked at me as we surveyed the rest of our little group – we'd done pretty well at spotting the Ramblings.

One person was missing: a gentleman Myrtle said, who'd booked too late to secure a seat on the scheduled plane. Instead, he'd taken an alternative flight from Gatwick, which was due in just twenty minutes. So we waited and gossiped, sizing each other up. Twenty of us in total – well, nineteen. We were still waiting for the Gatwick gent.

Chapter 61

Lee

The missing traveller's flight was delayed, so we spent nearly an hour hanging around the concourse of Pisa airport before he finally showed up. He was apologetic and grateful.

'I thought you'd go without me and I'd have to take a taxi,' he said, shaking hands with Myrtle.

'Oh no,' she said. 'Nobody minded.'

Well, I did. I was tired and grumpy – Teri had picked me up at 4 a.m. to make the check-in at Leeds-Bradford and I was annoyed with Myrtle who, having herded us together, wouldn't allow us to leave the group for a cup of coffee (or tea) and a sit down. So, we'd stood listlessly and, mostly silent having run out of polite inanities. The exception was my Heathrow pal, who'd finally introduced himself as Maurice Entwhistle-Moody, and who talked virtually non-stop. He was playing another game: guessing the occupation, which he claimed he could do by studying faces. He couldn't – he thought I must be a care home worker and the chap, who he identified with certainty as a medic, was a forklift truck driver in a meat factory. I eyed my companions and wondered who else was fantasising about wringing his neck?

At last, the missing traveller breezed in, completely oblivious to the gathering ill-humour. 'Dan,' I said. 'What are you doing here?'

Dumb question: walking and cooking, obviously.

'Lee,' he said. 'What a lovely surprise.'

Hmmm – when Teri said 'look out for Dan' I didn't think she actually meant it literally.

But at least now we could make the coach transfer to our hotel – and my first introduction to the unspoken rules of rambling. Rule one: couples sit together, singles on their own. So Dan sat behind me and Maurice in front, and the pair of them conducted a blokey conversation about the walks they'd been on while I played Billy-No-Mates in between.

Rule two: dinner is always preceded by a group briefing that included an outline of the next day's programme, and an invitation to join Myrtle on an after-dinner tour of the town. 'You'll love the cemetery,' she gushed. 'The locals light lanterns every evening at dusk to commemorate the dead. And the dragonflies are like little fairies lighting up the night.'

'I think I'll give it a miss,' I said. But that wasn't an option because rule three says there's no opting out of optional extras.

And so to rule four: dining room etiquette is to eat each meal with a different group of 'friends'. Which forced me to break the ice with a couple of other members of the group. But I like to choose my friends rather than have them forced on me.

Finally – for the evening, at least – rule five demands that Ramblings walk leaders must swallow a guidebook ahead of every expedition and must recite it ad nauseum.

'Here's the Town Hall – it was built in the mid-15th century and extensively renovated in the 1960s,' Myrtle said, indicating a nondescript stone-built mausoleum. 'And this little shop has a good range of postcards and some nice regional gifts.' Oh, pleeease – it's cheap tat. 'And this lovely little square is home to the village market on Tuesday and Fridays. But you have to get up early,' she warned, 'because the market opens at 7 a.m. and everything is all packed up by noon.' No thanks, there's be no wandering around half a dozen-or-so flea-bitten stalls for me.

Unless Ramblings had a rule about that, too.

Maurice, of course, lapped it up. 'Oh my,' he said. 'Oh my, isn't it lovely?'

No! It's a very ordinary town square, not dissimilar to umpteen thousand other squares scattered all over the Mediterranean and beyond. I was in a minority of one though, because everyone else seemed to think the place was delightful. Maurice almost had an orgasm when we got to the church. Pre-Renaissance, naturally.

Dan wasn't much better; for the first time I was reminded of how sceptical, disapproving even, I'd been when Teri grumbled about his endless good nature. Now I could see what she meant – someone who always looked on the bright side could be a real pain in the backside.

Chapter 62

Teri

Declan's behaviour got me thinking. I didn't want to repeat that awful night in March, but I did take to popping round to Leyland Road on certain nights when Declan said he was either working late or taking his kids out somewhere. And on those nights when you might not expect to see his car parked near his flat, it generally was. Even I found it too tiring to organise reasons and excuses as to why this might be. Nor could I explain the blonde-haired woman who parked her Mercedes SLK outside Number 12 and walked up to the door to ring the buzzer. I could only watch as Declan stuck his head out of the top-floor window, wave and throw his keys down to her so she could let herself in and save him from having to come down several flights of stairs.

It wasn't so much the blonde hair or the flash car; it was the way Declan seemed so relaxed and pleased to see the woman. He chucked down the keys in that familiar, trusting, loving way he used to do for me.

That woman was clearly not his mother, aunt, or sister – not that I'd ever met any of his relatives apart from sitting behind his mother in church at the Christmas before last, but I was on a champagne-fuelled giggly high then and hadn't taken much notice of either her or Declan sitting beside her.

I very much doubted the blonde was a work mate. You don't lean out of a window and laugh unless the person below is someone with whom you have done this before. It's just… well… too familiar.

****

I wasn't handling the Declan situation very well, and I don't think I handled the David Greenspan business very well either.

It was supposed to be harmless enough. The second semester was coming to an end and, as usual, the students had planned a May Ball. It was a chance for the boys to dress up in their rented tux and the girls to spend Mummy and Daddy's money on ludicrous, skintight, bosom-revealing ball gowns. They arrived at the university's Thomas Packenham Hall in their stretch limos, giggly with all the booze they'd drunk beforehand.

A few lecturers went. In fact, Lee and I were planning to go together until she decided to go on her madcap holiday instead. Declan refused to go – typical – so I found myself climbing the steps up to the grand hall entrance on my own in a rather stunning hot-pink gown with a be-jewelled peplum and mermaid skirt. Entering the foyer, I could see a mass of colourful gowns ahead of me in the grand hall. But among the wave of bobbing heads and coiffed hair, one person with a shaggy, blond head, and long, lean limbs stood out: Gorgeous Greenspan. I'd only ever seen him in scruffy jeans and T-shirts and here he was in a slim-fitting, contemporary one-button dinner jacket with a black bow tie and looking every inch the sharp hero of a James Bond movie. He looked a knock-out.

'Well, hiya, David,' I said, running my hand up, and down an expensive sleeve. 'Don't you look the part?'

'You look pretty amazing yourself,' he said, eyeing my breasts rounding over the top of the hot-pink bodice, before collecting himself and adding, 'Shall I get you a drink?'

I said a white wine would be great and off he loped off in the direction of the bar, leaving me wondering what the heck I was doing.

The hall became crowded as more and more people arrived. I was nudged and bustled by those coming in behind me, so I moved over to the wall on the right-hand side and hoped David would find me. I must've waited about ten minutes, nodding hello to various people who looked my way. Then, horrors, I saw Mike Orme bearing down. Of course the old tight fist wasn't wearing a dinner jacket but a dark blue jacket with trousers that didn't quite match, with a white shirt, and university tie.

'No tank top tonight, Mike?' I said. He looked at me oddly as though he had no idea what I was talking about.

'Are you here on your own?' he asked, leaning slightly towards me, his glass of red wine slopping dangerously at the edge of the glass.

'No, I'm waiting for someone…'

'Lucky man,' he leered. 'My wife won't come to these dos, so I'm here on my own,' he added.

'As I said, Mike, I'm waiting for someone, so please don't let me hold you up.'

Mike shambled off, and I stood on tiptoe to try to see over the heads of the crowd for signs of David returning with my now much-needed drink. No sign. I headed off in the direction of the bar, bought myself a bottle of white wine and found an empty table at the edge of the hall and sat down. I needed a couple of glasses to fortify me before I went in search of the arrogant boy.

Heartened after drinking, fairly quickly, nearly the whole bottle of Pinot Grigio, I edged my way through the crowd and back to the bar for another. With the new bottle in one hand and two glasses in the other, I spotted him. I'd recognise that trim back view anywhere.

'Hi, David.'

He turned and as he did so, I noticed the girl he'd been talking to. He quickly turned back to her and said something I couldn't hear. She looked at me and laughed, then nodded, and David turned back and walked towards me.

'Sorry… I was meant to get you a drink, wasn't I, but I see you managed…' he said, looking at the bottle.

Something about his lazy insolence annoyed me. You don't offer to buy me a drink and then leave me waiting, I thought, but swallowed my pride and said, 'Look, come, and help me finish this bottle and then we'll get another.'

'I've got a lemonade, thanks,' he said, raising a half-pint glass.

'Well, come anyway,' I said rather more harshly than I meant to.

Poor lamb, off to the slaughter. We found a table. We chatted. I can't remember what about. I was just so happy to be with someone who clearly liked me and who wasn't Declan. Before I knew it, I'd drunk about half the bottle; David was still sipping at his beer.

'Look, Teri,' he said. 'Don't you think you've had enough?'

Cheeky little snot.

'Oh, I've hardly started. Come on, David. Have another drink.'

'I don't drink much,' he said. 'I had a bad experience with booze and…'

'Oh, for God's sake, David, lighten up,' I snapped, slopping more wine into my glass. I took a huge slug, placed it back down carefully on the table then reached over and took one of his hands. I raised it to my lips and kissed it, or rather (I hate to think about it) it was probably more of a slobber.

'Wha…?' he said, snatching his hand back.

'Oh, come on, David… We're both adults. What's wrong with you?' I stood up and in one fluid movement swung round the edge of the table and into his lap. Which is not easy to do when you're wearing six-inch heels and a mermaid skirt. I put both arms around his neck and nudged my face into his and kissed him firmly on the lips. At this stage his arms should've gone round my waist, all the better to pull me in and closer to him, but instead, he put two large hands on either side of my hips and pushed me away. It was only my holding on to the back of his neck that stopped me from slithering to the floor albeit I was balancing precariously on the edge of his knees. I yanked myself back into his lap and tried again. This time he stood up, and I did slither to the floor. Not a good look, whether in hot-pink, or not.

'You're drunk, Teri,' he said. He reached down and pulled me to my feet. One of my shoes had come off, so I stood there doing a sort of dance as I balanced first on one high-heeled foot and then the other shoe-less one. A small knot of people had witnessed the whole thing, including the daft girl David had been speaking to earlier.

Suddenly, little miss found a voice. 'David,' she yelled. 'Are you coming with us?'

'Will you be all right?' he asked, looking doubtfully at me.

'Oh, fuck off, David,' I said.

Chapter 63

Lee

Italian plumbing leaves a lot to be desired – in small, rural hotels in the Tuscan hills, anyway. The water pressure was so poor the shower amounted to little more than a trickle, and there was barely enough water flowing from the bath taps to extinguish a lighted match. The electrics weren't much better – my travel adaptor 'suitable for use throughout southern Europe' wasn't compatible with the hotel plug points, making both my hair dryer and mobile phone charger redundant. While drip-drying my hair could be borne, not having a phone, and access to my apps could not.

Breakfast was a mixed bag – cold meats, yoghurts, and muesli, plus pastries, fruit, and bread. David Greenspan would have been horrified by my food choices. 'Never eat fruit at breakfast,' he'd always said. 'Interferes with the digestion.'

Maybe. But indigestion is preferable to constipation.

No prizes for guessing what he says about pastries.

Things perked up after breakfast. I walked the short distance into town with Jean, a Cockney lady holidaying with husband, Sidney, who'd was 'finishing getting ready' – while she bought the ingredients for a sandwich lunch. We found a nice grocery – which, to be fair, Myrtle had pointed out the previous evening – where we bumped into another walker, Christian, a blond, bearded Scandinavian, who was surveying the deli counter when we arrived. 'Ladies,' he said, gesturing to us to step ahead of him. My order was pretty straightforward – well, when the choice is bread filled with cheese or bread filled with ham, and you don't like cheese, there's not much to procrastinate about – but Jean couldn't decide whether Sidney would prefer Parma ham or prosciutto, and would he want Dutch Edam or a hard local cheese or…? And then there was the question of bread: plain focaccia or tomato and rosemary or, perhaps, cheese, and onion bread? And should she buy a small tub of green olives? Or black? Or would figs be nicer? Talk about indecisive.

'I'm so sorry,' she apologised. 'I'm holding you up.'

'Not at all,' Christian said. 'It's important you consider all the options.'

I glanced at him, unsure whether to take his words at face value – or what? Jean had no such inhibitions and promptly asked his opinion of the various breads on offer. They'd tried continental black bread at dinner yesterday, she said, and Sid'd been none too keen on it. 'Didn't agree with him at all,' she said. Christian raised his eyebrows. 'Had a bit of a funny effect on his digestive system,' Jean elaborated, circling her hand in the direction of her lower tummy region. 'He was up and down all night.' Christian nodded sympathetically, which was all the encouragement Jean needed to expand on the subject of poor Sid and his dodgy belly. 'Went through him like a dose of salts—' she started.

'Heavens, woman, I said, under my breath, 'at this rate, we'll be here all day.'

I'd spoken rather more loudly than intended.

Useless to try to apologise or pretend the words had come out wrong when clearly they shouldn't have come out at all. Jean, though, bless her, didn't take offence. 'Too right,' she said. 'I need to get a move on.' And she briskly bought one ham and one cheese sandwich on large flat ciabatta bread, a couple of loose tomatoes, and a small bunch of black grapes, together with a bar of milk chocolate, which melted into a disgusting mess long before lunchtime.

'I'll have to come shopping with you again,' she said as the three of us walked back to the hotel. 'No time for dithering when I'm with you pair.'

You pair – I peeked at Christian. I liked the sound of that.

From then on, our days followed a similar pattern. A post-breakfast walk to the grocers, followed by assembly at the front of the hotel, and then a hike into the countryside surrounding our little town. Most days we covered between ten and twelve kilometres – slightly less on cooking afternoons when we returned early to stuff courgette flowers (delicious), transform stale bread into a more-ish Panzanella and butcher a rabbit to make a chasseur (not to be recommended).

Whether cooking or walking, I teamed up with Christian (originally from Copenhagen, but now teaching modern languages in Huddersfield) and Dan and Maurice. Ramblings probably had a rule about this – thou shalt not enjoy the company of likeminded people – but Myrtle found it impossible to properly police the walks, and hotel owner, Cinzia, who ran the kitchen, didn't care who we teamed up with so long as nobody chopped off a finger.

Teri's dire predictions about it all being dull and dreary were wide off the mark although she was right about one thing – most nights I was tucked up in bed by 9.30 p.m., and asleep almost before my head hit the pillow, which hadn't happened in a long time.

Chapter 64

Teri

I never thought I'd say it, but I was not looking forward to the summer's holiday. For a start, I hadn't any money apart from my salary. Dad hadn't put any cash in my account – again. *I'll have to ring him and chase it up*, I thought. And so I couldn't really afford to go anywhere. Declan didn't seem interested in any of the long weekends or days out I suggested, in fact, since our trip to the Lakes, he'd been distinctly chilly, and only been round to the flat once or twice for a bit of hot sex, which, given the mood he was in, was still surprisingly good. We could lose ourselves in our passion, I suppose. But he rarely stayed overnight and never arranged when we were going to meet again. I'd just get a text saying something like, *U free 2nite?* and, as there was very little else going on in my life, I texted back, *Yes.*

I'm not proud of that.

And another thing, there'd be no one about. Most of the lecturers would bugger off to their cottages in Cornwall or rustic gîtes in rural France, and there'd be nothing to do. God, I was bored. And angry. Usually, I'd been able to rely on Lee, but she'd let me down big time.

She was on that ludicrous holiday with my ex-husband. I mean, for goodness' sake. What the hell was either of them doing on a damn cookery holiday?

Because Dan and I still texted each other now and then, I knew he was going to Tuscany, but he hadn't elaborated, so I imagined it would be for the galleries and architecture not walking and cooking. With Lee.

I never for a minute imagined they'd meet up, far less become best buddies. But when Dan texted to say, *Guess who's here?* I couldn't believe it.

It's typical of both of them: bugger off and enjoy themselves while I'm having such a rotten time.

****

Holidays had once been great. There was one time I'd been staying on the Greek island of Paxos and met up with Vasillis, the son of a taverna owner. He spent so much time showing me the delights of the Ionian islands when he should have been working in Papa's place, that Mama – finding us brushing up Anglo-Greco relations in an olive grove – turned nasty. I caught the first boat taxi back to Corfu where, instead of hopping on the first flight out of there, I met up with some yachties in a bar on the waterfront who were looking for crew. 'Can you cook?' one of them asked. 'Cook? Me? Sure,' I lied. How difficult could it be?

Every two weeks we picked up a new set of clients from the northern tip of Cephalonia for a fortnight's sailing, swimming, and snorkelling. I stayed with the crew for three months and learnt to cook along the way thanks to the chef, Carlos, whose body was tanned and taut, and who taught me a hundred and one things to do with eggs in the galley and some nifty tricks in the cabin bunk too.

Back home, I enrolled on a catering course and did some cheffing here and there, before Lee decided I was wasting my time and persuaded me to get a degree as a mature student. From there I got the job at Wharfevale – and eventually, at central Yorkshire – where life was supposed to take a turn for the better.

Chapter 65

Lee

The last night of the holiday was a little sad – after dinner the whole group, plus Myrtle, congregated in the hotel garden and reminisced about our adventures. One or two people pulled out diaries and address books with promises to keep in touch. Not Jean. 'I've had a lovely time, dear,' she said, 'and I've enjoyed getting to know you, but there's no point exchanging addresses. Holiday friendships are like holiday romances.' She cast a sly glance at Christian. 'Best packed away with the suntan lotion.'

I wondered what she meant – Christian was undeniably attractive, but there'd been no hint of anything remotely lovey-dovey.

Maurice, unsurprisingly, was determined to keep in touch with all and sundry. He went methodically around the group and painstakingly collected home addresses, phone numbers, mobile and landline, and email addresses (work and home) too. 'We'll have a reunion,' he said.

The flight home was strange. We boarded the aircraft as a coherent group and alighted as individuals. Passport control was rushed, and I got separated from Christian, Maurice, and Dan and, though I managed a quick goodbye to Jean and Sid, my connecting flight was already being called, and there wasn't time to wait for the others, who all had train connections. Oh well, perhaps Dan and I might meet up now and again, and Christian wasn't too far away either, while Maurice was already planning a trip to what he called the 'north country' although he was a little worried about the bull terriers which he'd heard were the pet of choice among working folk. 'Nasty brutish creatures,' he'd shuddered. 'The dogs,' he clarified, seeing my raised eyebrows. 'Not the people.' As my plane taxied down the runway I was wondering whether he'd ever brave the journey to Yorkshire when a message from Dan pinged into my inbox. *Bon voyage*, it said. *Fancy meeting for a coffee in a week or two?* Well. I'd prefer tea to coffee, but it was a nice idea. Two other messages, one from Maurice, and one from Christian followed swiftly. *See you soon*, Maurice said.

Fancy a night at the opera? Christian asked.

No, I didn't. But I did want to see him again. *Sure*, I messaged back.

Chapter 66

Teri

With nothing better to do, I decided to check out the new John Lewis store on the outskirts of town and have an afternoon shopping. Would my credit card stand it? Oh, blow it, a girl's got to enjoy herself. I was driving towards the ring road when I realised I was passing the dull grey concrete block that contained the throbbing news-gathering offices of the *Evening Leader*. I'd never been inside; Declan always warned me off.

'It's a miserable, soul-destroying place with no windows. The newsroom is a vast, open-plan arrangement, like an aircraft hangar, where sad-looking gits spend their days staring at their computer screens.'

'You make it sound so welcoming,' I said.

There's a small visitors' car park at the front of the building and, on what instinct I don't know, I pulled in, and parked up. I turned off the engine and sat, looking at the double glass doors with *Evening Leader* etched in large lettering on the front.

One of the doors swung open inwards and an elderly woman, holding her long tweed coat tightly closed at the front, stepped out, having, presumably, just placed an appeal for her lost cat. Right behind her came a young girl with long hair, which she flicked back from her face as she stepped, laughing, into the paved area between the doors and the car park. Cassie! Yes, it was definitely her – last seen at the tyre factory fire. Behind her came a youngish-looking man, someone I assumed was another reporter. And then Declan. I gasped. Why was I surprised? It was lunchtime. They were off for lunch. But then the youngish man waved and strode off, and Declan reached out, and put his arm around Cassie's shoulders and steered her away in the opposite direction.

I watched as they walked up the road, away from the car park, and disappeared around the corner. Oh, for goodness' sake, I told myself. You are not going to follow them. Besides which, it's all perfectly innocent. She's a junior reporter; he's her boss. They're probably working on a story together.

I got out of my car, locked it, and marched quickly, following them. When I got to the corner, I could see the road stretching ahead, but no sign of the two of them. There was a pub, The Old Duke, on the left, and I strode up to the first window and looked in. Declan leant on the bar with Cassie beside him. It was a lunchtime drink for two colleagues. A working lunch. Innocent. So why did Declan still have his arm around her, and why was she giggling so much?

Part of me wanted to believe there was nothing in this encounter. Declan's a friendly bloke and he's just being nice to a junior reporter. The other part of me wanted to scream. Wake up, girl. Of course he's cheating on me. Anyone can see he's cooled; for a start there are no more constant text messages of undying love and he's had other women at his flat. The old Teri would have confronted him and bawled him out. So why don't I do that? I'm worth so much more than this. Come on, Teri Meyer. I dredged up some resolve. The next time I see him, I'm going to challenge him. I think.

****

When Lee finally came back from her holiday, I decided not to tell her about the illicit lunchtime drink incident because I didn't want her thinking I was spying on Declan. And I left it a while before I told her about the May Ball. I explained how David and I had both got drunk and been a bit silly before I sent him packing.

'David doesn't drink,' she said. It crossed my mind to ask her how she knew that, but I had more to say.

'Anyway, off David goes with his friends and then Mike Orme came to my rescue.' Lee looked interested and quizzical at the same time.

I didn't go into detail, but it's true. Mike had seen the whole thing and came over, marched me to the foyer from where he called a taxi to take me home. My knight in a shiny blue jacket and ill-matching trousers.

Nor did I tell Lee that the following Monday I had to go into uni to deliver some mark sheets. She would have 'tutted' that I'd left it late. While we do all the marking and inputting of results online via a slow-moving and electronically clanking system called MarkItIn, for some reason the mark sheets themselves had to be signed by individual lecturers and handed in personally. So much for the paperless society. Admittedly, the mark sheets should've been in earlier to give the admin team time to collate them and let the undergrads know their final scores, but I'd been so miserable I hadn't had the energy to mark anything. I must say, when I logged into the system and realised how many essays there were, I panicked. I whizzed through each one, adding the odd comment here and there to make it look as though someone had read the stuff and gave each one a mark I felt roughly suited whichever student the work belonged to. When it came to David Greenspan's essay, I hovered between a good First and a poor Third and ended up giving him a decent 2:1.

I went up the carpeted corridor that contained Peter Heron and Mike Orme's offices and the admin department. There were four girls working in admin with Chrissie, and they all looked in my direction as I entered. I noticed a plastic container of chocolate and cream eclairs open on one of the desks, pointed at them, and laughed. 'Forever on the hips, girls,' I said, but their expressions were icy. I tried again with a cheerful, 'Here you go…' and waved the mark sheets.

Chrissie stood up, and unsmiling, walked over, and took them. 'We've been waiting for these,' she said in a tone of self-righteous tolerance.

'Well, they're here now,' I said.

'Yes, but we've collated all the other marks – apart from yours – and we're going to have to stay late tonight re-doing everything.'

'Good luck,' I said, leaving the office, relieved that all my academic responsibilities had been dealt with until September – and bumped straight into David Greenspan. 'Hi, David,' I said. 'I'm glad I've bumped into you. Can we have a little chat?' He shrugged and nodded and, before he had a chance to retract, I grabbed his hand and pulled him along to the far end of the corridor where there was a leather couch and coffee table at which visitors sat while waiting for their appointment with Peter or Mike, and where Chrissie, and her mates sometimes sat to have their sandwiches and, no doubt, eclairs.

I sat down and pulled David down beside me. 'I'm so sorry about the May Ball—' I began.

'Look, Teri, it's okay,' he said. 'You'd had a bit too much to drink… it happens…'

'No, listen,' I said. 'I've been going through it since my divorce and everything and, well, I've been feeling down, and you cheer me up. I know you like me and I'm not that much older than you and—'

'Teri,' he interrupted. 'I do like you, honest. Who wouldn't? But you're not my type. I have a girlfriend… Let's just leave it at that.'

'What do you mean, leave it at that? David,' I said, bristling. 'I'm sitting here telling you I like you and I think we could be good for each other…'

He stood. I looked up and seeing the exasperated expression on his face, something inside me broke. I rose to face him and said, rather more loudly than I'd intended, 'David, I have to warn you that I've just marked one of your final Level 1 essays, but the mark can be changed. It could be a Fail…' Even I knew as I said it that I'd gone too far.

'Oh, do your worst,' he said. 'You're pathetic.'

And as he strode off back down the corridor to the admin office, there was Chrissie, standing in the open admin doorway looking at me with a knowing smile on her face.

Chapter 67

Teri

'Look, sweetheart,' Declan said, stretching the word 'sweetheart' into a lazy drawl. Very patronising. 'We're both single people. We're not married. We don't own each other.'

'Yes, but,' I replied, 'we are in a relationship… or so I thought?'

'Hardly a relationship, is it,' he snapped back, 'if you're forever following me, checking up on me?'

'So why do I feel I have to do that?' I demanded. 'You never tell me what you're doing, or who you're doing it with. How can I trust you?'

'Oh sorry,' he said. 'I didn't realise I had to check in with you every day.'

'Don't be so ludicrous.' I rounded on him. 'You don't. But it would help if you were honest with me.'

'Honest? What do you mean?'

'Well, all these other women you're seeing. You tell me you're not seeing anyone else, but you are! Just tell me the truth, Declan, that's all I'm asking.'

'Tell you what? What other women?' He sounded genuinely offended, but for once, his little boy lost look, his defensive reasoning, had no effect on me.

It was some time after I'd seen the woman parking up outside his flat in her Mercedes. As I looked at Declan, a sudden thought of Dan came into my head, and I felt a tinge of sadness. Dan would never have treated me this way. Why hadn't I gone on that Christmas holiday with him, even if it had meant taking the wretched daughter along? I would've been with Dan, looked after, and cared for. I certainly wouldn't be sitting here now, in my duplex on a rare visit from Declan, demanding to know who all these other bloody women were, especially the blonde who I very much doubted was a workmate. You don't lean out of a window and laugh as you chuck your keys down unless the person below is someone with whom you've done this before.

I'd steeled myself for this visit – demanded he came to see me – and was determined to either sort things out between us or finish it completely. I reeled off facts and dates starting with the awful weekend in March when I kept going back to his flat, filling in with the night of the blighted casserole and his illicit lunchtime soiree with Cassie, and finishing in triumph with the blonde and her bloody Merc.

He just glared at me. Gone was the sorrowful, pity-me-I'm-only an-innocent-puppy look, and in its place, a look not of anger at having been caught out, but of rebellious determination. He didn't even try to reach out and touch me and I was glad, because what I didn't want to do was listen to his pathetic excuses, forgive him, and melt into his arms. Lee thinks I'm completely clueless sometimes, but on this occasion, I knew exactly what I had to do, and, I thought, Lee is going to be proud of me. Although what it had to do with her, I wasn't sure, given she hardly had any time for me. Last time we spoke she was crowing about finally getting over Mike – getting over Mike! God. She should never have got into bed with that idiot in the first place. But now it's all Christian, Christian, Christian. I must say, though, she's pulled a stunner there. He's not half bad and, if I hadn't been so wrapped up in the Declan situation – and, of course, if Lee hadn't been going out with him – I could've quite fancied Christian myself.

Perhaps if things didn't work out between him and Lee…?

But no, I had the Declan situation to sort out and while I was trying to be articulate and reasonable, Declan shook his head in a sorrowfully pitying way as though I was the one at fault and he was trying to be patient with me. That made me see red. He was trying to say he'd already explained about the March weekend and the night of the casserole; the drink with Cassie had been just that – a drink; and the blonde – well, she was a secretary at *The Leader* who'd been delivering something.

It was pathetic. He was pathetic. Did he honestly think I was going to believe this crap?

'Oh, for God's sake, Declan,' I shouted. 'Do you think I'm absolutely stupid?' And then I had some sort of out-of-body experience and wasn't really there saying what I was saying as I leapt to my feet to look down on him sitting on the sofa, staring up at me intently, defiantly. I shouted a lot of things mainly to do with him being a two-timing, lying bastard who took what he wanted and used people, then just threw them away. The defiance bled from his face and he tried to interject but I hammered on, shouting, and swearing, tossing my head in rage, throwing my arms in the air until finally my heart pounded. Light-headed, my whole body burnt, and if I didn't do something soon, I would slump on to the sofa, crying. So with one almighty effort I screamed at him, 'FUCKING well get out of my FUCKING life you FUCKING moronic bastard.' And I stretched out my left arm to indicate the door, Declan rose wearily from the sofa and, with head low, he walked slowly, quietly – and, I like to think, shamefacedly – out of the room, out of my duplex, and out of my life.

Chapter 68

Lee

Inevitably, as Jean had predicted, my little thing with Christian didn't survive our homecoming. I'm sure it was kind and thoughtful of him to buy surprise tickets for a gala performance by Calderwood Choral Society, but if he'd asked first, he might've saved himself a lot of money. And I'd have been spared one of the most ear-shatteringly awful evenings of my life. Definitely not my cup of tea.

I wasn't over-keen on our night at the opera, either. I've nothing against Northern Dales Opera per se – but my goodness, they do make a dreadful racket.

And the best thing about our evening watching the latest avant-garde offering from the Ptarmigan Ballet Company was Teri's surprised appreciation of my new beau. 'Ey up, lass,' she drawled in a mock Yorkshire accent when we bumped into her in the foyer. 'What have we here?' And she gave a knowing wink as if to say: 'You're batting above your weight with this one.'

No, Christian was aesthetically pleasing – not on a par with David Greenspan perhaps, although close – but on his home turf the dry humour that had been so amusing in Tuscany turned out to be little more than Scandinavian pedantry. And I didn't think I could take very many more nights at the opera. Or anywhere else even remotely highbrow, for that matter. I might be an academic with a string of erudite papers to my name, but that didn't mean I was a cultural snob. In fact, quite the reverse. Give me Spiderman the Movie over Die Fledermaus any day.

So, by mutual consent, we downgraded our relationship – in other words; we made a couple of half-hearted efforts to arrange to see a film or visit the theatre but, sadly, our diaries were incompatible, and gradually we became sort of friends. The sort who don't mind bumping into each other, but can't be bothered to make the effort to actually arrange anything. Dan and Maurice, though, were a different kettle of fish. Both messaged regularly and Dan and I met up a few times for drinks and a pizza. He was a funny mix – sweetly charming to viewers who approached him for an autograph, but otherwise quiet and self-effacing. He was always immaculately turned out – smart casual was not in his vocabulary – and he was the only man I knew, apart, perhaps, for Peter Heron, whose nails were neatly manicured. Up to now the Dan I'd known was the version painted by Teri, this new Dan was altogether different.

Maurice, who'd eventually steeled himself to venture north, telephoned to say he'd booked into a little bed-and-breakfast and was hoping Dan and I'd show him some of the sights. So, of course, we did, and he swooned over the Tudor-Jacobean mansion house at Temple Newsam and gushed over the Palladian country house at Harewood, and afterwards Dan treated the three of us to dinner at an Italian trattoria that he said had been a favourite of his and Teri's. He looked a little wistful when he said that.

'Do you miss her?'

He sighed. 'Not as much now.'

Poor Dan. I'd never really experienced the sort of passion he and Teri shared. He tried to explain. 'She's so like…' His voice trailed off and he appeared lost in thought. 'Quicksilver,' he said eventually.

Quicksilver?

'Mmm – sort of. Captivating, I suppose, and fascinating, and ethereal and…'

Ethereal? I stifled a giggle. I'd heard Teri called many things in her life and granted, she was slim and graceful, and, at a pinch, might be described as delicate and light. But other-wordly? No, definitely not. I've never met anyone more grounded in the here and now. But he was so serious and trying so hard to find the right words. I just felt unbearably sorry for him. He must've really loved her.

'Damned hard work, though!'

What?

'Oh, I know you two are still good friends and you wouldn't hear a word against her. But don't you sometimes think she can be a little self-centred?'

A little self-centred? Are we talking about the same woman here?

He was definitely in a reminiscing mood. 'And she could be very sharp tongued.'

Had to agree with that.

'And very intolerant.'

She could, indeed.

'Not to say downright nasty if she doesn't get her own way.'

This conversation wasn't going the way I'd expected at all.

Maurice interrupted. 'She doesn't sound like a nice person.' Neither Dan nor I said anything. I thought Dan should be the one to contradict Maurice and, presumably, he thought it was up to me.

'Actually,' Dan said, 'the first time we met, it was Lee I had my eye on.'

What!

He smiled at me. 'You had such a lovely sense of humour and I thought it was really kind, and smart, of you to make a joke to save your friend embarrassment.'

Maurice frowned. 'So why on Earth did you end up with the other woman?'

'Dunno.' Dan shrugged and considered. 'I suppose, I was flattered. She was probably the best-looking woman in the room—'

I coughed. But Dan continued, oblivious to what he was actually saying. 'I couldn't believe my luck at first.'

'You mean, lucky escape,' I interjected.

'Eh? Pardon?' Dan asked.

'If Teri hadn't lured you away, you might have ended up with me. Wouldn't that have been terrible?'

I was peeved.

Thank goodness for Maurice. 'I don't see how it was a lucky escape,' he said. 'Sounds like the most awful bad luck.'

'You're right,' Dan said. 'I think I began to suspect even before the wedding that we weren't quite right for each other.'

So why did you marry her? Poor Teri – she'd really been given a bum's rush. 'It wasn't really kind or smart of you to get married if you were having doubts.' I deliberately echoed his earlier words.

'I know,' he acknowledged, 'But Teri can be quite forceful and it's hard not to be carried along. And,' he added, almost as an afterthought, 'it was quite exciting.'

'It sounds clichéd,' he said. 'But she swept me off my feet.'

He was right – it did sound clichéd.

'Dumb too,' Maurice said, who'd been following the conversation with interest. Absolutely, I thought. Good old Maurice.

'I know,' Dan agreed. 'But it wasn't until after the wedding that I really began to wonder if I'd done the right thing. She wasn't nice to Victoria, you know?'

Well, I did, of course, but Maurice didn't – though he wasn't surprised, he said.

Dan was knee deep in reminiscences. 'I'm sure she wanted a tropical beach wedding because she didn't want Victoria to come on honeymoon.'

'Can hardly blame her for that,' Maurice butted in.

Dan ignored him. 'It was very tempting. A simple ceremony, just us, and a couple of witnesses. Golden sands. A cooling sea breeze. The sun setting over a pale turquoise sky. Waves lapping.' Dan sighed. 'But I couldn't exclude Victoria, and I really don't understand why Teri didn't want us on holiday with us.'

Because it was supposed to be your honeymoon.

'Sounds like a load of twaddle to me,' Maurice spoke briskly. 'There'd be sand everywhere, and almost certainly the wind'd be blowing a gale. And, when you got home, all the nearest, and dearest who weren't invited would have your guts for garters.'

Dan appeared pained. 'Well, I definitely didn't want a repeat of my first wedding. It was the most elaborate and costly shindig it's ever been my misfortune to attend. And I picked up the tab for most of it because neither my parents nor Sara's had two ha'pennies to rub together.'

Well, he got his wish. A shabby wedding in a drab register office.

Dan gave a theatrical shudder. 'And two of the twelve white doves Sara insisted should be released as we emerged from the church got themselves electrocuted. One of them nearly knocked the best man for six as it dropped to the ground.'

'You don't seem to have had much luck with the marrying lark,' I said.

'Next time, I'm going to do it differently,' he promised. *Next time? He should quit while he was ahead.*

Chapter 69

Teri

I blame Dan. If he'd listened to me and tried to understand what I was saying, we'd never have got divorced. But he wouldn't listen, would he? If he'd only opened his eyes to what that little vixen of a daughter of his was doing, he'd have seen the light. That little she-Devil broke up our marriage. Well, I hope she's satisfied. If it hadn't been for her, Dan, and I would still be together. And if Dan had only considered me – his wife – and not treated me so inconsiderately, I wouldn't have felt the need to go off with Declan.

And I blame Declan. If he'd behaved responsibly instead of going off with every other woman he saw, we could've made a go of it. But, no. Any lips on sticks in a skirt and whoosh, off he goes. Can't keep his prick in his pants. I wouldn't mind, but he's the one who started it all. 'I love you, Teri… I can't live without you, Teri…' If he felt like that, why the hell did he feel the need to go off? Typical bloody man.

And if Declan'd come to the May Ball with me, like I asked him to, the business with David Greenspan wouldn't have happened.

And what was wrong with that little creep? Immature pseudo-intellectual little dick-head who couldn't see a good thing when it happened to him.

Chapter 70

Lee

I met up again with Dan and Maurice for Sunday lunch. L'homme-vert. Very expensive. Silver service. And waiters with faux French accents.

'Didn't you used to take Teri here?' I asked.

'No,' Dan said. 'I booked a table once, but we had to cry off.'

He caught my eye – and I remembered. Oh, yes, Teri hadn't been best pleased.

'I'm sure you took her somewhere equally nice,' I said.

'Most definitely – she talked about it for ages afterwards.' And we both roared with laughter.

Maurice looked puzzled. 'What's the joke?'

'Nothing, nothing. It's not really funny at all.' Dan frowned. 'Water under the bridge.'

Okay – if you say so.

Maurice was studying the menu. 'What's the difference between chicken liver parfait and chicken pâté?'

I looked at Dan. 'You're the gourmet.'

'About five quid,' he quipped. 'You'd get pâté in a cheap and cheerful bistro and parfait in a banged-up-to-the-nines brasserie.'

'And potted meat in a greasy spoon,' I added. And we both roared with laughter again. Why? I don't know – the joke wasn't especially funny but somehow, I felt in a giggly mood.

Maurice was not amused. 'You two are being silly.'

'All right,' Dan said. 'I'll be serious. Lee, do you like ten-pin bowling?'

Maurice gave him a dirty look. 'How's that being serious?'

We ignored him. 'No,' I said. 'I don't like ten-pin bowling…'

'Now you're not even making sense,' Maurice interrupted.

'But I do like ten-pin bowling with my nephew Ritchie. I love his excited little face when he scores a strike.'

'And I bet you don't mind burger and chips in the café afterwards.'

'Actually, I'd rather not. But Ritchie does – so we usually do.'

'Exactly,' Dan said, as if he'd proved a point.

'Still not making sense,' Maurice said.

Oh, but I think he was. For possibly the first time in my life, I was being compared to Teri – and coming out on top. I could get to like this.

Afterwards, Dan suggested driving across to Westchester. Maurice should see the new internationally acclaimed museum and sculpture gallery, he said. But Maurice, who'd rambled all over Europe, had barely ventured north of Watford Gap and was nervous about leaving the comparative safety of our metropolis. 'Isn't it a bit rough there?' he asked.

Whatever gave him that idea? 'I'm sure there was something on your programme last night about an illegal dog fight near Westchester.'

'That was in East Grimley,' Dan said. 'Different class of people altogether in Westchester.'

I'd seen the same news item too – and decided against pointing out that two of the three pit bull breeders who'd been arrested were Westchester born and bred. Although I did suggest the sort of people who went in for dog fighting tended not to be arty types and were most unlikely to be counted among the million or so visitors who'd visited the museum since it opened.

But Maurice said he got car sick after a big lunch – the wimp – and instead we made the short journey to the nearby ancestral home of the local gentry and strolled around the rhododendron gardens for a couple of hours until it was time for his train back to London.

'Be careful,' Dan warned him as we waved goodbye at the ticket barrier.

'Careful? Why?'

'The first stop is Westchester.'

****

Maurice texted when he got back to London. He'd had a terrible journey, he said. Having secured a front-facing corner seat with a table, he was looking forward to a quiet couple of hours working on the *Sunday Telegraph* crossword when a group of postal workers boarded the train at Doncaster. They were heading for the England vs India test match at Lord's the next day and, having spent the afternoon in the pub, were in party mood. Maurice, it appeared, did not share their good cheer, and several times declined their hospitable offer of a can of lager from one of the several carrier bags now piled on their shared table.

They kept calling me cock, he texted.

It's a term of endearment, I texted back.

No, it isn't, he replied. *It's a very rude word. And I didn't get to finish my crossword.*

Clearly, the north was a foreign country.

I showed Dan the message – he'd suggested a drink after we'd seen Maurice on his way and, more than two-and-a-half hours later, we were still sharing a communal table and bench in the low ceiling, floor-boarded basement of a wonderful bar and charcuterie round the corner from the railway station. It's one of the city's lesser known gems, although, these days, since a critic in one of the Sunday supplements gave it a big thumbs-up, it's not quite such a well-kept secret. Tonight the place was heaving and the noise and banter from the other punters so loud it was almost impossible to hear oneself think – let alone whatever it was Dan had just said.

'Pardon,' I leant closer. 'I can't hear you.'

He leant closer too and, brushing my hair aside, almost bellowed in my ear. 'Fancy ten-pin bowling?'

And the chatter, which had been rising, and falling all evening, did what chatter always does at such moments and dropped several decibels.

The silence was deafening, and the old fellow nursing a Belgian beer bottle on the bench opposite winked. 'Great chat up line, mate.'

Dan blushed and looked away.

'I thought it might be fun… if you're free next Saturday.'

Damn! 'I can't,' I said. 'I'm looking after my niece and nephew – their mum and dad are going to York races. I've got the kids all day and overnight as well.'

'Bring them along,' Dan said. 'It'll be fun.'

Fun? He hadn't met Fee, who was toddling around now and turning into a little terror. 'I don't know…'

'I like small children,' he insisted.

'You do? Even ones you've never met before? You're mad.'

'Go on, love.' The old fellow raised his bottle in Dan's direction. 'Can't you see he's smitten?'

Who's mad now?

I demurred at first – the combination of me, the region's premier autocue reading media tart (his words, not mine), a seven-year-old, and a nearly two-year-old seemed a recipe made in hell.

But both Dan and the Belgian beer bloke were adamant.

'Give him a break,' the beer bloke insisted.

'I was a little boy once,' Dan said.

What's that got to do with it?

In the end, I capitulated. It was the peck on the cheek as we left the bar that did it. And the warm hand that grasped mine as we stepped into the street.

'I'd better hold your hand,' Dan said.

'Why?'

'The Sunday supplement critic who recommended this place said this street was only used by those trying to leave town or locate someone to mug.'

'When did he say that?'

'Didn't you read his review? It was mostly complimentary. But he was a bit rude about this part of the city.'

'Oh,' I said. And I didn't need to tell Dan that my 'Oh' meant, yes, hold my hand.

Of course, I'd forgotten about Teri.

Chapter 71

Teri

There's some software on the university central computer system called LookItUp that allows lecturers and admin staff to gain access to individual student's personal details – home addresses, next-of-kin, medical history, that sort of thing. If you were a personal tutor – and we were each allocated a certain number of Level 1 students to whom we had to act in this capacity, for instance, helping them to settle into university and cope with homesickness – you were automatically given two passwords. One was to gain entry to LookItUp, and the second was specific to a particular student. We all had the initial password to access LookItUp but, under the Data Protection Act, University Rule Securities, or some privacy nonsense like that, you weren't allowed the second password unless that individual student was one of your personal tutees.

David Greenspan hadn't been on my personal tutee list and, as a reasonably mature student, I'm not entirely sure he would've needed a personal tutor to help him cope, anyway. I did, however, have his mobile phone number because he was in one of my tutorial groups and one way of keeping in touch with those I taught directly was to text them. So, shortly after my carpeted corridor debacle with him in May, I texted David, ostensibly to apologise. I'm not sure if I had any ulterior motives at the time, but there is something about being snubbed by a man that doesn't sit easy with me and I was determined to get back on to – if nothing else – a level footing with him.

Hi. Just wantd 2 apolgse. How u doing? I texted. But he didn't reply. So I rang him. And the phone went on to voicemail. So I left a message. *Hi, David. Hope you got my text okay. I just wanted to apologise for being such a prat. Can I buy you a drink to show there are no hard feelings? Ring me back.* He didn't ring back.

I left it for a few weeks, but then popped into uni. Universities are a bit like the *Marie Celeste* during the summer holiday given there are no students other than those attending summer schools, and very few staff other than those in admin.

It was lunchtime, and I hovered at the end of the carpeted corridor in the hope Chrissie and her admin mates weren't going to assemble their fat little bums on the sofas to eat their carefully prepared home-packed plastic tubs of salad preferring instead to head off into town where they could have some proper food by way of a long lunch at the local pizza place. And as luck would have it, all was quiet, and I was able to nip into the office without having to think up an excuse as to why I was there. The only person on guard was a little work experience girl who looked up nervously as I entered.

'Oh, hi,' I said. 'I need to get in touch with one of my students, and my computer's packed up at home. Can I use one of yours? Oh, by the way, save me looking it up. Have you the password for LookItUp as I've left my address book behind?'

'Er,' she said. 'I'm not sure I can…'

'Oh, don't worry, I'll use this one,' I said, plonking myself down at Chrissie's desk, switching the machine on, and logging in as quickly as the very slow antiquated system would allow. 'Now, the password?' I said, looking up expectantly. The little love pulled a file from her drawer, opened it, and read out the main password. I entered the system. 'Ah, damn,' I said, thinking how convincing an actress I would make. 'I've forgotten David's password. Have you got the one for Greenspan D?'

'Oh, I'm not supposed to…'

'It's okay, love,' I reassured her. 'I just need something quickly and then I'll be gone.' She wilted in the face of my authority and read out the password to David's personal file. I keyed it in and up popped everything I needed to know. Would you believe it? There was an address on Leyland Road – Number 22, Flat 4. He lived just a few doors down from Declan. All those times I was round there, and I'd never known Gorgeous Greenspan lived just a few yards away. I made a note of the address, exited LookItUp, and then remembered to log off and shut down the computer. That was clever of me: I didn't fancy Chrissie coming back and discovering I'd been using her PC.

It wasn't an entirely proud moment when I realised I was driving slowly up and down Leyland Road once again. The last time had been trying to find out what Declan was up to. This time I was looking for an altogether younger model.

I parked the car, walked up to the front door of Number 22, looked at a list of names with separate buttons against each of them, saw the name Greenspan, and pressed. It was one of those intercom systems and shortly after my buzz, I heard David's voice saying 'Hello?'

'Hi, David. It's me. Teri. Can I have a word?' He should've responded by saying something like 'Oh, hi. Yes, come on up,' and pressing the buzzer that would let me in, but he didn't say anything at all, and he clearly didn't press the entry buzzer.

'David?' I queried.

Then he spoke. 'Look, Teri, whatever it is you want, can you please just forget it?'

'But I only wanted to apologise.'

'I don't want or need your apology. Just, please, leave me alone.'

'Oh, come on, David. I only want to talk.'

'I'm sorry, Teri…' Just then the front door swung open, and a resident emerged. I stepped forward, through the door, and into the foyer. Ahead of me was a flight of stairs and I assumed, rightly, that Flat 4 was on the first floor. Sure enough, at the top of the first flight was a battered-looking brown door with the number '4' roughly scrawled in white paint. I knocked. If a door can open angrily, this one did.

'What the fuck?' David glared at me.

'Like I said,' I said. 'I've come to apologise. You weren't answering my messages, so I thought I'd better come to check you were all right.'

'I did get your messages,' he replied. 'But I chose to ignore them. Teri, can't you get the picture? How can I put this? I'm not interested. I don't fancy you. I don't want us to be friends. I wish you would just fuck off and leave me alone.' And he slammed the door in my face.

Chapter 72

Lee

The days leading up to what I hardly dared think of as my 'date' with Dan were fraught with tension. Logically, there was no reason why Teri should object – she was the one who'd filed for divorce after all. Who was I trying to kid? Teri would blow a gasket. Just because she'd dumped Dan didn't mean she'd look kindly on me muscling in. Besides, I was breaking the cardinal rule of friendship: hands off a mate's ex. So I cravenly spent the entire week actively avoiding her – which was easy enough since we were now in the close season, waiting for the new academic year to begin. Technically, I was on annual leave, which removed the possibility of bumping into Teri at work, and I carefully screened phone calls, not picking up when she rang.

She left a couple of voicemails, but they were inconsequential, gossipy messages. She was clearly at a bit of a loose end and though, under normal circumstances, I would've enjoyed a long, wine-fuelled lunch while she let off steam, but not right now. Once, when I popped to the supermarket for a few essentials, I spotted her browsing through a copy of *Harper's Bazaar* in the periodicals aisle. I dumped my basket and fled. Which was a bit of a nuisance, because I then had to drive to the Sainsbury's Local at the petrol station near the university, and they were clean out of Muscadet, so I had to settle for Pinot Grigio. And, yes, I know it serves me right – and it's a hard life when you have to make do with Pinot Grigio – but what would you have done? She'd have been bound to ask about my plans for the weekend – one of her voicemails had suggested lunch at Romilee's in Harrogate – and, even if I fudged, and said I was looking after Ritchie and Fee, she'd probably guess I was hiding something. She always does. She can read me like a book. Damn her!

When I got home, another voicemail was waiting. Teri again.

Lee, sorry. Change of plans. Can't do Romilee's after all. Something's come up. Can't tell you now but watch this space.

Phew! That was me off the hook. But the ambiguous message could mean only one thing – another man was on the horizon.

Felicity and Euan dropped the children off at my house just before noon. We had a light lunch, then Fee had a nap and Ritchie settled himself at my PC and spent a couple of hours saving the world from prehistoric monsters, vampires, and extra-terrestrials with two heads and multiple arms. He wasn't best pleased when I told him a friend of mine was planning to join us at the bowling alley.

'It's bad enough having to bring Fee,' he said with one eye still on his computer game. And he wasn't over-impressed when I played what I thought would be a trump card.

'He's off the telly.' No, the only acceptable him-off-the-telly in Ritchie's eyes was either a soccer presenter or a motor racing commentator. And, once it was clear Dan was neither, his status dive-bombed. Still, Ritchie accepted the inevitable, and went back to saving the world. And I attempted to while away the time with a book. I might as well have tried to fly to the moon; I could barely keep my eyes off the clock. What time should we leave? Should I wake Fee?

'Don't,' advised Ritchie. 'She's grumpy as hell if you wake her up before she's ready.'

'Don't swear,' I said.

And Fee carried on snoring in her buggy in the hallway – Ritchie had pushed her out there because, he said, she was disturbing his concentration – and I carried on trying to read and the clock crept slow as a snail and the butterflies in my tummy danced a clog dance.

At last – long, long last – Fee, who'd been grizzly earlier, woke sunny, and refreshed. So, once I'd changed her nappy and cleaned her up – ugh! – the three of us got into the car and headed for the bowling alley.

I suppose parents take the packhorse element of travelling even very short distances with small children for granted. But, for me, it was a bit like a poorly executed military operation – I struggled to get Fee's car seat fastened properly and, then, once it was secure-ish, I struggled to manhandle Fee into it and, in the end, almost drove off with her baby bag, change of clothes, and emergency toys and rations still sitting on the roof. Thank God for Ritchie! After several pantomime minutes, he elbowed me aside and, clunk-click, the seat was safely secured, and another clunk-click, and Fee was also securely stowed. And, just as I turned the ignition, he remembered the baby paraphernalia. Shame he forgot about the baby buggy, which we'd left sitting in the hallway. But never mind, we'd only gone a couple of miles when he reminded me, and if we hadn't then got stuck behind a funeral procession, we might've arrived at the bowling alley promptly at 4 p.m. as arranged.

He wasn't there. Obviously, he'd got fed up with waiting; we were twenty-five minutes late, after all. I could've cried. I hadn't realised until that moment just how much I'd been looking forward to it.

'Where's your friend?' Ritchie asked.

I shrugged, determined not to spoil his afternoon as well as mine. 'I expect something else cropped up and when we weren't here on time, he had to go.'

'We're not that late,' Ritchie said, looking at his watch, and doing some mental arithmetic. I smiled – Ritchie had a somewhat elastic sense of time. 'You'd have waited at least half an hour for him, wouldn't you?' Actually, I'd probably have waited a lot more than half an hour – in fact, if I was being strictly honest, I'd been waiting several years for a nice man like Dan to take me on a date. Even a date with a couple of kids in tow.

But never mind, we could still enjoy the bowling. Well, Ritchie would enjoy it, and, for his sake, I'd pretend to be having a good time, despite the heavy lump of disappointment sitting in the middle of my chest. I'd go through the motions and Fee would come along for the ride. She was already mesmerised by the flashing lights and blinking noises from the gallery of soft machines banked against the side walls of the entrance lobby.

'Let's pay and get our shoes,' I said, hunting for my purse.

'Lee, I'm so sorry we're late.'

We're late? Who? I looked and standing behind Dan was a young blonde woman – Victoria.

'It's my fault,' she apologised. 'I missed the bus to Dad's house, and he had to come and pick me up. And then we got stuck behind a funeral procession and Dad, stupidly, followed it all the way to the cemetery, instead of turning off towards the bowling alley.'

'Who are you?' Ritchie asked. He looked at me accusingly. 'You didn't say he was bringing a girl.'

'I wasn't,' Dan said. 'But Victoria wants to be a children's nurse, so she offered to come and help look after Fee.'

'And my friends call me Tory. Nobody calls me Victoria,' she said, giving Dan a filthy look.

'I do,' he protested.

'And I wish you wouldn't.'

'I know what you mean,' Ritchie said. 'My nana always calls me Richard – it's such a sissy name. I pretend not to hear her. But she told my mum I needed to get my hearing tested and when Mum said there was nothing wrong with my hearing, she dragged me out of footy practice and took me to the doctor's herself.'

Yes, she had. Fliss had been furious. And so had Mammy. The doctor diagnosed a severe case of selective deafness.

'I'd been going to pretend to the doctor I was deaf too,' said Ritchie. 'But then I thought if I did that, there'd be more tests and more tests, and if Dad had to pay for an expensive hearing aid that I didn't really need, he'd be furious.

'And I was really worried that our footy coach would drop me from the squad if he thought I couldn't hear him shouting from the sideline.'

Dan looked at him in awe. 'And does your nana call you Ritchie now?'

'Naw. She still calls me Richard.'

'And do you still pretend not to hear her?'

'No.' Ritchie's shoulders drooped. 'Dad said I had to stop being rude, or he'd ban me from footy.'

'Well, I think he's mean,' Victoria said. 'Parents can be such a pain in the backside.'

'Victoria!'

She gave Dan a cheeky grin and she and Ritchie swaggered off together towards bowling lane number thirteen.

'Mine's a Diet Coke,' she said over her shoulder.

'And so's mine,' Ritchie said.

Chapter 73

Lee

Until the bowling alley trip I'd met Victoria perhaps a handful of times and my view of her had been very much coloured by Teri's one-sided, somewhat biased, opinions. I'd never quite believed she was the Devil child of Teri's imaginings, but, even if only half the things Teri said about her were true, she was undoubtedly a remarkably spoilt and self-centred young person. How wrong can you be? She was, perhaps, a little young for her age but she and Ritchie hit it off straight away and Fee, who doesn't take easily to strangers, fell passionately in love, climbing onto her lap, and sharing her post-bowling plate of nuggets and chips. Dan watched the pair of them feeding each other fries with a funny look on his face. He looked wishful and pleased at the same time.

'Penny for them?' I asked.

He took my hand and shook his head. 'It's nothing.'

He dropped my hand abruptly as the waitress arrived with another round of drinks. Fizzy stuff for Dan and the kids, and mineral water for me.

'Nice kids, you've got there,' the woman said. 'Makes a change to see a family what likes each other.'

And she was wiping down the next table before we could put her straight.

I did like Victoria though, and when Dan said he had to work the following weekend – a regional business conference – and Victoria pouted and said, 'But what about me? Mummy's at a spa all day Saturday.' It seemed perfectly natural to suggest she spend the day with us instead.

'It'll be boring,' I warned, 'but you'll be very welcome.' And when Ritchie added his voice to mine and Fee slapped a whopping great kiss on her forehead, she accepted gratefully.

She mucked in as if she'd known us forever, elbowing me aside at the supermarket checkout to repack my shopping. 'Lee,' she said, 'put the fridge stuff in one bag and the veg in another. And don't mix store cupboard stuff and toiletries.'

Fliss, who was doing her Saturday big shop with me, raised her eyebrows. 'Bossy boots,' she mouthed. But I noticed she was quite happy to let Victoria play peek-a-boo with Fee, who was holding court in her buggy, while she packed her own shopping. And she didn't mix store cupboard and toiletries or fridge and veg stuff either.

Afterwards we went for ice cream – well, Ritchie and Fee had big chocolate fudge sundaes, and Fliss and I sipped polystyrene mugs of tea while Victoria 'helped' Fee with her sundae. Helped is a deliberate euphemism. 'One for you,' she said in a sing-song voice as the spoon followed an aeroplane trail through the air into Fee's open mouth. 'And one for me,' she said as she popped a scoop into her own mouth. Fee giggled delightedly. 'Again, again…'

'Sorry,' Victoria said. 'I'm eating rather a lot of her ice cream.'

'No worries,' Fliss said. 'You need the calories more than this little fatty.' And she tickled Fee's chubby pink feet.

Victoria blushed. 'I'm much better at eating now than I was.'

Startled, Fliss and I exchanged a look of surprise.

'Last week I put on a whole pound.' She said it as if this was something to celebrate.

'And Lee lost another two pounds at her Slimmer's Nation weigh-in,' chipped in Ritchie.

'Slimmer's Nation!'

'Shush, everyone can hear you.' I glared at Ritchie and the family at the neighbouring table, who momentarily stopped shovelling fries into their mouths.

'You never told me,' Fliss accused. 'And how do you know?' She turned on her son.

'Because I thought he could keep a secret,' I answered.

'I can. I can,' he protested. 'I didn't tell when Tory sicked up her chips last weekend. Or when Mummy was sick before breakfast.'

'Ritchie!' It seemed to be his day for letting cats out of bags.

'More drinks all round,' I said. 'Tory, come, and help me. Give Fliss the ice cream. Sounds like she's the one in need of extra sustenance.' And I gave my little sister a meaningful glance.

We joined the counter queue, behind a gaggle of young teens who'd clearly just been released from the matinee performance of the season's mini blockbuster at the nearby multiplex.

'Don't tell Dad,' Victoria pleaded. 'I hardly ever do it now. And I was on my period and I had a really, really bad bellyache.' She sniffed. 'I've been trying so hard and Dad…'

'Here.' I held out a paper tissue.

She dabbed at her eyes. The queue inched forward. Every one of the blasted kids was ordering separately and paying with pennies and tuppences from their piggy banks. I dug out my own purse and started counting coins. I needed time to think. 'I can't not tell your dad,' I said at last. 'He needs to know.'

'No. No. He doesn't.' She sounded desperate. 'It would just be worrying him when there's nothing to worry about.' The tissue was now a mangled sausage, twisted around her twitching fingers.

'Isn't there?'

'No! I'm cured now.'

'How do I know that?' I felt quite desperate myself. This was the first time the spectre of anorexia had raised its head and I felt out of my depth. And just a little angry Dan had never mentioned anything. It was like struggling to put the lid back on a can of worms I'd never wanted to open in the first place.

'What do you mean by cured?'

'I keep a photo of Teri next to my bedroom mirror.' Her tone sounded as if she was stating the bleeding obvious when it was about as clear as mud to me.

'It was sort of Dad's idea,' she explained and then stopped – we'd reached the front of the queue. I ordered the drinks and, Slimmer's

Nation be damned, some muffins too. I needed a sugar hit if no one else did.

Ritchie grabbed one as if he hadn't seen food in a month of Sundays. 'Yum,' he said, spitting crumbs across the table. 'Thanks, Auntie Lee, you're the best.' And he gave a thumbs-up.

Whatever Fliss said to him while we queued didn't seem to have dampened his spirits.

'You and I need to talk,' I said.

'No, we don't,' he replied. 'Me and Mum have already talked.'

'Yes, and I need to talk to your mum too.' I looked at Fliss.

Victoria coughed and tapped my arm. 'And we ought to talk a bit more too,' she said.

'We all need to talk,' Ritchie said. He started to sing in a high-pitched pidgin falsetto, 'Happy talk, keep talking happy talk. Talk about things you'd like to do.'

I should never have taken him to see South Pacific last Christmas.

Later, as we ambled back to the cars, Victoria tucked an arm through mine. 'I wouldn't lie to you, Lee. I am better.'

Fliss, who was pushing the baby buggy on my other side looked across at her and shoved the buggy in her direction. 'Tory, darling, be a love, and strap Fee into her car seat.' She fumbled in her pocket and zapped the keys in the direction of the car. There was a satisfying click. 'It's open,' she said and pulled me back as Ritchie and Victoria raced ahead.

'Take her out for a drive,' she whispered.

Eh?

'Anywhere. Doesn't matter. Just go somewhere this afternoon that involves a long-ish drive. She'll open up in the car. Kids always do.'

I grasped on to the one bit of this statement that made any kind of sense. 'But she's not a kid.'

Fliss harrumphed. 'She's the youngest sixteen-year-old I've ever met.'

True. It was one of the things that struck me last weekend. It was partly why I struggled to understand why Teri had been so intolerant of the child. But perhaps that was it – Teri saw a burgeoning young woman and expected her to behave accordingly. And when she didn't… my musings were interrupted by Victoria. 'What are you two muttering about?' she asked.

'I was just asking Fliss if she fancied a mooch around the new out-of-town shopping complex,' I improvised.

'But I can't,' Fliss said. 'The kids would hate it and Euan is playing golf this afternoon so I can't dump them and run.' She smiled affectionately at her son, who looked distinctly unimpressed at the prospect of an afternoon being dragged around the shops. Then his face brightened.

'It's okay,' he said. 'You can go. Dad's not… Ouch!' He squealed. 'Mum, what did you do that for?' He rubbed at the bright red pinch mark where Fliss had grabbed his arm.

'Because Dad is playing golf this afternoon,' she said with heavy emphasis, and frowned at Ritchie. 'Why don't you go instead, Tory? I'm sure Lee would enjoy the company.'

This was my cue – but I'm afraid I missed it.

Instead, Victoria, who clearly didn't quite buy into the golf charade, gave us both a sceptical look. 'You're plotting something,' she said. 'What?'

Thank God for Ritchie. 'I know,' he shouted. 'Mum wants Auntie Lee out of the way this afternoon so she can finish icing her birthday cake. She's trying to be subtle.' Birthday cake? Since when had Fliss baked birthday cakes for me?

'It's for her surprise party next weekend.' Trust Ritchie to spill all the beans.

Fliss laughed and pushed Victoria in the direction of my car. 'Tory. Lee. Go.' So we went.

****

For a Saturday, the traffic was relatively light. However, Fliss and her confident prediction 'she'll open up in the car' proved misplaced.

'I wish I had a sister to plan a surprise birthday party for me,' she said as we eased out of the car park and didn't say another word until we reached the outskirts of town.

I tried a couple of times to start a conversation, but it was like trying to get blood out of a stone. Her responses were monosyllabic and almost sulky. I gave up in the end and switched on the radio and caught the tail end of *Any Questions*?

Victoria folded her arms and glared out of the window. Hmm – was this Teri's Devil child?

Eventually, with a theatrical sigh, she closed her eyes and pretended to nap. I might've been fooled, except a couple of times I caught her eyeing me speculatively. I said nothing. Whatever Fliss might say, there would be no 'happy talk' on this car ride.

We got lost. My fault. You'd think I could find a brand-new retail park on the outskirts of town, but I got confused on the ring road and we started going round in circles. 'This isn't right,' I muttered as I made a second circuit. Victoria, who'd dozed off, jerked awake as I did an emergency stop at a pelican crossing. Bloody pedestrians.

'Are we there?' Victoria tried to get her bearings. Me too. I recognised the railway station – I ought to, I'd passed it twice already. 'Pull into the car park,' Victoria ordered. 'Okay, don't,' she said as I sailed past the entrance, unable to envisage indicating, braking, and turning into what looked like a narrow entrance in the nanosecond available. 'Just keep driving and I'll get some directions.'

How? Where? I was beginning to feel stressed. I'd already taken a wrong turning down a one-way street – fortunately Victoria was still asleep at that point, although the beeping horns from oncoming drivers and my own panicked expletives as I executed a hasty three-point turn were loud enough to wake the dead.

Thank God for Victoria. She pulled out her mobile phone, googled a satnav app and, in almost no time at all, had us heading back out of the city and in the right direction.

As it happened, the new shopping centre was well-signposted – once we were on the right road – and busy. We weren't the only ones to fancy a Saturday afternoon potter around the shops. Victoria's nap seemed to have done her a power of good, though. Nice Tory was back.

'What's so special about John Lewis?' she asked as we strolled across the car park.

'I liked their Christmas ad,' she mused. 'But it didn't make me want to rush to the store and start spending money.'

I agreed. The last time I really enjoyed shopping I'd been perhaps seven or eight. I spent most Saturday afternoons with Mammy and Fliss exploring the delights of the old Victorian indoor market in town. Even then, the big attraction wasn't the shopping but the old-fashioned sweet stall we visited for cola cubes or pear drops. We'd get the bus home and if the conductress knew Mammy she'd take our fares but give lots of change in coppers and small silver. My mother got off the bus with exactly the same sum as when she'd boarded. The conductress said she was 'looking after her own'.

But here we are at the new, giant retail park, looking for John Lewis because, whatever Victoria's phone app said, we couldn't see it. 'It's over there somewhere,' she said, pointing vaguely. Phone app two provided much better directions than number one. A couple of minutes of brisk walking and we entered the hallowed portals of the newest temple to retail therapy. It was a bit of a disappointment, if I'm honest. Although I did pick up a tunic, I'd had my eye on for a while but hadn't been able to find in my size and which was reduced in the sale too.

Victoria though had the shopping attention span of a gnat – clearly a girl after my own heart – and made a beeline for the first-floor cafeteria. 'I'm starving.'

Starving? It was barely a couple of hours since she'd last eaten. And didn't she have an eating disorder? You wouldn't have thought it judging by the speed with which she polished off her share of our cream tea. She was right. She was cured – or, if not completely cured, well on the mend. And I followed her to the ladies' loo afterwards and listened carefully for any puking noises.

She pulled a face at me in the washroom mirror. 'You're dying to ask, aren't you?'

Ask what? I had so many questions I didn't know where to start.

Victoria didn't wait for an answer. 'Teri and the picture on my bedroom mirror?'

It seemed as good a place to start as any. So we headed back to the car and, on the drive home Victoria talked, just as Fliss had predicted she would.

'Dad suggested I put her photo on the mirror. He said it would be a daily reminder.'

It sounded bloody bizarre to me.

'He has this theory about Teri.'

Oh, yes?

'I suppose, I shouldn't tell you this… you're her friend after all.'

Don't let that stop you. I'm agog.

'Dad reckons Teri is a bitch because she's always starving hungry.'

Pardon?

'Have you ever seen her eat a proper meal?'

Actually, no, come to think of it, I hadn't. Not recently, anyway.

'She picks at things and pushes them around her plate.'

Yes, that's right, she did. Does. In fact, the only thing I'd ever seen her eat with any degree of enthusiasm was a rocket salad. And she always eschewed the dressing. Oh God. Had she been ill all these years, and I'd never noticed? What sort of friend was I?

'Dad doesn't think she's anorexic or bulimic.'

Huh! When did he qualify in medicine?

'Because she never gets any thinner. Her weight stays more-or-less stable.'

Thank God, yes, that's true.

'But proper anorexics, like me, do. Get thinner and thinner, I mean.'

You know something? I was really beginning to wish I'd never taken Victoria to the supermarket with me that morning. If I hadn't chivvied her into coming, if I'd just left her slumped in front of reality show repeats on the TV, I wouldn't now be confronting unpleasant truths that, quite frankly, I preferred not to know.

Slowly, I pieced the whole story together. Victoria had become anorexic and bulimic shortly after she moved from her safe, non-threatening primary school to high school. Dan, despite his status as a high-profile television presenter, was a firm believer in comprehensive education, so he'd insisted Victoria attend the local academy, as I suppose we should now call it, rather than the expensive, exclusive private girl's school preferred by his wife.

Almost inevitably, Victoria had been bullied and, in an effort to make herself invisible, had stopped eating.

'I managed to keep it hidden for a couple of years,' she said almost proudly.

How? Didn't her parents notice the shrinking schoolgirl hunched over the dinner table? Apparently not. Dan was busy at work and her mother, who sounded like she could have been Teri's secret twin, was too busy being a lady who lunched. Hell's bells! She even went to my gym. How many times had I heard women like her moaning about their selfish husbands and stroppy teenagers? Poor little Tory.

Obviously, I'm paraphrasing a bit here. Victoria insisted her parents were blameless. 'I got really good at skipping meals and pretending I'd eaten before they got home.' She used to rustle up healthy-ish suppers, like beans on toast. She'd cook the beans and butter some toast and dish it up on a plate and dirty a knife and fork. And then flush the whole plate of food, untouched, down the toilet and load the dishwasher with the 'used' saucepan, crockery, and cutlery.

'I once nearly blocked the loo. I didn't know to cut the toast into chunks so it would flush away more easily. The toilet almost flooded.' She chuckled. I'm afraid I didn't see the funny side. 'And beans float horribly,' she said. 'I used to pour tonnes of bleach down the loo trying to get rid of them.'

Eventually, of course, Dan and his wife realised what was happening and so began an endless round of quarrels and recriminations and trips to the doctor and long spells in therapy and special care.

'It was awful,' Victoria said.

At some point, the marriage broke up. Her mother, apparently, went to the hairdresser one day and, as well as a new cut and blonde highlights, acquired a boyfriend, and packed a suitcase for Dan and booked him into the Herriot Hotel in the city centre. And there he stayed until D'reen from work sorted him out with a two-bedroom apartment in town.

Victoria, of course, blamed herself. 'They wouldn't have been arguing if it wasn't for me,' she said.

Possibly? More likely there would've been another catalyst. Chez Caine didn't sound a very happy ship, even at the best of times.

And Sara, her mother, behaved badly. Despite the fact she'd instigated the breakup and subsequent divorce, she wasn't very happy when Dan started getting his life back together. And drip, drip, drip, she fed Victoria little bits of nastiness. 'Your father has always been unfaithful… he never wanted children… this isn't the first time he's walked out on us… he was too mean to send you to a decent school… I told him you were ill, but he said you were a spoilt brat… I've begged him to come back but he says he hates us both…'

And Victoria, who was battling the demon of being a teenager alongside the twin evils of anorexia and bulimia, was a mess.

The Dan she saw on his weekend and mid-week access visits was just as he had always been – genial and loving and indulgent. And the Dan her mother described was a penny-pinching monster who couldn't wait for her to grow up and get out of his life. Throw in puberty and her periods starting and her body changing shape and it was no wonder she was confused. Teri, of course, didn't help.

'I don't think I was very nice to her,' Victoria said. 'But she made me feel as if I was really greedy and always wanting Dad to buy new things. And she treated me as if I was a naughty child who kept getting in the way.'

Which was exactly what Sara was telling her?

But none of this really explained the photograph of Teri on her bedroom mirror. Dan, it appeared, had fairly quickly realised the marriage was a mistake.

'On the rebound,' Victoria said unnecessarily. It didn't take a genius to work out he'd jumped from the frying pan into the fire. So, he wasn't quite as heartbroken as Teri had thought when they too divorced but had employed a very effective bit of cod psychology to help Victoria manage her eating disorders. 'He said to take a good hard look at Teri every morning. He said people who don't eat have no heart.' So she started eating again and, though she still had bad days when she gave in to the temptation to sick up her supper, these were becoming rarer and rarer.

I guess you could say Teri cured her. She'd have been thrilled.

Chapter 74

Teri

'You did what?' I could hardly believe what Lee was telling me.

'I've been ten-pin bowling,' she repeated.

'Yes, so you said. But you went with Dan?'

'Well, yes. We're friends… he suggested it might be fun. We took the kids, you know, my niece, and nephew… and Victoria.'

'I can't believe this,' I said. 'Honestly, Lee, I can't believe you did that. Going with Dan behind my back. It's ridiculous.'

'Why is it ridiculous?' Lee was indignant. 'And we're not doing anything behind your back. You and Dan are divorced. He's a free agent to do what he likes.'

'Yes.' I stormed at her. 'But not with *you!*'

I wish now I hadn't managed to get through to her. God knew I'd been ringing and ringing, but she never picked up. I needed to talk to her about the David Greenspan business, but I kept getting her voicemail and there was no way I could tell her the ins and outs of it all in a message, so I kept it light and chatty – suggesting lunch instead – and she still didn't call me back. Then I had a brainwave and left a message suggesting we go to Romilee's for afternoon tea at the weekend. It's a fabulous little place that does every blend of herbal tea and exquisite little iced cakes. Just the sort of thing Lee goes in for. That would get her talking to me. But no, still no reply. So I rang back and left another message saying I couldn't do afternoon tea now. Something had come up. She wouldn't be able to resist ringing me now to find out what was going on. Unfortunately, nothing was going on.

There was one odd thing, though. I was in the local supermarket, having a quick scan at the expensive magazines and, out of the corner of my eye, I thought I spotted her, but by the time I turned to have a proper look, she'd scarpered. Can't have been her, but it was certainly someone who looked just like her from the back.

It'd been an odd few weeks. I suppose the David Greenspan situation had taken my mind off the Declan situation. Maybe what I thought I'd felt about David was a reaction to what had happened with Declan: was I on the rebound, or was it some sort of love transference? Anyway, even I could see I hadn't behaved particularly well with regard to David but, although I thought about trying again to apologise to him, I decided against it. He'd made himself fairly clear. So David was off the list then. Lee broke up with Christian some while back and when I jokingly suggested he'd be free to go out with me now, she hadn't thrown a wobbly as I thought she would but laughed instead. 'He'd bore even you to death,' she said. Even me? I didn't ask for clarification; she can be so sarcastic sometimes, but generally she means well. Lee seemed a lot happier now she'd finally got Mike out of her system and, while I thought she'd have clung on to Christian, she didn't seem that bothered they'd split up. But this business about her and Dan 'walking' each other really got up my nose: who the hell did she think she was?

Lee finally deigned to ring me.

'Where the hell have you been?' I demanded. 'I've been trying to get hold of you for days.' She wittered on about this and that and how busy she'd been and then, finally, she told me about her little family outing with my ex and his wretched daughter – to the bowling alley of all places. God, I was furious. I'd told her about the time Dan and I went bowling, and she'd obviously decided this was the sort of thing she had to do as well. Scheming little cow.

Chapter 75

Lee

Fliss cornered me after Mass. I'd given Mammy a lift there and was waiting to run her back home while she sorted out some finer points with Mrs O'Brien relating to Tuesday's UCM meeting. Fliss swanned over just as Mammy, business finally concluded, leant towards Declan's mother and, with a conspiratorial inclination of the head towards Marnie, who was awkwardly navigating the church steps, said, 'Won't be long now.'

Sunday after Sunday, I'd chartered the progress of Marnie's ballooning stomach with an equal mix of fascination and horror. If it came to banging bellies with a sumo wrestler, she'd win, hands down. I shuddered, thinking of the blood bath that'd ensue when she and Teri found out that Declan was stringing them both along. Not for the first time, I wondered whether I'd been right to keep my own counsel. To be fair, I wasn't overly concerned about Marnie, but maybe I owed it to Teri to put her in the picture? No, every conversation about Declan ended with us arguing and I was done banging my head against a brick wall.

In the meantime, there were things afoot on my own doorstep requiring attention. I stared at Fliss, who had the grace to look slightly embarrassed.

I grabbed her arm. 'Mammy,' I said over my shoulder as I pulled Fliss in the direction of the church hall where the St. Vincent de Paul ladies served after Mass tea and biscuits. 'Fliss and I are going for a cuppa.'

'My treat,' I said, throwing a couple of pound coins into the collection box being rattled by Sister Mary, who was in charge of the teacups. She tutted. 'The proceeds go to helping the poor and needy, Lee. You could be a little more generous with the pennies from your fat university income.'

What? I'd just paid two quid for two cups of stewed tea. If that wasn't generous, what was? I was about to answer back when Fliss took out her purse and dropped a £2 coin in the box. 'Will that do?' Sister Mary, who seemed to have forgotten she was supposed to be a sister of charity, sniffed most uncharitably. 'Biscuits are extra,' she said.

Keep your bloody biscuits, I thought – but said nothing and smiled politely instead.

'Pardon?' she asked.

Oh my God. I'd done it again and spoken aloud when I should've kept my mouth shut. Giggling, Fliss hustled me away.

'She'll tell, Mammy,' she said. 'You wait and see.'

We elbowed our way through the crowd – Declan, who hadn't been at Mass, must've come to pick up Marnie and the kids, and was sipping tea with them at a window table. Their son stared moodily at his mobile phone while their little girl sat on Declan's knee, twiddling the hair at the back of his collar. I almost choked. I remembered Teri telling me how much she liked to curl up on his lap and nuzzle his neck and twirl her fingers through his hair – which, I have to admit looked temptingly lush and twirl-able.

I was tempted to go over and say *hello*. It'd be interesting to see how Declan reacted, but Fliss waved from the other side of the room. Oh well, perhaps later.

'Me first,' Fliss said as I sat down. 'What's this about Slimmer's Nation? And Victoria. Come on' – she crooked her finger and waggled it – 'tell your little sister…' Hang on a minute. I've got some questions of my own.

But Fliss was having none of it. 'You tell first.' She always was a bossy little bugger.

She listened with sympathy as I told her about Victoria. 'Poor little thing,' she said when I finished. 'But she's not cured, you know. Not yet. It's not that simple.'

That's what Dan had said last night. He wanted to tell me, he said, but it was Victoria's secret (Ha! Ha!) and he felt it had to be her decision about what and when and if she told me. Okay, I got that – it was early days, and we were all still getting to know each other, but I still felt just a little hurt he hadn't trusted me enough. Fliss patted my hand reassuringly. 'It's a control thing. It always is with eating disorders. Sufferers feel helpless about the big things in life, so food becomes a way of getting some power back. Even if it's just over what they do and don't put in their mouth.'

Hell's bells. This was getting profound. 'So Dan—?'

'Was absolutely right to leave it to Victoria to tell you herself.'

'And it's a big compliment that she felt able to tell you so early in the relationship.'

Okay, I got that. But he might have given me a hint – he'd left her in my care for a day and it was a big responsibility.

Fliss was exasperated. 'She's not a child, even if she might seem like one. And don't be so bloody self-centred. You're beginning to sound just like Miss-the-whole-world-revolves-around-me-Meyer.'

Fliss! She's not that bad.

'Oh yes, she is,' Fliss said. 'You can't see it… you never have. But even a baby like Fee shows more consideration for other people.'

That was a bit of an exaggeration. Fee could be pretty single-minded when she wanted something. But, on the other hand, she was still in nappies and Teri… well, Teri wasn't. But talking of babies. 'Your turn now.'

'There's nothing much to tell.'

Stop being so coy.

'You mustn't tell anyone,' she said. 'Especially not Mammy. Ritchie hasn't even put two and two together yet. Euan and I want to keep it a secret a bit longer. At least, until I've had my first scan.'

'But you're having another baby?'

'Yes.'

Wow. Another niece or nephew. I stifled a little twinge of jealousy.

'I'll tell you more later,' Fliss said. Mammy stood in the doorway of the parish hall, having a word with Sister Mary, who – Holy Cow! – had abandoned her teapot and was clearly tittle-tattling. Fliss nodded in their direction. 'Quick, Slimmer's Nation?'

Nothing much to tell. Why does anyone join an organisation whose raison d'être is helping people lose weight, get active, and eat healthily? Same reason as most other people – I wanted to get into a posh frock for a special engagement, of course. Don't jump ahead – this particular engagement was about Victoria, not me.

'It was David's idea – I've told you about Gorgeous Greenspan?' Fliss nodded. Yes, David, who sometimes seemed to forget I was the grown-up one in our relationship and who constantly nagged about what he described as my 'unhealthy' diet. Sometimes he could be very patronising. 'A healthy diet is more than just eating five fruits and veg a day,' he preached. 'It's a way of life.'

Huh! I'd seen his idea of a healthy diet – boiled eggs and nutrition shakes for breakfast, dinner, and tea. Practice what you preach, mate. But blow me down. The little sod signed me up at a Slimmer's Nation group run by his auntie Joyce. I was initially furious with him. 'I ought to smack you good and hard,' I said. But he just grinned and – do you know what? – he turned up on the night of the first meeting and frog-marched me to my first group. 'You've lost weight,' he said as he deposited me at the door. 'You're active.'

'And,' he added, pushing me into the room, 'now you need to square the final side of the triangle and learn to eat healthily, and, this is as good a place to learn as any.'

Don't even get me started on the ridiculousness of his mixed metaphor.

But hey-ho. He was right. I did have a lot to learn about healthy eating and, though I still enjoyed French fries and greasy burgers as much as the next woman, I cut out a lot of the rubbish that previously characterised my diet – although I hadn't yet had the willpower to completely give up on the dry white wine. And I'm not sure I ever will.

Glasses of Muscadet withstanding, I'd almost finished the transformation that started with Ritchie and our bike rides.

Chapter 76

Lee

Frankly, Teri lied about her encounter with David – I know, because when he eventually told me his version of events, it had a far more convincing ring of truth to it. More importantly, his account tallied with the one Chrissie said she'd been reluctant to draw to my attention because she didn't want to cause trouble but…

There was no bloody 'but' about it. She loved every minute. And made a meal of spitting out the facts.

'…as deputy head of teaching and learning, I think you need to know that Ms Meyer is guilty of professional misconduct.'

I groaned. It sounded like she too had heard about Teri and David's drunken fumble – there was, I suspected, a bit more to it than Teri had implied when she confessed he'd made a drunken pass at her. A drunken David? I'd like to have seen that. But, nevertheless, it sounded like nothing more serious than a consensual bit of misplaced drunken fumbling.

'I wouldn't say it was quite as serious as that,' I said.

'Wouldn't you?' Chrissie was surprised.

'It's not as if he was just out of school,' I said. 'Technically, he's a mature student – old enough to look after himself.'

'What's his age got to do with anything?' Chrissie asked.

God! The woman was a moron. 'Because he's not a kid. He's been around the block a few times. Kissed a few princesses and his share of witches too.'

Phut! Chrissie made a rude noise. 'I don't care who he's been kissing. Although if he's been snogging Ms Meyer, he's dafter than he looks.'

How unkind.

'But I do care that Ms Meyer threatened him with a Fail grade if he didn't respond to her sexual advances. And her module marks were days late. And, contrary to what she might think, it does matter. And they very nearly weren't ready in time for the award board. I'd bet my bottom dollar too that none of her scripts had been second marked or internally moderated either,' she ended.

Good God!

'Sit down,' I said, pulling out a chair. 'Tell me about it.' And I felt my stomach twist in a cold knot of fear as she did – at length and in damning detail.

She really hadn't wanted to cause trouble, she said, again. She was just a little more convincing this time – perhaps trying to justify the long delay between overhearing Teri's foolish outburst and finally coming to someone in authority about it.

Why me, though?

'You know what it's like over the summer, Lee. Can't find an academic on the premises for love nor money.'

I knew I should've stayed away, but it was the first day of Clearing and duty had called. Damn. Damn. Damn. But Mike and Peter were both in today – I'd seen them. So again, why me?

'I really didn't want to cause trouble,' she repeated. Heavens. She was like a broken record. 'I've worried about it all summer and I thought at first when the module marks seemed broadly in line with what students were getting on other modules that maybe I should let it go.'

Well, why hadn't she?

'It just seemed wrong. If a male lecturer had propositioned a female student…' The sentence trailed off. She didn't really need to finish it.

And she'd come to me because she thought I'd be sympathetic and, basically, she was kicking the ball into my court. She'd raised her concerns with 'someone in authority' and if I did nothing, it would be my neck on the line if the whole thing blew up. Huh. I wasn't having that.

'Hang on,' I said. 'You need to speak to Mike.' Chrissie wasn't the only one who could pass the buck. But God help Teri, though.

Predictably, Mike wanted to call David in and interrogate him then and there. With difficulty, I persuaded him to hold fire. Let me talk to David off the record, I said. No point launching a full-scale inquiry, with all the ramifications that were involved, until we were sure of the facts. 'Okay,' Mike said. 'No need to involve Peter Heron, and Human Resources, just yet.'

It was a breathing space.

Chapter 77

Lee

If I'm honest, I'd hoped I could persuade David to let sleeping dogs lie – which, yes, was unprofessional of me. But old habits die hard and protecting Teri's back was almost a reflect action.

I decided against speaking to David on university premises. Instead, I thought I'd raise the matter casually at the gym. I didn't get a chance. David had been mulling things over and, before I could say a word, he dropped his own bombshell.

We were running side by side on neighbouring treadmills. 'More companionable,' he said and, in deference to the fact our relationship had irrevocably changed after the miserable evening when he spewed up all over my car, he no longer charged me personal trainer rates either. 'We're gym buddies now,' he said. 'You're almost my second mother. I can't take money off you.' Thanks, I thought. I'm now officially old.

I knew what was coming as soon as he started to speak. 'I don't want to bother you,' he said, 'but…'

'But…?' I asked.

'I need advice,' he said. 'Tutor to student.'

Aagh! Why did he have to say that? If I'd been able to keep things off the record, I might've been able to keep a lid on this. Now though, I hadn't a hope in hell. Without an official complaint from David, it was Chrissie's word against Teri's – and Teri was the best liar I knew. But those three little words, three little words! – tutor to student – made the whole damn thing official. F***! F***! F***!

I'd suspected Teri wasn't being completely honest when she said she and David had been 'a bit silly'. Teri never stopped at being 'a bit silly' and, that one time aside, when David got drunk as a skunk over his silly little hairdresser, I didn't think he'd ever been 'silly' in his entire life. He was too damn earnest – and romantic. He had some very old-fashioned ideas about how to treat a girl and taking advantage of a drunken woman just wasn't in his DNA. And it went without saying that Teri would've been drunk. In the old days she had a rule: she didn't drink until the sun dipped below the yardarm – these days the sun seemed to go down earlier and earlier. 'It's half-past six somewhere in the world,' she would say when she telephoned at 4.30 p.m., already ever so slightly the worse for wear and bang on about her many real and imagined grievances. It was impossible, and I tried, believe me, to distract her. I never thought I'd say this about Teri, but she was becoming a complete and utter bore.

I stopped the treadmill. 'I think we'd better find somewhere a bit quiet,' I said. So we went and sat in the coffee lounge – which wasn't terribly private, but it was almost deserted and would have to suffice.

David was prepared to overlook her drunken advances at the May Ball. 'It was the booze talking,' he said, which was generous because he must've been embarrassed. He wasn't even concerned about her little overture outside the admin office or her attempted apology at his flat. 'I'd rather forget about it,' he said. But he couldn't ignore her threat to amend his essay mark if he didn't comply. 'That's the bit that's nasty,' he said. 'And isn't it against the rules? Aren't we supposed to be marked on academic merit? Not favouritism.'

He'd got it in one – David might want to forget about propositions one, two and three, and, at a pinch, the university could overlook them too. But demanding sexual favours in return for a good mark, for that's what it amounted to, was practically a hanging matter. Good God, Chrissie was dead right. If a male tutor had made a similar suggestion to a female student, he'd have been hung out to dry with his professional reputation in tatters. And, for the life of me, I couldn't see how Teri could escape the same fate.

I felt a little shaky and trembly – it was precisely to avoid this sort of conflict of interest that I'd ended my own burgeoning relationship with David. And I'd made sure both Mike and Peter Heron were aware I knew him socially outside the university and – just to be doubly careful – when he signed up for my semester two first-year module, always invited one, or other of them to double mark any assessed work he completed for me. Teri, damn her, had mocked. 'What are you afraid of?' Fool! I was covering my back. If only she'd had the sense to do the same.

'What should I do?' David asked.

I sighed. 'It's out of both our hands now.'

'What do you mean? I don't want a big fuss.'

'It's not really up to you,' I said. 'It's not up to me either.'

Chrissie, I told him, had already raised the matter with me, and with Mike. Chrissie hadn't filed a formal complaint yet, but Mike, I felt sure, would insist she did so. He liked things to be neat and tidy. There would have to be an investigation – it was a very serious accusation and, if true, would have serious consequences for Teri.

'Oh, Lee.' He patted my shoulder. 'I'm so sorry – I know Teri's a good friend.'

Huh! With good friends like her, I was rapidly running out of the need for enemies.

Without corroboration, I told him, it would've been a simple case of Teri's word against Chrissie – impossible to prove either way.

But now that we'd spoken, and he'd confirmed Chrissie's version of events, the case was cut and dried.

'Can't you pretend I never said anything?'

No! I wished I could – but no! 'Things don't work that way.'

'I'm sorry,' he mumbled. 'I'm so, so sorry.'

I gave him a hug. 'It's not your fault,' I reassured him. 'You're the innocent party here.'

'What happens next?'

I explained.

Once a formal complaint was received, he'd be invited in to speak to Mike and probably Peter Heron, too.

'The dean?' David asked. 'It's that serious?'

'Yes,' I said, 'but don't worry.' I hugged him again. 'I'm sure Teri will wriggle out of trouble. She usually does.'

Who was I trying to kid? Peter Heron would have a field day when Chrissie's complaint landed on his desk. Talk about fastening your own noose and sticking your neck in it. Teri couldn't have done a better job if she'd tried.

Chapter 78

Teri

I decided to pay a surprise visit to Lee as she'd been playing silly buggers and not answering her phone. I took a bottle of her favourite Pinot Grigio (I prefer Sauvignon myself, but you can't account for other people's tastes). Previously, she'd have smiled in delight at seeing me waving a bottle of wine, and she'd drag me inside, grab the bottle opener and two large glasses, and we'd plonk down on her sofa to gossip. But this evening she seemed distracted and not entirely delighted to see me. I thought for a moment she wasn't going to invite me in, and I stood on the doorstep feeling slightly foolish, but then she relented, stood aside, and I strode past her into the kitchen to uncork the wine.

'What are you up to?' I asked, trying to lighten what seemed to be a tense mood. 'Oh, before you tell me,' I continued, 'did I tell you I went to the new retail park, you know, the one on the outskirts of town, and guess what I found? The most wonderful Georgia Le Riska skirt. It's the most heavenly shade of—'

'Yes,' Lee interrupted, 'I've been there.'

'Where?'

'The retail park—'

'When did you go?' Frankly, I was surprised. Lee doesn't go shopping on her own, and she'd be too nervous to go to a big new store like that without me.

And then she told me how she'd been quite recently – with Victoria – and went into a spiel about how Victoria had been having it tough and needed help sorting her problems out. When I tried to remind Lee about how spoilt that child was, she started doing her disappointed-shaking-of-head at me and I just said, 'Oh fuck it. It's nothing to me what that wretched girl does. I'm just sorry you've been sucked into it, Lee.'

It was bad enough when I found out Lee was playing happy families with Dan, but now she tells me how well she and Victoria are getting on.

'Lee, you must have the patience of a saint,' I told her. 'What did you do with her? What did you talk about?' The idea of having a conversation with Victoria left me puzzled; she could never string two sentences together when she'd been with me.

'Well actually,' Lee said, 'the girl's had to put up with an awful lot. And she's not had an easy time of it—'

'Oh, play me the violins,' I said.

Lee suddenly snapped. 'Look, Teri, you don't know anything about her situation and frankly, you never bothered to find out when you had the chance. But take it from me, the kid has problems, and I thought a trip out shopping would be just the thing for her.'

'Very noble,' I snapped back. 'But I don't remember her ever being short of shopping trips when I knew her. And Dan usually gave her thousands of pounds to do it with, if you remember?'

Lee shook her head in that way she has when she can't think of anything fast, funny, or clever to say.

I wasn't sure, but Lee looked as though she was about to cry. I took a quick swig of my wine, hoping to encourage her to do the same. I had so many problems of my own, I wasn't in the mood to start hearing any more of Lee's sob stories. Yes, she'd been through a lot, but was over all that now: the abortion, Mike, Christian, and everything. I'd tried to be supportive, but, hell's bells, she shouldn't still be filling up all the time.

'Come on, Lee. What's up?'

'Nothing…' But it really didn't sound like nothing.

'Well, okay,' I tried again. 'What have you been up to?'

'Oh, this and that,' she said.

'What is it, Lee?' I said in as concerned a way as I could muster. 'I know something's wrong. You're not answering my calls. I hardly ever see you.'

Lee looked at me as if considering something. Then she said, 'It's nothing, or, rather, I've got a lot on my mind and I can't talk to you about it at the moment.'

Now I was intrigued. 'That's ridiculous. What can't you talk about?'

Then she shrugged and pulled her shoulders back.

'Oh, Teri.' She sighed, exasperated. 'If you must know, it's about the David Greenspan business.'

'What about it?'

'Well…' She checked herself and then added, 'Have you thought about what would happen if David makes an official complaint?'

'Oh, for goodness' sake, Lee. He's not going to do that. I told you, it was all very innocent. We got drunk and one thing led to another—'

She held up a hand to shut me up. 'Teri, can we please not talk about it? It's putting me in a very bad position.'

I couldn't quite see why what happened at the May Ball would put Lee in a bad position, and I told her so. I also added that whatever had gone on between David and me was my business and nothing to do with her. And anyway, it was all months ago, nothing happened, nothing was going to happen. But when she started shaking her head and looking pityingly at me in the way she does, I saw red. How dare she look at me like that? It wasn't bad enough that she had cosy meals out with my ex-husband, but she tried to muscle her way in further by taking his darling daughter off shopping, and now she was interfering in my relationship with David or rather, my non-relationship with David. I slammed my glass down on the draining board, told her I couldn't be doing with her superior attitude – especially not after the way she was behaving – and stormed out.

Chapter 79

Teri

I was so cross with Lee I drove home perhaps a little too fast. One of those dratted speed cameras on the A615 got me, as I was aware of a sudden flash. But I was angry and couldn't be bothered. Let them fine me. Just try it. Who cares?

I got to the flat, still angry and shaking, and went straight inside to open another bottle. After the first glass, I felt a bit calmer and picked up my mobile to call Lee. I wasn't going to apologise. Why should I? But I shouldn't have stormed out. She was only trying to help. But as I tapped the contacts button to get her number on screen, the phone beeped with a message. Hah! I thought. Lee texting to apologise. But it was Declan texting to ask if he could come in.

Obviously, I texted back. *No*, but he came straight back, saying he was sitting outside and needed to see me. *No*, I texted again.

Please, please, please, he texted again.

No, I texted back.

Then my doorbell rang.

Why did I answer it? Why did that lost-puppy-look cause me to crumple? Why did that lopsided grin make me smile? Why did I let him reach out for me, pull me into his chest, kiss the top of my head, push me against the wall, running his hands up and down the sides of my body, and then pull me gently to the floor? Why?

'I've missed you so much.' He breathed into my ear as we lay, later, on the bleached hallway floorboards. 'And I've missed this.' He laughed, waving an arm to take in the reclaimed wood hall dresser and soft vanilla surroundings.

I got up and reached down to pull him to his feet. 'Declan, what are you doing here?'

He looked serious. 'I've missed you. Pure and simple. It's been a bloody awful couple of months. I can't live without you. I had to see you. I've been so lonely. I love you, Teri, and I only realised just how much when I could no longer see you.'

'But what about all the other women?'

'Oh, come on, Teri. You know all that was innocent stuff. I explained, but you wouldn't believe me.'

We went through into the lounge, and he picked up the bottle of wine I'd left on the coffee table, poured some into my empty glass, and took a drink. 'Make yourself at home.' I smiled and went into the kitchen to get another glass.

As conversationally as I could, I added, 'Talking of home, are you still at Leyland Road?'

He looked sheepish. 'Ah, no,' he said. 'Got a bit expensive what with paying the rent and the mortgage on the old house. So, I… er… had to move back in with Marnie.'

'You're back living with your ex-wife?'

'Well, technically, she's not my ex, as we never got divorced. But it's not what you think. I sleep in the spare room. We live in the same house, but separately. It's just the cheapest option. Cheaper all round until the divorce comes through and we can sell the house. Plus, I get to see the kids.'

'It can't be very pleasant, having to dodge round your wife all the time.'

'Oh, it's not that bad. Anyway, I don't want to talk about her when I've got you… come here and tell your uncle Declan what you've been up to.'

Reason, experience, logic – all those – should have told me to stop it right there. But I was still angry and emotional from my row with Lee – and hurt, to be honest. I needed some love and affection in my life. But, honestly, what could I have been thinking taking up with Declan again when he'd not only been unfaithful to me with several other women but clearly lied to me on numerous occasions? And now he wanted us to get back together again even though he still lived with his wife in the marital home.

I could just hear Lee's voice in the background telling me what an idiot I was. But I knew how happy Declan could make me. He told me how much he'd missed me; he even admitted he'd taken me for granted before and now realised what a fool he'd been. He never wanted to let me out of his sight, out of his arms, out of his life. We were meant to be together – didn't I realise that? – and he would do anything to prove to me he was a changed man. He was getting a divorce – didn't that tell me how serious he was?

And idiot I am, I believed him.

He didn't stay that first night, although we made love again – in the bedroom this time – and we met for lunch the next day. Over the next two weeks, he would dash round to the flat during the day when he was supposed to be out on a job; I went to meet him when he finished work; he spent his time off with me. If he couldn't see me, he rang and texted, even sending late-night messages on his mobile like he used to do.

'I love you,' he said.

'I love you too – and I can't live without you,' I replied.

It was a glorious couple of weeks.

Chapter 80

Teri

And then the doorbell rang.

I didn't recognise the woman standing there. She was small, plump-faced, and despite not wearing much make-up, fairly pretty. Her hair was a nondescript brown in an equally nondescript style. But what I noticed immediately was how enormous she was and how her belly stuck out in a most unattractive way from between an unbuttoned brown, boiled wool coat. She breathed heavily as though she'd run up the stairs to my flat and leant towards me with one hand on the doorsill as if to prop herself up and the other laid on top of the bulge in that odd way pregnant women do as they absent-mindedly rub their bump. I wondered if she was one of the other residents in my block and perhaps the baby was on its way, and she needed help. I stared at the bulge, praying that no waters were about to break. Hell, I didn't want her having her bloody baby on my hall floorboards.

'Yes,' she said, still rubbing her stomach, 'you might well look surprised.'

And there was something about the voice that jolted me. I'd heard that voice, that slight accent, a couple of times before – on the phone. Marnie. And she was heavily pregnant.

I'm no judge when it comes to guessing how many months gone women are and, to be honest, the sight of them heavily pregnant in close-fitting puma cotton tops, leggings, and cheap, gaping coats makes my stomach churn. She must've seen the quizzical look on my face because she said, 'Six months. And it's twins.'

'Oh, my God,' was all I could manage.

'And you might want to know… they're Declan's.'

'Yes, but…'

'While you were playing your fancy games with him, you obviously didn't know that Declan and I were attempting a reconciliation?'

She made it sound like a question but didn't give me time to answer. Instead, she went on. 'You might also want to know that we had a fairly romantic weekend of our own at his flat. That's when this happened.' She pointed at the frankly obscene bulge. 'And we didn't take kindly to you coming round and continually ringing the bell. You clearly didn't recognise my car, or perhaps that would have been a hint?'

The SUV!

'But from what Declan tells me, you're a bit of a stalker. I wanted to call the police then, but he wouldn't let me.'

I was speechless. She barged past me into the lounge, still breathing heavily with the effort, went to the sofa, turned slowly and, like a rather large walrus, lowered herself down, one hand on the armrest, the other still laid over her stomach, which from that position, looked fit to burst.

'So you two…?' Was all I could manage.

'Yes, despite your little games, we're still very much together,' Marnie said, looking me in the eye as I sat opposite her on the matching chair.

'But what about all the other…?'

'All the other what? Women?' Marnie said, finishing my sentence. 'Oh, I've always known about women who throw themselves at him, and I know he can't resist the odd shenanigans. I've been married to him for long enough. He goes off and does his thing and gets it out of his system, but he always… *always*… comes back to me and the kids.'

I wanted to say something about how demeaning this must be for her, but something about the determined look on her face stopped me.

'You probably think I'm a naïve, stupid little wife who lets her husband get away with murder,' she said, as if reading my thoughts. Well, yes, I was going to say, but thought better of it.

'But what you don't understand, pet,' she said. 'Is that when two people love and understand each other, their relationship can stand the odd indiscretion.'

I must say, I thought the poor woman was deceiving herself and I suddenly wanted her out of the flat. God, what if her waters broke? But she had more to say. 'You might think that Declan loves you, but he doesn't. I know he's been seeing you over the last couple of weeks.' She held up her hand to stop my denial. 'Don't worry,' she said. 'He told me. He told me about your attempted suicide and how he had to come round to look after you…'

'What…?'

'Yes, another of your tricks. I don't suppose you had any intention of killing yourself. More's the pity,' she snapped. 'You just wanted him here on whatever pretences you could find. Frankly, pet, I find that a pretty low thing to do. You worried the life out of him, ringing him like that, and saying you'd taken all those pills. You should be ashamed.'

'But I never…'

'He's told me how you manipulate him, how you threaten him by saying you'll make a complaint against him to his editor. Well, lady, do it; do your worst. He wants rid of you once and for all, so we don't care what you do. But I'm asking you… no, I'm telling you… get out of our lives and stay out. If you ever come near my husband, me, or our children ever again, I shall call the police and have you arrested.'

The drama of her final statement was lost to some extent by the effort it took her to drag her fat body off my sofa and waddle across the room. But I'd got the message, so didn't argue, and neither of us said anything as she struggled down the hallway to the door. There she turned, probably to get her breath, but so as not to waste the moment, she added, 'I mean it.'

'But I never tried to…'

'I don't want to hear it,' she said as she pulled on the handle, opened the door, and lurched out as tidily as all that extra weight she was carrying allowed.

She headed towards the stairs, thought better of it, and walked towards the lift as I watched, speechless. When I heard the familiar 'ping' of the lift announcing its imminent arrival, I woke from my stunned silence and shouted, 'Declan's told you a complete pack of lies. He's done nothing but lie to you, me, and every other woman he's ever met throughout his whole sad little life. He's a womaniser, a total bastard who just uses women. And you're stupid and gullible if you believe any of his crap. If I were you, *pet*, I'd get the hell out of it before you have those bastard twins of his.' And I slammed the door shut.

I strode up the hall, into the lounge, and over to the window. I don't know why, but I wanted to make sure Marnie was off the premises. Confronting and rowing with me was enough to induce labour, and I didn't want any bloody O'Brien offspring being born in my block of flats.

I pulled up the white wooden slatted blinds and looked down into the car park and saw Declan's VW and Declan leaning against the closed driver's side door. He was looking intently at the mobile phone in his hand as if he had some important call to make, but then he looked round at the entrance to the flats and the beached whale that was his wife waddled out and across towards him. He rushed round to open the passenger door and I could see by the way Marnie angrily wagged her finger at him he wasn't going to be able to make that call.

Chapter 81

Lee

The first few weeks of the academic year are always stressful, and this year was no different. Getting back into the swing of teaching is straightforward enough but there is always an endless round of minor problems: timetable anomalies, new staff – who haven't been set up on the email system (despite filling in the required forms in triplicate) – and umpteen departmental meetings – some of which are useful and some of which, frankly, aren't. Unfortunately, it's hard to know which you can miss (without missing out on something vital) and which are desperately important (and not to be missed at any cost). As a result, I end up attending them all and, more often than not, find myself doodling on the back of the minutes and wishing I was somewhere else.

It all settles down eventually but, usually, not before I've begun to think about a career change. Digging coal sometimes seems a preferable alternative.

This year was worse than usual because always in the background was the pending complaint investigation. Nothing happens quickly at a university – they're like oil tankers and movement requires careful consideration and planning and always happens at the pace of a geriatric snail. And so it was with the complaint against Teri. The relevant authorities had been notified and due process had begun, although God only knew when a decision might be expected. My nerves were wrecked – at best I thought Teri might escape with a severe rebuke and, at worst… suspension? A downgrade from senior to junior lecturer level? Transfer to another department? I don't know why I was worrying – Teri certainly wasn't.

'Pah!' she said. 'Who's going to take a silly complaint like that seriously?'

Quite a lot of people.

'Pah!' she said again.

And that was it. She flatly refused to cooperate with the investigation, and I couldn't decide whether she was burying her head in the sand because she was too scared to contemplate the implications, or because she genuinely thought there was no case to answer. Either way, it wasn't comfortable.

No, she preferred to blether on about me and Dan and not to raise my hopes in that direction. Raise my hopes? How old did she think I was?

I tried pointing out he was a free agent and could choose his own friends, but she wouldn't listen. Instead, she started moaning about Victoria and, while I know the poor kid's no saint, and, yes, had sometimes behaved like a spoilt brat, there were, I thought, extenuating circumstances. Not in Teri's book. 'Play me the violins,' she sneered. So, I simply downed my glass of Pinot Grigio – and wished for the millionth time she'd stop trying to educate my palate and simply stick to

Muscadet – and changed the subject. Which was a waste of time since she was clearly spoiling for a fight and, since I was fed up with listening to her moans, I obliged.

Cheers, I thought, as she slammed the door behind her. And good riddance, too.

Afterwards, I wished I'd been a little more tolerant. Let's face it, I'd spent donkey's years not letting Teri wind me up. What was so different now? Dan, of course. It's the golden rule of friendship, isn't it? Except not dating Teri's exes would seriously restrict the pool of available men in our neck of the woods. So, feeling thoroughly guilty, I resolved to offer an olive branch at the first available opportunity – as it turned out, the following morning in the ladies' loo at work where she caught me doing my hair and make-up, and offered advice on the benefits of a good blow dry.

'I've just been to the gym,' I said.

She wasn't listening – instead she picked up the mini tube of face cream, which I'd left by the side of the washbasin, and squeezed a pinch onto her finger. She sniffed it. 'It doesn't smell too bad,' she conceded, 'although it's really not a good idea to use hand cream on your face.'

It's not bloody hand cream! It's a handbag-sized tube of the not inexpensive super-concentrate paraben-free face cream I use night and day because it doesn't bring me out in hives – unlike the heavily perfumed fungi stuff she'd gifted me last Christmas.

'But why don't you use that lovely truffle serum I bought you for Christmas?' she continued.

Because I'm allergic to it, and if I'd told her once, I'd told her a thousand times. But did she listen? Of course, she didn't.

She didn't wait for an answer now either – she poked around in my make-up bag instead. She held up my eyeliner and inspected it. 'Have you ever tried…?'

'No,' I snapped, snatching the eyeliner out of her hand and bundling the make-up bag back into my handbag. Today, of all days, I had neither the time nor inclination to engage in a discussion about my sartorial shortcomings.

Yes, it's true I can't blow dry my hair like the girl at the hairdresser – but who can? And I know I'm never going to be Teri-svelte and streamlined because I'm not about to half-starve myself like she does.

And it's been months too since I wore a pair of jeggings.

But none of this mattered, because if Teri wasn't worried sick about the Greenspan business, I was. And, it was far more important to tactfully let her know that she really ought to be on her best behaviour and not give people additional ammunition to fire at her, because if I'd noticed she was idling away her time in the powder room at 9.45 on a Monday morning when she should be mid-lecture with her Level 2 Renaissance literature group, it was a safe bet that other folk had too.

A dead safe bet – a toilet flushed and Chrissie, from admin, emerged from the cubicle.

She nodded at me, but ignored Teri until she'd finished washing her hands. She gave them a hasty wipe on a paper towel and, as she dropped it into the waste bin, asked in a disinterested voice, 'Lecture finished early, Teri?'

She didn't wait for a reply and, as the door slammed behind her, Teri launched into a tirade about 'pen-pushing Chrissie' who, it seemed, had the temerity to 'invite' Teri to a 9 a.m. meeting with Peter on Wednesday. And, further, had refused to tell her, A) why she needed to meet Heron at such an early hour, and B) why she needed to meet with him in the first place.

'Do you know what he wants, Lee?'

Oh, for goodness' sake! It didn't take a genius to work out the Greenspan powder keg might be on the agenda. Not to mention the departmental restructure that had been on the cards for a month of Sundays.

'Perhaps it's a promotion?' she suggested and got quite cross with me when I pointed out the little matter of David Greenspan had still to be resolved.

'That's a storm in a teacup,' she said. 'The boy's got the mark he deserves and I'm not going back on it just because he's got an inflated sense of his own intelligence.'

I couldn't agree – and this storm in a teacup had all the makings of a full-blown hurricane.

'I really think there was no need for you to get involved, Lee,' Teri said.

At that point, I lost patience with her. It was her funeral after all, and if she chose to go around with her head in the clouds, there was no point in wasting time and energy trying to offer unwanted advice. And, for almost the first time in our long friendship, I stomped off in a huff.

And, just like yesterday when we rowed over the Pinot Grigio, almost instantly regretted it. But there was no chance to apologise and offer another olive branch because the rest of the day was pretty full-on with teaching and meetings and other stuff. It wasn't until I finally got home that I had five minutes to myself and, of course, started fretting. Poor Teri; lately she seemed to have lurched from one mess to another. And I knew I wasn't responsible but felt guilty I hadn't been more supportive.

But what to do? Especially as whatever Peter Heron planned to discuss with her on Wednesday, it was a dead cert today's missed lecture would come up – along with so many others she'd missed or cancelled.

Should I ring her? Would she listen to some advice? And then there was the little matter of my own piece of news, which she needed to know sooner rather than later.

My news? Oh yes, something rather wonderful happened. Three nights ago, over dinner at L'homme-vert, Dan pulled a little gift box out of his pocket. He'd just got back from Ireland where he'd been filming a series of packages about James Joyce's Dublin to kick-start a new *Ridings Today* book programme. He had a little present for me, he said, when he called from the airport taxi to tell me to meet him at the restaurant at 7 p.m.

I'd grumbled a bit – I was tired and didn't feel like getting all tarted up to go somewhere posh. L'homme-vert is not a baggy jeans and T-shirt sort of establishment. But Dan insisted and, after a glass of wine and a sharing platter of charcuterie and figs and crusty French bread, I was in a much better frame of mind.

That's when he produced the gift box. It was clumsily wrapped. 'Christmas paper?' I queried.

'Couldn't find anything else. Open it,' he urged. Easier said than done. Dan belongs to the 'you can never have too much sealing tape' school-of-wrapping. 'Here,' he said, snatching the box as I fumbled with the tape. He pulled at the wrappings with his teeth. 'There,' he said, handing me the mangled package again.

I pulled at the paper and stroked the velvety box. 'What is it?' I looked at him. 'Not the pearl earrings I was looking at last weekend?' I felt touched by his kindness. The earrings had been outrageously expensive, and I'd balked at shelling out the asking price. 'You darling,' I said, leaning across the table and kissing him.

'Open it. Open it,' he said again.

I lifted the lid and gasped at the gold, bejewelled Claddagh ring nestling inside.

'Do you like it?' he asked.

I was lost for words. When Mammy and Daddy married, they exchanged the traditional Irish ring, representing love, loyalty, and friendship. 'It's lovely,' I said, unsure if he understood the symbolism.

'Try it on. Does it fit?'

I slipped it on the third finger of my right hand, the heart facing inward. 'You've captured my heart,' I told him.

'No,' he said. And taking my hand, he pulled the ring from my finger and slid it gently onto the third finger of my left hand, heart facing outward. 'Have I got it right?' he asked. 'This way round, it means you're engaged?'

Me? Engaged? To Dan? I wanted to cry. I was crying.

'I'm sorry, I'm sorry,' he said, wiping away my tears. 'Don't cry. I didn't mean to upset you. It's too soon, I know, but I love you so much…' He looked miserable. 'I'm sorry,' he repeated. 'I don't know why I thought you might want to marry me. I know I'm second-hand goods.'

'Third-hand,' I corrected.

He groaned. 'How could I be so stupid?'

'You're not stupid,' I said. 'I'd love to marry you. I can't think of anything nicer.'

I'll draw a veil over the rest of the evening – some things should not be shared with third parties.

Reality, of course, kicked in the next morning. Teri. It didn't take a rocket scientist to work out we could expect explosions. If she didn't take happily to us being 'good friends' she'd be apoplectic at the notion of a replacement Mrs Caine. Especially as I had a feeling she still held a candle for Dan. She'd hinted as much a few times. 'Don't get too attached to him,' she warned. 'I've only got to lift a finger and he'll come running back.' She hugged me. 'We've got unfinished business, Dan, and me. He's on the rebound at the moment, but it won't last, and I don't want you to be hurt.'

How kind. Deluded, too.

Nevertheless, she was definitely a fly in our happy little ointment.

Chapter 82

Teri

I looked at the pile of essays waiting to be marked in my office and decided it could wait. I was going home. It had been a bad day from the start. First, I slept through the alarm. Had one or two glasses of wine last night to cheer myself up, and they must've knocked me out because I slept like a baby for the first time in months. I'd had an awful time of it since my marriage broke up, and Declan started playing his tricks again. And that damned student, David Greenspan… well, let's not go there right now.

Anyway, it all seemed to be swirling round in my head. No one understood the pressure I'd been under. I was late getting into uni, and of course, today was the day I was supposed to give a lecture at 9 a.m. – Rochester: The Enlightened Poetical Hero of the 1600s. But by the time I got there, half the students had buggered off. Level 2 students, for God's sake. They pay all that money in tuition fees and then don't bother turning up for lectures.

Then I got a message from Peter Heron – and what a prick he was. Anyway, the message, sent via Chrissie in admin, said could I see him on Wednesday at 9 a.m. Why can't he tell me himself, I asked Chrissie?

He's away at a conference, she said. Conferences. That's all these academics here do – go to conferences to talk about Deep Seated Learning Environments in the Digital Age.

I'd no idea what plonker-Heron wanted, so thank you, because I would now be worrying about that.

Then Lee was in a mood about something that morning. All I did was try to give her some advice about her make-up and she got uppity when I looked in her bag to see what she slathered on her face nowadays.

You know, I spent £85 on that truffle serum I gave her for Christmas, and she didn't even use it. I sometimes wondered if she cared about her looks. She went to the gym for a while, but I couldn't tell if it did much good. I thought I detected a bit of weight loss, but she wore those baggy tunics so you couldn't really tell what was underneath. No, she didn't make the best of herself. I told her that, for someone like her who's carrying a bit of extra flab, it could be disguised with a well-cut dress rather than those awful jeggings and shapeless tops.

I tried to talk to her about what Peter Heron might want me for, but she went all evasive and huffed off.

What a relief to get back to my flat. I love to shut the door and unwind. My style is minimal; I don't over-furnish or fill the place with objects. Everything is pale and subtle. I can relax here; it's calm and restful – monastically aesthetic.

I plonked the tote on the sofa, eased off my shoes, and walked into the kitchen, opened the fridge door, took out a two-thirds empty bottle of white wine and poured the remnants into a wineglass plucked off the drainer. I went into the sitting-room, sat down wearily, reached for the zapper, and pressed the TV button.

Ah! A shopping channel and a prancing, over-made-up girl having orgasms about a handbag as she opened the flap to point out the 'mechanics' of the zipped section inside.

Flick to another channel and… oh! It was Dan staring back at me. Well, not so much staring at me as reading the latest news on *Ridings Today*.

Seeing my ex-husband. That's all I needed.

Chapter 83

Lee

My phone had been red hot all evening. First, Fliss warning me to expect a call from Mammy. 'Act surprised,' she ordered. And hung up.

The phone was hardly back on its hook when it rang again. Mammy herself, cooing over the prospect of a new baby and delighted to be the first to tell me the good news.

'And you really didn't guess?' she asked.

I told a little white lie. 'No, hadn't a clue.'

No need though to act surprised, or anything else for that matter, because I could barely get a word in edgeways. 'Due date blah, blah, blah… first scan blah, blah, blah… don't mind if it's a boy or a girl blah, blah, blah.' I was only half-listening, feeling just a little sad. But no point dwelling on might have-beens.

She rang off eventually, and two minutes later Fliss was back on the line again.

'I've been trying to get through for ages. What did Mammy have to say?'

Did she want the short or the long answer? 'A lot.'

'Such as?'

Oh, Fliss. What do you think she said? 'She's thrilled to bits, of course. Expect lots of fussing,' I warned.

I could almost hear her grimacing.

'It's your own fault,' I said. 'I thought you weren't going to say anything just yet?'

Seems she'd seriously underestimated Ritchie and his ability to put two and two together. He'd blabbed when Mammy did her usual Tuesday tea-time school pickup, utterly delighted at the prospect of a little brother. 'Because God couldn't be so mean as to give me another sister.' Oh, the innocence of youth. God could, and might well, do just that.

Fliss was on the phone, talking babies, even longer than Mammy.

Next to call was Declan, also grumbling about my line being engaged. 'I tried your mobile too,' he said.

Yes, I'd seen the missed call but could only hold one phone conversation at a time.

'Don't be sarcastic,' he said.

Feeling a bit touchy, Declan? 'What do you want?' I really couldn't be bothered with the pleasantries. Nor could he.

'Have you spoken to Teri recently?'

Daft question. 'We work together,' I said. 'We're best friends. What do you think?'

'Okay. Okay. You're joined at the hip… I get it.'

Now who's being sarcastic? But I held my tongue. No point in quarrelling.

There was a short silence. 'How's she taking things?'

What to say? She's a mess? You broke her heart? She's barely coping?

'Couldn't be better,' I lied. 'In fact, I think she's got her sights set on someone new.' Well, if she hadn't, it wouldn't be long before she did. 'You know Teri, she doesn't let the grass grow under her feet.'

Another silence. 'Declan?'

'I wanted to call… tell her I was sorry… try to explain…'

'Why didn't you?'

Silence again. 'I daren't.'

For God's sake. Why ever not? She won't bite you.

'Marnie,' he said. 'I know she's checking my phone – that's how she found out about Teri in the first place.'

I sighed. Teri and her 'cheeky' text messages. It made sense.

'Marnie said she'd kill herself, and the babies, if I didn't come back.'

What? That wasn't what Teri told me.

'She's crazy, Lee. It's the pregnancy – hormones or something. I don't know.'

Huh. Trust a man to blame a woman's hormones. 'And who got her pregnant?'

'She said she was on the pill,' he wailed.

Idiot. You wouldn't think he'd be stupid enough to fall for that one.

'Call her bluff,' I said. Sorry, but he wasn't getting any sympathy from me.

'Would you risk it?'

'It's not my call.'

'You're a cow, Lee,' he growled. 'I only called because I was concerned about Teri and wanted you to pass on a message.'

'Don't believe you. And, no, I won't.' No sense in beating about the bush. 'She's well shut of you and if you think I'm going to pave the way for reconciliation so you can break her heart again…'

'Break whose heart?' he asked.

'It doesn't matter. Do your own dirty work. Ring Teri yourself – if you dare.' And,' I added, 'I don't bloody believe you about Marnie.' I slammed the phone down so hard it practically bounced back off the hook.

The liar. Serve him right if Marnie did commit suicide. Oh, how horrible of me? I crossed myself and muttered Mammy's favourite prayer: 'God forgive my body spoke not I.'

But Declan's call left me feeling thoroughly churned up and fretting even more about Teri than I had been earlier. I knew I should ring her but, at the same time, it was getting late and I was tired and didn't know if I could face another long, drawn-out conversation listening to someone else let off steam. It was about time someone listened to me for a change.

Fat chance. The phone rang again. Dan. *What did he want?* Sighing, I picked up the receiver. 'Can I come round?'

I knew what that meant. He was still running shy about coming clean with Teri. I sympathised, but he was her ex-husband, and it wasn't fair to expect someone else – me! – to do his dirty work. He was supposed to break the news that afternoon – he texted earlier to say he'd decided not to put things off any longer. And I'd texted back, *YOU'D BETTER!!!* And I knew damn well because Teri was just about the only person who hadn't telephoned tonight. He'd chickened out again.

'You bloody coward,' I said as he walked in, his face still shiny from scrubbing off his studio make-up.

'I know, I know.' He held up his hands in a gesture of surrender. 'Don't shout. I didn't dare.' Men! First Declan, now Dan.

'Man up,' I said.

He said nothing, just poured himself a glass of lime cordial.

'What do you want to do?'

He shook his head. 'Don't know.'

Mentally, I slapped myself. Don't be unkind, I thought. Or smug. Doesn't suit you.

And I remembered that when the chips were down, Teri had been there for me. Okay – I opened the fridge and extracted a bottle of Muscadet. Dan had already got the glasses. I filled them both almost to the brim.

'I'll speak to her tomorrow,' I said.

'Promise?' he asked.

'Promise,' I said.

Chapter 84

Teri

I stared out into a lecture theatre full of students; most offered blank, bored faces. True, there were some expectant looks, but these were from the handful of 'mature' students treating their Eng Lit BA as a lucky dip in which they got to read books they should've read when they were younger. In the main though, the students were dull looking; not interested and not bothered. Some even had their heads down, staring at their laps. 'Could you turn your mobiles off,' I instructed. Do they think I was born yesterday and didn't realise half of them were Tweeting or Facebooking?

'Rochester,' I said as authoritatively as I could. 'He's a fallen lyric poet, obsessed with the poignancy of absence, loss, and fear.'

I'd said those words before (hell, why rewrite your lectures every year?) There is no better way of describing Rochester. Love, for him, is linked with pain. For him and for his lovers.

But now, standing in front of Level 2 and repeating the well-worn themes of love, despair, and wantonness, I shivered. I was describing the libertine, the rake, the masochistic poet for whom sexual activity and conquering the woman was the only way of coming to terms with morality. 'Rochester is tortured by the increasing gap between the love that he believes is divine and human love which he finds impossible to achieve,' I said.

Something snapped in my brain. Hang on, I thought. What am I talking about? A man who needs to put flesh on flesh like no one else; a man who treats women as his personal playthings and whores. Why does this remind me so much of Declan? Surely, I thought, I must've seen this before. Declan, the womaniser, the libertine, the rake. What irony. The man I'd been researching all my academic life and the man I'd had as my lover were one and the same. Rochester the poet and libertine; Declan the writer and rake.

I felt dizzy with the sudden awareness. Bastards. Both of them.

I must've looked spaced out for a moment because there was a general rustle of anticipation as Level 2 realised I wasn't speaking, but staring into the ether.

David Greenspan broke the spell. He was leaning back – comfortably – in his seat and ever so lazily raised an arm. It would be him. Damn him. 'Yes, David?'

'Aren't you over-egging this idea?' the impudent little sod asked. 'Wasn't he just one of those blokes who liked a good time?'

Who, I thought, confused for the moment: Declan or Rochester?

Half a dozen faces lit up. There were some nudges as some of the more half-asleep students realised something had happened and they wanted to know what. Another half dozen looked up from their texting to see what all the fuss was about. Suddenly, I had everyone's attention.

'If blokes behave the way he does, then they're not very nice people,' I said. 'For Rochester, sexual activity is a momentary act of need. Something that offers instant gratification.'

'Yes, but it's not just men who are like that, is it?' Greenspan suggested. 'Can't women be just as predatory?'

'I'm not saying Rochester was predatory. In fact, I don't believe he needed to be. He was wanton, and he made no secret of his pleasure-seeking.' (Hah, Declan, again.)

'Oh, so you think it's wrong to make a secret of pleasure-seeking. Rather like stalking?' Greenspan put much emphasis on that word stalking.

'I don't know how we got to talking about stalking,' I stammered. 'Rochester was debauched, but he never stalked anyone…'

'Unlike some modern-day heroes… and heroines?' Greenspan said.

My brain churned. How was I going to get this back on track? I had everyone's attention now. They didn't realise what was going on, but they were delighted something was.

'I mean,' Greenspan said, 'what would you say about a woman, ooh in her forties, being a bit of a libertine with her students?'

That certainly sparked a few bums to wriggle in their seats.

My head became suddenly hot. I could feel tiny globs of perspiration breaking out on my top lip and, worse, running between my breasts. Oh hell. I can't get damp patches on this silk shirt.

'But we're not talking about a female libertine, David,' I offered as reasonably as I could. 'We're talking about a Restoration man who wrote pornography, often about his king, and managed to not just satirise a licentious seventeenth century court but roister neck deep in it as well. Here was a man for whom relationships with women amounted to as much sex as he could get but with non-permanence as the overriding feature.'

The full force of it hit me. It was Declan. I was talking about Declan. How that bastard had used me. Declan: the only man I'd ever loved… how had it got to this? Self-pity slathered over me like hot oil from an overhead caldron. It knocked the breath out of me and my whole body weakened.

I reached for the front of the desk on which my notes and bottle of water stood. The room span as I leant forward. Oh, God, no. Don't let me faint in front of Level 2. I grabbed the bottle, twisted the top off, and took a swig. The room settled. The students were silent. Watching. What sport, they must be thinking. One of the mature women students shifted forwards in her seat as if ready to lunge in my direction to catch me should I fall.

I needed to say something, but I couldn't get my breath. Was I having a heart attack? I tried to drag some air into my lungs. No. Couldn't breathe. I clenched my fist and thumped it against my chest, trying to make the action seem as natural as possible, but in fact, hoping that some self-administered chest compressions would restart my heart. Which was ludicrous as my heart was thumping so loudly I was surprised the daft little twerp with the Mohican haircut at the back of the hall couldn't hear it drumming.

'Basically, David Greenspan,' I managed to say at last. 'Men like that are bastards. Fucking evil, selfish, time-wasting bastards. And you'

– I added, glaring at him with all the venom I could muster – 'are the male equivalent of a prick tease. A pretty boy who's trying to play with the big boys. Only you picked the wrong woman, didn't you?'

'Very literary,' I heard him say before I turned from the lectern and ran out of the room.

Chapter 85

Teri

It's not like me to have panic attacks, and I can only assume that's what it was. I certainly wasn't having a heart attack, and I didn't pass out, but all I'd been able to think about was getting out of that lecture theatre and away from those inquisitive little faces, enlivened by the idea that something pretty catastrophic was happening to their English lecturer.

I was supposed to be running a couple of seminar groups later in the day, but there was no way once I got out into the staff car park and into my car I was going back into that university.

I drove straight home, parked the car, went into the flat, and poured myself the remnants of a bottle of white wine I'd left in the fridge the night before. As I sloshed it into a glass and knocked it back, there was that satisfying warm glow starting somewhere in the gut I always get when I have a drink. So what that it was just after 11 a.m.? So what that I'd not had breakfast? So what if I was going to open another bottle. So what if it meant I would probably spend the rest of the day lying on the sofa, slightly drunk, and watching mind-numbing programmes on daytime television? So what? Who cares?

Dan would care, I told myself later having polished off a couple of glasses from the next bottle of wine. He was the only one who ever cared for me – at least; he was the only one who ever cared enough to marry me. Why didn't I realise earlier what a lovely, kind, patient man he was? I mean, look how nice he was being to Lee. He realised how lonely she was and, to be honest, she'd had a bit of a bad time of it what with that creep Mike Orme and the abortion and then the love affair – or whatever it was – with Christian going belly up. It was nice of Dan to be so concerned; he was such a softy. I just hoped Lee wouldn't get the wrong idea and think Dan fancied her or something.

Dan and I had some good times, didn't we? We were good together, weren't we? Why did I let him go? He'd be round like a shot if he knew how bad I was feeling. He'd want to come and take care of me. He'd look at me lying here on the sofa, my eyes red from crying, and he would take me in his arms. 'Darling, Teri,' he would say, softly kissing away my tears. 'You were the only one for me. Take me back.'

Oh, get a grip, girl, I told myself. You're sounding like a Mills and Boon novel. But it would be nice to talk to Dan. I rang his mobile.

'Hi, Teri,' he said. (Bless him, I was still in his contacts list.)

'Oh, Dan, I'm so glad to get you.' The relief at hearing his voice turned my words to sobs. 'Please help me, Dan. You're the only one who can.'

'God, Teri. What's happened? What's the matter?' He sounded alarmed.

'Something awful happened today…'

'Are you all right? Have you had an accident?'

'No, no, nothing like that. It's just that things have got out of control. I need to talk to you, Dan. I need you.'

'Oh, Teri. I'm just about to go into a pre-record for tonight's programme—'

Of course, once again, the programme took precedence; that was how it was throughout our marriage. I resisted the desire to tell him to forget it and instead said weakly, 'Oh, of course, you must do the programme. I'm sorry, I'd forgotten how busy you are. Don't you worry about me, I'll be all right.' And I clicked my mobile off and left it switched off.

It worked. Thirty minutes later, the doorbell rang, and I walked gingerly to open the door and let Dan in. He took one look at me and slipping an arm around my waist he gently guided me back to the sofa. 'God, you look awful,' he said.

'I feel awful,' I told him.

'Listen, I got someone else to do the pre-record, and I'm here now. Tell me what's wrong.'

'I just realise what a fool I've been,' I said between breathy sobs. 'I behaved really badly towards you, and I forced you away, and I'm really, really sorry. Ever since we split up life has just got worse. It's all crap… shit.'

I told him in short, sharp sentences how Declan had let me down; how I made a fool of myself over David Greenspan, and how he, Dan, had been the only man to ever truly love me. 'I need you, Dan. I want you back.'

I looked at him appealingly, probably aware that my mascara was running down my cheeks and making me look ridiculously pathetic, but not caring – for once – about how I looked. There would be plenty of time for looking more like me again once Dan was back in my life.

But Dan shook his head reluctantly. 'Teri, I'm sorry,' he said.

'Why are you sorry?' I asked, reaching a hand up towards him, aware that he was still standing over me instead of nestling down where I lay slumped and panda-eyed on the sofa.

He took an intake of breath. 'Teri, I did have enormous feelings for you, but come on, you've got to admit it, it didn't work out between us. We wanted different things. Different lives. We simply couldn't live together. We rowed constantly.'

'I could change,' I pleaded. 'I will change. We'll do things together. We'll work it out. I'll be different…'

'No, Teri,' he said.

'Please, Dan. I'll do anything…'

'No,' he repeated, wiping his brow with the back of his fingers. 'I'm sorry, love, but it's too late. After Sara and then you, I felt as though I was never going to have a relationship that worked. But I've found someone else and we're really good together…'

'Who…?' I demanded, pulling myself upright.

'Well… er… look, who she is isn't the point. The point is, it's never going to work between you and me. Even you've got to see that. I think you're just feeling sorry for yourself at the moment but, hey, this is Teri Meyer we're talking about and what does she do best? She pulls herself up and gets back on with it, and this is exactly what you'll do. In a couple of weeks' time you'll be laughing at the idea that you and I could ever get back together. That's how you are, Teri. You want instant gratification but when you get it, you're still not satisfied. You always want something else. Something more. If I agreed to come back now, it would be good for a day or two and then – pow! It would be all over again. I'm right, aren't I?' He smiled down at me. 'I'm going to make you a cup of strong, black coffee,' he said. 'Then I will leave you to drink it while I hotfoot back to the studios. When I've gone, I want you to have a shower, scrub that make-up off that gorgeous face of yours because it doesn't need all the slap you put on it, slip into something comfortable that isn't silk, short, or tight- fitting, put the wine bottle away and give yourself a night off from stressing about your life. Will you do that?'

I nodded sadly. 'I might even watch your programme and look out for skateboarding ducks,' I told him.

86

Lee

David pushed open my office door. 'I think you should know there's been a little upset with Teri…' He left the sentence dangling, shuffling his feet in the doorway. *A little upset?* As David recounted their verbal exchange and Teri's headlong rush out of the lecture theatre I upgraded the status of the *upset* from little to catastrophic. Especially in light of Teri's impending face-to-face with Peter Heron. 'David.' I sighed. 'What were you thinking?'

He shrugged and stared at the floor. 'Dunno,' he said. 'She just wound me up. I mean, she's paid to teach us and yet the lecture's hardly started and she goes off into a moonstruck daydream.'

He had a point, but I wished he'd kept his gob shut because now I had to find someone to cover Teri's afternoon seminars. 'We'll talk about it later,' I said, turning to my pc and pulling up the staff schedule to see who might be free.

Ping! A message from Dan. Teri'd called. She'd sounded frantic, and he was nipping out of work to check on her. He promised to call as soon as he got a chance. I groaned, wondering why she'd called Dan rather than me. Aagh! A quick scan of the timetable revealed I was the only member of the English team with any free hours. Great. Most of what I knew about Rochester could be written on the back of a postage stamp. Still, at least there was one task I could off-load onto someone else… I texted Dan, *TELL HER ABOUT US!!!* And I knew darn well he wouldn't.

He didn't. Or, at least, not directly. 'Don't be angry,' he said. 'I *did* tell her there was someone special. Just not that it was you. She was almost hysterical, and, I just couldn't kick her when she was already down.'

Chapter 87

Teri

'Ah, come in Miss Meyer.' Peter Heron looked suave in a pale blue, heavy linen jacket with darker blue trousers and a crisp, white T-shirt. I thought, nice combo, but at the same time wondering, why Miss Meyer, and not simply Teri?

Oh, the prat is playing at being formal; we're going to get lots of Heron-buzz-speak.

He'd come to the door when I knocked and now stood on the threshold holding it open for me, which surprised me as normally he likes to stay seated behind his great desk and call 'Come' in the way senior managers do when they think they're above saying 'Come in.'

I stepped into the office and saw someone else in the room, sitting at the very boardroom table where two years previously I'd sat for the interview for my job. The someone else was Tim, the rather good looking, and only bloke in Human Resources, the rest of them being simpering girlies who did nothing but ask staff to fill out forms demanding to know which training courses they'd been on – although why Man Handling and Understanding Fire Extinguishers was on the list of training courses is beyond me. Tim looked up and didn't return my smile. He appeared a bit glum.

'Oh,' I said, turning to Peter Heron. 'Shall I wait outside while you finish with Tim?'

'No,' Peter said. 'Tim is in on the meeting. I thought it advisable that someone from Human Resources was here. Have you not brought anyone with you?'

Ah, this was either going to be a promotion or something else, and I remembered with not inconsiderable alarm something Lee suggested when I told her I had a meeting with Peter. She'd adopted that concerned look and said, 'You know, Teri, it might be something and nothing, but, whatever, why don't you take along someone from the union?'

'Why on Earth would I want a union rep with me?'

'Well…' She hesitated. 'It's always useful to have another pair of eyes and ears in any sort of meeting, whether it's about something good or bad.'

'What do you think it could be about?' I asked her, rattled now.

Again, she hesitated. Then she said, 'I don't know,' in that resigned tone she reserves for people who aren't thinking sensibly.

'Well, anyway,' I retorted, suddenly angry with her. 'I'm not in the union. I never joined. Didn't see the point. They're always spouting a lot of hot air and taking days off on strike, and I just can't be doing with them. So I doubt very much any of the reps will want to sit with me if I'm going to have my hands slapped.'

For a nanosecond I wondered about asking Lee if she'd come with me, but then dismissed the idea. Ever since that bloody Tuscan holiday she and Dan went on, she'd been insufferable. They'd become best buddies, for goodness' sake. They saw themselves as each other's 'walker', all very palsy, and platonic and friendly. I mean, what the hell were they playing at? Dan would never fancy Lee in a million years. And, anyway, from what he'd told me last night, he'd met someone else and, although he wanted to keep it hush-hush, it sounded serious. Lee was in for a surprise when she found out. She obviously thought she was in the running with Dan. Hah! Well, it served her right for being so treacherous; anyone who pals up with their best friend's ex is frankly asking for trouble. Dan would have to drop her like a ton of the proverbial when this new woman was made public. She wouldn't want pally Lee around.

So I wouldn't give Lee the satisfaction of asking her for any help. But what could Peter Heron be planning that required armed back-up? Okay, so I'd missed a few lectures and my research had ground to a halt and the ungrateful undergraduates were giving up on my Moral and Monarchical Panics of the 1600s in droves. But what's the worst he could do to me?

'Ah, sit down, Miss Meyer,' Peter said, using the formal tone again and indicating a seat on the other side of the boardroom table to Tim, who now looked closely through a pile of papers stacked in an open green file. Peter sat down next to him, opposite me, with a similarly sized stack of papers in a similarly open green file.

'Looks ominous,' I joked.

'This is a serious matter,' Peter said, taking a sheet of paper from the top of the file and examining it. 'Let's start here. Cancelled and missed lectures…'

Ah, I could see where this was going, so I leant forward and started to say something about how there were reasons… and everyone cancelled or missed… but Heron ignored me, raising a hand with his palm flat out in my direction in the way of a bored dictator who wants to silence a rebellious insubordinate before he has him taken out for execution.

He read off a list of dates starting with one in December two years ago and ending with yesterday's. My mind whirred. December? Oh yes. That was the day of the RTS awards dinner, and I'd taken time off to get ready. The other dates went on… and on. Heron took his time, enunciating clearly and crisply. When he got to yesterday, I interjected, 'I was ill…'

'I'm sorry, Miss Meyer,' Heron said, again dismissing me. 'There are too many dates on this list to warrant any kind of excuse. Missed and cancelled lectures. Group seminars where you started late or finished early or simply did not turn up. Individual tutorials, similarly. While I accept that illness, traffic delays, and urgent meetings can affect delivery of some lectures, seminars, and tutorials, there are, quite simply, far too many dates on this list in which you failed to turn up, failed to offer a reasonable excuse for your absence, and abdicated your responsibilities to your students who, I might add, pay a high price for attending this university and expect to be treated with a larger degree of respect than you seem able to offer.'

'Ah, but…' I tried to say, but he went on.

'Next, we turn to mark sheets.' He lifted another sheet of paper from the pile. 'Mark sheets never handed in on time and you do not need me to tell you how inconvenient this is to not only the admin staff who have to collate hundreds of marks from across the faculty at one of the busiest times of the whole academic year, but to the entire teaching cohort on whom final marks are crucial to the awarding of overall student results.'

'Oh, it was just…' I tried to say, but he went on.

'And, even more seriously, on examining the marks on the mark sheets that you eventually handed in in May, this year, for example, we find huge inconsistencies in the comments you make and the results you award.'

'The marks were all…' I tried to say, but he went on again.

'And when we had the marks that you awarded subjected to second marking and external scrutiny, we found, interestingly, that while the second marker and the external examiner both agreed their marks, the results were vastly at odds with the marks that you, yourself had awarded.'

'Well, no two examiners always agree entirely—'

'You're right, they don't, but the inconsistencies between the marks of the second and external examiners and your own are of such variance that we've had to come to the conclusion that your judgment in these particular results was highly… how can I say… *Suspect.*'

'Are you accusing me of—'

'We are not accusing you, Miss Meyer, we are telling you: if you award a student a mark of seventy-five, which equates to a good First, yet both a second marker and a respected external examiner award that same piece of work a fifty-one, which equates to a low 2:2, what are we supposed to deduce?'

I decided not to deduce anything. I looked down at my hands, neatly folded in my lap. It was a fair cop. Of course I remembered rushing through the marking I had to do back in May, but how many lecturers haven't done the same? Who hasn't skimmed the surface from time to time?

But Heron had more to say. 'And now we come to an even more serious matter,' he said, leaning forward with yet another piece of paper from the pile. Tim hardly dared look at me. 'We have received a serious complaint from a student…'

'What—?'

'…from a student who alleges that you made a quite specific threat to him regarding his mark…'

Gorgeous Greenspan!

'It wasn't a serious threat… I just—'

'Miss Meyer, the allegation is that you made a serious threat regarding a student and one of his end-of-year marks. You threatened the student that if he didn't behave in a particular way, and I won't go into the details here because I think we all know what we're talking about, you would reduce his mark from what would have been deemed a Pass to what would then be deemed a Fail. We consider this to be totally unacceptable as well as unprofessional and, frankly, outrageous behaviour from a member of staff.'

'I really don't think—' I stammered, wondering how Gorgeous Greenspan could possibly have taken me seriously, but Heron cut me off again.

'You might be relieved to hear that the student in question was extremely reluctant to make a complaint against you, but your threat was overhead by a member of staff who felt under a professional obligation to report the matter albeit after a period of time while the said member of staff considered the implications of her doing so.'

Fucking Chrissie. Trust her to open her big mouth.

'Now look…' I began, but I wasn't sure where I was going, which was not a problem, as Heron had even more to say and cut me off.

'I come to another matter which, while it was something that occurred outside of the university campus and outside the usual university hours, is still of grave concern given that it involved the same student, who is the subject of the existing complaint, and yourself at an event in which dozens of other undergraduates were present and who, I'm sorry to say, witnessed what happened.'

The May Ball!

'We take an extremely dim view of any member of staff behaving in a drunken, lewd manner, whether it's on university property, in university time, or not. We do not expect our members of staff to do other than behave professionally at all times and set a good example to the young people studying at our institution and, on this occasion, what they witnessed in your behaviour, Miss Meyer, did not attain the highest standards that we endeavour to achieve in our professional capacity as capable and responsible examples to, and leaders of, young people.' He went on. 'As Dean of the Faculty of English and Media, I need to be quality focused and while I have parked various of your indiscretions during the two years you've been with us—'

'Parked indiscretions?' I asked, genuinely surprised.

'Yes,' he replied. 'Let me explain. Your research, for example. You were awarded a place at this university partly on the strength of a research bursary of £30,000 that you gave every impression was expected to be awarded to you by the Association of English Educators. But it transpires that it was several months after that bursary was awarded to another academic at another university, in fact, a competitor of ours, that you chose to reveal you had failed in your application and that, in fact, you had not attained the bursary. Keeping this knowledge to yourself, as you did, you continued, nonetheless, to give every impression that the AEE had not made the award and that you, yourself, were still being considered for it.'

'Ah, there was a reason—'

'Whatever the reason, Miss Meyer, we offered you employment partly based on the understanding you would be enriching our research facility with a major piece of academic work, and it was your responsibility to inform us the minute the wherewithal for said same research was withdrawn. As I said, this was one of those indiscretions that we chose to park, giving you the benefit of the doubt. But may I ask, what has happened to your research?'

'I—'

'I'll tell you.' He went on. 'Nothing.'

'Miss Meyer,' he said, changing tack. 'As I said, I need to be quality focused, have clarity of purpose to empower everyone on my team, and while I have parked various indiscretions of yours on the cloud—'

Oh no. He wasn't going to go on – not using Heron-speak. 'Oh, for goodness' sake, Peter,' I said, brittle and stern. 'You don't need to go on. I know and you know that you've parked your so-called indiscretions because I was married to Dan Caine and you thought you had to keep me sweet, so I would put in a good word for you and your hopes of being a television star. And now that Dan and I are divorced you don't need me anymore, so I guess what's happening here is that you're trying to get rid of me. How's that for professional behaviour from a dean?' I looked at Tim for support, but he suddenly found his notes extremely interesting and wouldn't look up.

'Well, Mister Heron, I'm afraid your chances of being on the telly are extremely dim—'

'We're not here to talk about my future, Miss Meyer. We are here to talk about yours. And you are right, although your phraseology is somewhat amiss. I'm going to offer you the chance to resign, rather than be dismissed for gross misconduct, and, although your contract of employment allows you two months' notice of termination, I'm willing to let you go right away. Frank, the porter, is waiting outside and he will escort you to your office so that you can collect any items of a personal nature and then he will accompany you to Human Resources where I would ask you to hand over your staff badge and security swipe card, and then Frank will escort you to your car and off the premises. Unless you need any further clarity, or have any further questions, I shall expect a letter of resignation from you delivered by Recorded Delivery on my desk tomorrow morning. Thank you, Miss Meyer.'

I'm sure there should have been a thousand and one things I could've said. But rather than appeal, apologise, explain, or simply sob, I stood up – Tim and arsehole Heron stood too – and I made for the door and tried not to wobble too much in the six-inch heels I'd chosen for the occasion.

****

Bugger me, but Frank was standing outside with pure satisfaction stamped on his face. He was just about to follow me as I set off down the corridor when I realised Heron had snuck up behind.

'Er, one moment, Teri,' he said, gripping my arm, pulling me to a stop, and offering me a sickly smile. 'You'll be delighted to know that Richard Walker, you know, the MD of *Ridings Today*, came to see me yesterday to tell me that the idea for a Friday night books programme, which had been shelved, is back on again. And despite the very kind reference you gave him about me, he offered me the role of presenter. Thought you'd want to know.'

Frank stood in the doorway of my office as I opened and shut drawers and ran my hand along shelves, looking for any items of what Peter Heron described as *of a personal nature* that I needed to remove. Someone had left a clear Perspex box on my desk in readiness for the haul and, like Frank waiting outside Heron's office to escort me, I could see my leaving had been an anticipated and probably foregone conclusion to which there would be no appeal and for which I had been the only one not to have seen coming.

Odd, that after two years, there was very little accumulation of items of a personal nature. Certainly no photographs – I don't have kids, but, anyway, I wouldn't have been one of those women who needed pictures of their precious little darlings glued to the wall above their computers in the unlikely event of their forgetting what the progeny looked like. Nor did I have pictures of meaningful partners – I'd torn up all my wedding photos when Dan left, and Declan was always reluctant to have his picture taken (fearful, no doubt, they could be used in evidence should his daft little wife or his latest mistress find them).

My books? There was a limited demand for tomes majoring on the Restoration period, and I didn't have the energy to sell them on the second-hand book market. My research? It was all there: the libertine lying in wait in a big, black box file. I picked it up and dumped it in the waste bin with a loud clatter, which made Frank look across in my direction. 'You must be loving this,' I said to him.

'Actually, I'm not,' he said. 'I thought, earlier, outside Mr Heron's office, that you'd got your comeuppance, but when it comes down to it, I feel sorry for you.'

'Well, that's hunky dory of you,' I snapped. 'But I don't need your sympathy. I'm well shot of this place.'

Frank shrugged. I reached into the bin and retrieved the box file and put it in the Perspex box. Might come in useful at some later date, I told myself.

Once the humiliating trip to Human Remains and the formal handing-in of my staff badge and swipe card was over, my Perspex box containing my life's research and I walked out to the car park. 'I know my way from here,' I said to Frank, but he shook his head.

'Got to see you off the premises,' he said. I placed the Perspex box on the roof of my car while I fumbled around in my handbag for the keys and saw that my mobile phone was flashing a message. I'd check it once I was away from here. I put the box in the boot of the car, climbed into the driving seat, and closed the door, winding down the window. 'Bye, Frank. No hard feelings?'

He had the grace to smile. 'No hard feelings, Teri.'

I accelerated away perhaps a little too quickly and had to brake sharply to avoid someone stepping out into my path from between a row of parked cars. I recognised the plump and dumpy figure of Stella Lastings and cursed myself for stopping so suddenly. Better to hit and squash her to a pulp. She looked up, realised it was me, and inhaled a sharp breath. Oh yes, she knew, damn her.

'Yes, Stella,' I said through the open window. 'It's me, and I'm off.' She looked about to say something, but I beat her to it. 'Some advice for you, Stella. Try a diet, you fat cow!' Not the most erudite of farewells, but who knows, she might be glad of the advice.

As I pulled out of the main university entrance, my legs shook. My mind reeled. What just happened? Had I really been sacked? I checked in the mirror to make sure neither Frank nor Stella were watching, then pulled over into the lay-by on the other side of the gates and laid my head on the steering wheel to get my breath. I reached into my bag on the passenger seat for a small bottle of water I always keep at the ready.

I took a pull of water and breathed deeply once or twice until I felt calmer. Taking the phone, I saw the message was a text from Dad.

Ring urgently.

I scrolled down my contacts until 'Dad' featured on the screen and I pressed the green 'talk' button, eventually hearing the long tone that meant the battered old dial phone Dad preferred to a modern device was ringing somewhere inside an old, stone cottage whose walls were covered in a mix of wisteria and knot weed in the deepest rural France. I imagined him putting his book down on the ground beside him, pulling himself out of his wicker sun lounger on the back patch of grass and shuffling along the stone flooring of the kitchen to the old, wooden plant stand where the phone sat with its cord curled in tight corkscrews.

'Bonjour?' he said.

'Dad, it's me. What's up?' He never contacts me, so I guessed this was some emergency to do with him, Mum, or Charlie. As it happened, it was to do with all of them – and me.

'Bad news, love,' he said. 'We've gone bust.'

It turns out finances at the factory had been on the downward slide for months. Dad was saying something about being shafted by 'that bastard' and explaining something to do with a bad investment in new machinery at a time when orders were dwindling thanks to competition from cheap imports, but I couldn't take it in. 'What are you saying, Dad? Who's shafted us and is this something we can recover from?' I couldn't imagine life without the factory in the background turning out its sheets of metal and, more importantly, the money that kept this family going.

'Pranks has shafted us. And I'm saying that it's the end of the line,' he replied. 'There's nothing left.'

Dad said he'd assumed I realised something was wrong when my allowance had become more erratic; some months it was late and other months it didn't arrive at all. Well, of course I'd noticed, but what with all I'd had to put up with over the last couple of years, I hadn't chased it up as I might've done.

'I should have warned you,' Dad said. 'Pranks started laying people off to save costs and then, of course, when a big order came in, he didn't have enough people to process it, so we lost that too. The order book has been empty since then so everyone's been given the boot and there's no money to pay any redundancy so you can imagine how the workforce is feeling about that.'

'But surely there's some money left? What about the factory itself? Can that be sold?'

'Pranks sold it off two years ago,' Dad said, sighing. 'The idea was to capitalise on the property by releasing equity to put into the business and then lease the building back, but it seems Pranks didn't put any of the capital into the factory, and nor did he pay any rent or rates for the last eighteen months.'

'Didn't he discuss any of this with you?'

'Well, yes and no,' Dad said. 'He'd discussed selling the building, and I thought it was the right idea at the time, so I left it all to him.

Gave him the power… signed everything over to him to take full control. I was an idiot, but stupidly, I trusted him.'

'And where is Pranks now?'

'Ah,' Dad said. 'That's the thing. He's done a bunk.'

'Done a bunk?'

'Yes, he's buggered off somewhere with all the money from the sale of the factory, plus what he should've been paying in rent and rates, and the entire company pension fund. He had full financial control over everything, you see.'

'And can't we find him? Stop his bank account? Do something?'

'Sorry, darling. I've been trying everything for the last couple of weeks since I realised what was going on. Pranks has been planning his getaway for years. The police said he's probably gone abroad somewhere, created a new identity for himself, and opened accounts under a new name. They doubt we'll ever find him. Meanwhile, the creditors are circling, and I'm going to be made bankrupt.'

'So what does it mean for us?'

'It means there is no money left.'

'But, Dad,' I wailed. 'I've just been sacked. How am I going to manage?'

'I'm sorry, darling, but you're on your own.'

I switched off my mobile and sat, blindly staring at nothing at all, trying to take it all in. I hadn't been able to think; to move; to do anything. A sudden knocking on my driver's window made me jump, and I looked to the right. A figure was bending down, looking into the car. Stella fucking Lastings was tap-tap-tapping on the window. 'Teri…'

she mouthed. I wound down the window so I could hear what she was saying.

'Are you all right?' she asked. 'You've been sitting here for ages. We were getting worried about you.' I noticed Frank behind her, shifting his weight from one leg to the other.

I couldn't speak; I wanted to yell, to scream, to cry, even to laugh. To do anything other than sit here while Stella and Frank took in the sight of me, pathetic, and broken; a sad fool who'd clearly had some sort of breakdown and was now unable to move or say anything.

Stella reached into the car with her podgy arm and gently stroked my shoulder. 'You've had a shock. Why don't you come back into uni with me and I'll get you a cup of tea or something?'

I stared in her direction but couldn't focus. 'I can't…' I said. 'Not allowed…'

'Oh, I'm sure it would be all right.' I looked more intently and took in her pretty, plump face. The rose-red lips formed in a compressed heart shape, which I read as being her concerned look. She smiled ever so weakly in the face of my suddenly focused scrutiny.

'Oh, God, Stella. Why are you being so nice to me?'

'Because you're upset and I'm worried about you.' With sudden clarity I realised she was being honest and genuine, and it shook me. I felt something give way – the iron grip around my middle that normally held me so tightly suddenly released. I took a deep breath and as I exhaled, the tightness round my stomach slackened even more. My shoulders dropped, my clenched fists loosened, and I slumped forward slightly and, for the first time for what seemed like years, I relaxed into my own body. Someone was worried about me, and it happened to be the one person I'd been so awful to over the last two years. I'd even shouted a totally offensive instruction at her after narrowly failing to run her down just minutes ago. 'Why? I mean, why are you worried about me?'

She looked nonplussed for a moment, and said, 'Because I think you need help.'

'Stella,' I said. 'Thank you…' I was going to add something cutting along the lines that I didn't need help and I certainly didn't need help from an oversized do-gooder like her, but in this new-found sense of grace that overwhelmed me, I couldn't. I felt she had been kind – more kind than I deserved – and I should try to reciprocate the feeling even if it meant giving her the satisfaction of knowing she'd done her good deed for the day.

'Look, I've just had some bad news. No, nothing for anyone to worry about,' I added, seeing her look of increased concern. 'No death or destruction. But I'm okay now. I'm on top of it. I know what I'm doing. I'm off now, but thanks again.' I pressed down on the clutch, switched on the engine, and pushed the car into gear. Stella withdrew from the window and stood back. 'Take care,' she said, as I accelerated away.

Chapter 88

Lee

Stella burst into my office, parked herself in one of the chairs I keep for visitors and burst into floods of tears. 'It's unbelievable,' she wept. 'So brutal.'

I swallowed, but the lump in my throat refused to shift. 'I suppose it was always on the cards…'

'No, no, no!' Stella's curls bounced vigorously. 'It's shockingly cruel.'

Even in the middle of my own distress, I was startled by her agony of grief. 'But you didn't…'

'…Like her?' She shook her head. 'Most of the time I thought she was simply horrible. But, today' – she paused and dabbed at her eyes – 'she seemed broken.'

My hands twisted in anguish, but before I could reply, Mike came in and slumped in the remaining chair. 'I'm sorry,' he said. 'I pushed for a suspension and behavioural awareness training, but Peter was having none of it.'

There was a knock at the door and Tim from Human Resources stepped inside. 'I just wanted to say' – his shoulders slumped – 'But, at least, she's able to tender her resignation. It'll look better on her record than an outright dismissal.'

Cold comfort. But I was touched they'd recognised my concern for my friend and taken the time to offer their sympathy. Tim, who'd perched on a corner of my desk, stood. 'Why don't you go home? Take some personal time.'

Mike nodded. 'Good idea. It's Wednesday. Student sports and hobbies afternoon. Nobody'll miss you.'

Stella wiped her eyes. 'I think I'll do the same. A few hours with my kitties and I'll feel right as rain.'

With difficulty, I suppressed a smile. Teri'd heave when I told her.

But she wasn't answering her phone, so I packed up my stuff and set off home, stopping off at the supermarket on the way. I felt an urgent need for something strong and alcoholic.

I was loading the bottles – buy six-get-twenty-five-per-cent-off so, of course, I'd stocked up – into the on the boot of the car when my phone finally rang. Heart in mouth, I answered.

Chapter 89

Teri

I was probably driving too fast as that bloody camera on the A615 flashed again as I went past, but I didn't care. I just needed to get home. If I could get home before anything else happened, I would be all right. As Dan said, I'd pull myself up and get back on with it. I just needed to think things through. Like what am I going to do for money? Will I get redundancy from the university? Probably won't get a reference. Besides which, do I want another academic job? Look where it's got me so far: nowhere.

I thought about Rochester lying in his big, black box file in the boot of my car – the lying libertine, the randy old rake. Then it dawned on me. I could write a book about him; I'd done enough research, I'd got enough material. I would explore Rochester's libertine philosophy, one of non-permanence, the breakdown of life's norms, and the dedicating of oneself to the moment – no matter how debauched that moment might be. It would be the ultimate story of a lyric writer constantly poised between a longing for Eden and a knowledge of its impossibility, writing poems of fallen sexual activity that remind us not of love, but of the world we have lost. *A Falling Friend* I'd call it.

I raced home, gathered Rochester into my arms, and slipped into the flat with a sense of overwhelming relief that, like Dan had predicted, I'd got myself together, had purpose again. I could hardly wait to start writing.

I switched my mobile back on. Three missed calls: one from my mother, who'd obviously surfaced long enough from her drunken reveries to digest the latest news; one from Charlie, same – although he'd have emerged from tending his goats; and one from Lee. She'd obviously heard about the great sacking and ejecting, no doubt from Frank or Stella – or from Peter Heron himself. So I listened to hers and ignored the other two. 'Oh, God. Teri. I'm so sorry. Why didn't you call me? Please ring me now.'

I rang. It took a few moments for her to answer and when she did, I could hear traffic noise and a sort of clanking in the background.

'I'm just at the supermarket, loading stuff into my car,' she said and added hastily, 'But I need to talk to you.'

'Well, let's talk now,' I said.

'Wouldn't you rather…?'

'No, I've got things to do tonight,' I said. 'Lots to digest. It's been quite a day.'

I gave her a potted, breathless version of my meeting with Peter Heron, launched into the dramatic saga of Edward Pranks and the missing millions, and finished off with my Stella-inspired epiphany.

Then I told her about Dan having rushed round to see me yesterday and how supportive he'd been. I didn't tell her he'd met someone else. In fact, thinking about it, I questioned how serious he could be about this other woman, whoever she was. He'd been so nice to me, so understanding. I told Lee I was sure he still had strong feelings for me, and what did she think? Was there a chance he and I could get back together?

She hardly said a word, but I could hear a rustling at the other end as she shifted the phone from ear to ear and packed bags into the boot of her car. 'Are you listening to me?'

'Yes, but Teri,' she said, 'there's something else you need to know.' Then what she said next was blurted out as though she'd been wanting to say this all along but been too nervous. 'I've just got engaged.'

'What?'

'Engaged. To be married.'

'Who to? Not that Christian chap? I thought that was all over.'

'No. Not Christian.'

'Who? For God's sake, Lee. Don't keep a poor girl in suspense.'

Acknowledgments

We are so grateful to all those people, friends and family, who have offered us support and encouragement during the writing of this book. So many of you have shown an interest, and it's impossible to name you all, but we're sending our heartfelt thanks.

We must, however, give special mention to a small number of people who have been particularly patient: Kevin, Geoff, Meg, Annie and Dandy.

As writers we draw a lot of inspiration from snippets of conversations that we overhear when we're out and about – at the supermarket, in cafes and restaurants, on the bus or train. Thank you to all those anonymous people who have inspired us more than they'll ever know.

Thanks too to our friends who remain our friends even though they know we're always listening – especially the lovely ladies of the Knitwits knitting group and Edie's book club.

We'd also like to mention all our author and blogger friends on Twitter and Facebook, who've been a much-valued source of support and encouragement.

Special thanks too to our editor Emma Mitchell, who has helped us revise and edit A Falling Friend, ready for its re-launch and re-publishing.

And of course, thank you, Lord Rochester, and those fabulous ladies: Teri and Lee.

About the Authors

Sue Featherstone and Susan Pape are both former newspaper journalists with extensive experience of working for national and regional papers and magazines, and in public relations.

More recently they have worked in higher education, teaching journalism – Sue at Sheffield Hallam University and Susan at Leeds Trinity.

The pair, who have been friends for thirty years, wrote two successful journalism books together – *Newspaper Journalism: A Practical Introduction* and *Feature Writing: A Practical Introduction* (both published by Sage).

They then co-wrote a novel, *A Falling Friend* – the first in their *Friends* series, which was first published in 2016.

Since then the pair have written two more books about best friends Teri and Lee: *A Forsaken Friend*, which originally appeared in 2018, followed a year later by *A Forgiven Friend.*

Sue, who is married with two grown-up daughters and two grandchildren, loves reading, writing and Nordic walking in the beautiful countryside near her Yorkshire home.

Susan is married and lives in a village near Leeds, and, when not writing, loves walking and cycling in the Yorkshire Dales. She is also a member of a local ukulele orchestra.

They blog about books at www.bookloversbooklist.com

You can find both Sue and Susan on Twitter @SueFWriter and @wordfocus

Printed in Great Britain
by Amazon

83054688R00210